The Right Kind of Unexpected

RAYNA YORK

ALSO BY RAYNA YORK

Everything I Knew to be True

When Life Gives You Lemons Instead of Lattes

The Right Kind of Unexpected

RAYNA YORK

Toad Tree
PRESS

Published by Toad Tree Press

167 Terrace View NE

Medicine Hat Alberta TIC-OA4

Publishers Note

This book is a work of fiction. Names, characters, places, and incidents are derived from the authors imagination. Any resemblance to actual persons, living or dead, business establishments, events or locales is entirely coincidental.

ISBN 978-1-9990951-4-7 (paperback)

ISBN 978-1-9990951-5-4 (ebook)

Cover design by Rocio Martin Osuna

Thank you to my family for the glorious ride we've shared. Live life loud and often.

CHAPTER 1

I RUSH to the bathroom at the side of the building and lock the door behind me. I can't deal with this anymore. I grip the sides of the pedestal sink and drop my head, breathing deep. In, out, in, out, fighting for calm.

Why? Why did I think this was a good idea?

Three days ago, Dax and I were on our way to a gallery opening when I mentioned I'd never been to Disney World. He said he hadn't either. I commented on how it would be fun to jump in the car and go. High school graduation was over, my parents were in Europe, I didn't have any plans for the summer, so the next afternoon we were on the road.

Bad idea.

Horrible.

The worst.

I lift my sunglasses to the top of my head and startle at the red-rimmed, brown-eyed zombie staring back at me. I haven't had a good night's sleep since we left, and I forgot to take my makeup off last night, then Dax was in such a hurry this morning.

Maybe our relationship was always a mess. I don't know. We've only been together for six months. In New York, Dax and I got along great. There were parties, restaurants, people, and places to fill our time. Now, without the distractions and being stuck together in mostly confined spaces, I realize we don't have as much in common as I thought. But it's more than that. He needs to be right about everything and nags me until I concede to his views. I never noticed him doing that before. There are a lot of things I didn't notice before.

I use a little soap and water on a paper towel and clean the black smears from around my eyes. It cleans the makeup off perfectly, but the dark circles and puffiness remain. I slide a hair elastic from around my wrist and pull my brown mop of humid-induced frizz into a messy bun.

With a deep sigh, I slide my glasses back over my eyes and push the door open into the bright sunlight. I take in the beautiful field dotted with wildflowers behind the gas station, then close my eyes and lift my face to the sun, disregarding the intensity on my pale skin. I breathe in the fragrant smell of green that only a sweltering heat can produce.

It's time to put an end to this impromptu adventure. It ceased being fun after the first five hours. And it's my car, my time, my money. With renewed strength, I turn on my heels, ready to confront Dax and get my car keys back. I'm heading home with or without my soon-to-be-ex-boyfriend. I can drop him off at a bus station if he wants to continue the trip.

I round the corner of the building. Wait, what? Where is it?

I walk to the two ancient gas pumps and turn in a circle,

taking in the white building with peeling paint, and everything else in the three-hundred-and-sixty-degree radius, but the car is nowhere in sight. I walk to the other side of the building, thinking he might have parked in a different location while getting something from inside, but the car isn't there either.

What the hell?

I hurry to the edge of the parking lot and look down the road both ways. I don't see my car anywhere.

Seriously?

He probably got sick of waiting and went into town to get us some food. I was in the bathroom for a while.

I walk back to the building and drop my butt on the edge of the crumbling walkway to wait. It's shaded by the roof's overhang, but with barely a breeze blowing, sweat trickles down my back and between my breasts. I stretch my legs out in front of me and lean back on my hands.

I could use something cold to drink.

Damn. My phone and wallet are in the car.

"What a dump," I mumble to myself in frustration.

"Don't let my mom hear you say that," a deep voice with a Southern drawl says from behind me.

I jump up, brushing my rear end off, and come face to chest with a large body in greasy coveralls. "Oh, I—what?" I didn't hear anyone come out of the building.

"My mother would take offense at you calling our family business a dump."

He stares down at me with stunning green eyes and a lopsided grin. "Sorry." I bite the corner of my lip, embarrassed at being called out on my rudeness. "I—uh, think my boyfriend, well . . . I don't know where he went."

"Just so you know . . ." The guy pulls apart his navy-blue coveralls, the snaps popping loose from neck to waist. "He didn't pay for the gas before he left." He slides his arms out of the sleeves, letting the material hang loose around his waist. "Damn, it's hot today." The gray T-shirt he's wearing underneath the coveralls fits snugly against his muscular arms and chest.

"He didn't . . ." I swallow hard at the passive sexiness of the action. "Pay?"

"No. He didn't. You okay? Your cheeks are a fiery red."

Holy shit, this guy is . . . *whoo, man.* He looks close to my age. Not that it matters, and the fact that he's sexy as all hell should be the last thing on my mind. I clear my throat. "You're right about the heat." I fan my face with my hand. Realizing how pointless it is, I drop it to my side. "He probably went into town to get something for us to eat, not realizing my wallet was in the car. I'll pay as soon as he gets back."

"He left over twenty minutes ago, so . . ." He lets the thought hang in the air for me to grasp.

"It's been that long?" I look down the road again, as if my car might suddenly appear.

"You can use the phone inside." He motions with his thumb. "You could call him."

"I don't have his number memorized."

He runs a hand through slightly messy, dark blond hair, looking like he's contemplating his next action.

"I'm sure he'll be back soon," I say, hoping I'm right.

"Well, you might as well come on inside. Dad will skin me alive if I let you stay out here and roast to death—even if you *are* a criminal."

"I am *not*"—I calm my tone—"a criminal." This whole situation is absurd.

He opens the door for me. "Guilty by association, then?"

I narrow my eyes up at him as I pass. Damn, he's tall. But then what do I know? I'm short.

"Wow." I stop in the doorway, sliding my sunglasses off for a brighter view.

"Could you, just, uh"—his fingers are on my back, nudging me forward—"move so I can get the door closed?"

"This is amazing." I take a couple of steps in.

I'm not sure what I expected, but this wasn't it. A gift shop with clean white walls and raw wood shelving—sort of rustic barn meets contemporary vibe—displaying paintings, jewelry, and small sculptures. I feel like a kid in a toy store. Art always gets my heart pumping.

"*That's* my mom. She's the artist. Me, I fix the cars." He points toward the restaurant. "My dad's the chef. Like I said . . . family business." There's pride in his tone. "Come on, I'll introduce you."

I want to stay and get a closer look at all the beautiful pieces, but the guy is moving on.

A pretty, young girl around nine, with long, dark hair, comes running out of the restaurant, skids to a stop and almost crashes into him.

The guy takes a step back, holding his hands out. "Whoa, kid, chill." She rolls her eyes in response. "This is Josie, my sister. Josie? Meet? Um—"

I smile at Josie. "Tess."

"Nice to meet you," she says politely, then whispers out of the side of her mouth to her brother, "Is this the thief?"

"Hardly," I say, choking on a laugh.

"Her boyfriend took off with her car keys."

"Some boyfriend," she says, her bright green eyes looking me over.

"*Josie.*" He gives her a look like, *Don't be rude.*

"He'll be back," I tell her.

"Let Mom know we'll be there in a sec." The guy jerks his head in the direction Josie came from.

"Okay," she bubbles, then runs off.

"What about your parents?" he asks. "Could they wire you some money? You know . . . if he—"

"He'll be back," I cut him off. Am I assuring him with this mantra or myself? "And besides, they're in Europe somewhere."

"You could call 'em though, right? You know, in case he doesn't, you know . . ."

"No. I can't."

"Why?" He looks surprised.

"Because, then they'll be right," I say on an exhale. Dax is the only guy I've dated that my father has met. He told me Dax wasn't a "quality person." One meeting and he knew. I guess being successful in business teaches you to read people on the fly. My mother hates everyone I date unless they are her choice, and will take delight in tearing me apart over this. It's one of her favorite pastimes. And when you've been ripped into as many times as I have, there comes a point when you don't want to hear it anymore. And I've reached it.

"It's fine. Dax won't leave me stranded."

"Uh-huh . . . I'm Colten, by the way." He holds out a large, grease-smeared hand.

I stare at the griminess and debate whether to take it. I don't want to be rude. I'm not a snob. It's just . . . *gross*.

He drops it and lowers his head with a sheepish grin. "Oops, sorry. I was in the middle of an oil change when Mom yelled for me."

Big muscular guy looking embarrassed. My insides glow with an *aw, how cute* moment. "Nice to meet you," I say. "And thanks for not being a jerk about all this."

"Yeah. No problem. Come on and meet my parents."

CHAPTER 2

I FOLLOW Colten into the restaurant. Country music plays on low in the background. Josie is standing next to a stunning woman with blonde hair pulled into a ponytail, who's got her glare on. That must be the mother.

Shit.

I take a quick look around. There's a man, probably the cook, behind the expo window, shaking his head. Other than a couple of customers scattered about, the place is mostly empty.

"You have a lot of nerve, young lady," the woman scolds, her crisp blue eyes burrowing into mine. I notice a couple of heads turn in my direction and instantly want to hide from embarrassment.

Colten takes a step forward. "Mom!"

She fists a hand on her hip and wags her finger at him. "Don't 'Mom' me, Colten Reed."

Josie covers her mouth, suppressing a giggle. I'm glad *she* thinks this is funny because I sure as hell don't. I've never felt this uncomfortable in my life. I should go. "Um—" I point toward the exit.

She turns her wrath back on me. "Um? That's all you have to say?"

My eyes go wide and I take a step back. "Sorry. I, uh . . . I'm sorry." I hold my hands up in front of me. "I didn't mean to cause any trouble."

Time to get out of here. I start to turn away.

"Where's that boy you came with?" She jerks her head toward the front of the building. "I've got a few things to say to him."

"Mom, lighten up," Colten says, looking stunned by her behavior. "He took off with her car. All her stuff's inside. She's thinking he'll be back shortly but . . ." I catch him shrug and give his mother a look that says he doubts it.

"What were you doing with someone like him, anyway?" she huffs. "Didn't your parents teach you any better?"

"Uh . . ." Holy shit! This woman. "I'm just going to wait outside." I turn to leave.

Colten touches my arm. "Don't go."

"Twyla!" the man from the kitchen barks out her name. "Give the kid a break. It's not her fault." He sends me a pitying look, which I return with a weak smile.

She scowls at him, then turns back, openly appraising me. Then, with a look of resignation, sighs. "He's right." Her features instantly soften. "I'm sorry. That was uncalled for." She rolls her eyes to the ceiling. "I just finished a hectic lunch shift. This situation is just one more thing heaped onto my pile." She points toward the kitchen. "That sweet man back there is my husband, Earl, and I'm Twyla."

I give her an awkward wave and Earl a grateful smile. "Tess." I shift my body nervously. "My—my, name. It's Tess."

"Where are you from, Tess?" she asks.

"Manhattan." And I wish I could just zap myself back home. This has been the weirdest day of my life.

"You're a long way south."

Yee-up. "We were heading to Disney World."

"And you say this boy of yours is coming back?"

"I sure hope so." I'd like to pay them for the gas and get out of here. Twyla hasn't been exactly hospitable.

The corner of her mouth lifts, somewhere between a smile and a smirk. "I heard you think my place is a dump."

Holy shit! I can't catch a break. Either the woman has bionic ears, or Josie was listening at the door and ratted me out. *Ugh.*

"Holy crap, Mom!" Colten's face turns bright red.

"Exteriors can be deceiving," I say, hoping to drive my point home. I mean, look at this place. The inside looks nothing like the outside. And I'm not a thief. I could get as much money as I needed, if I wanted to admit to my parents what happened— which I don't.

She pauses, then nods. "I suppose they are. Earl!" she hollers over her shoulder. "We need to get Sam over here to finish painting." She turns back to me. "He sandblasted the stucco two weeks ago and still hasn't put that fresh coat of paint on. I'm going to have to call him again."

I feel sorry for whoever Sam is. I imagine he's going to get an earful. "Your artwork is amazing, by the way." It's a random thing to say, but maybe the compliment will help smooth things over. And I'm not trying to suck up to her—well, maybe a little.

But it's not a lie. If this work is all hers, she's incredibly talented.

"Thank you." Twyla's face brightens. "It keeps me sane."

"I'll be right back," Colten says to me. "Gonna go wash up."

My eyes move to the art on the walls. "Are all these paintings yours?"

She glances over her shoulder. "They are."

"Brush or palette knife?" Curiosity for the art pushes me past the discomfort of being left alone with her.

She leans away, eyeing me up. "Palette. Do you paint?"

"Unfortunately, I have zero artistic ability, but I do have a love of art."

I'm rewarded with a beaming smile. Looks like I may have been forgiven. "Are you hungry?" she asks.

Shit. I am. And thirsty. "My wallet left with the car, but I'm good, thanks." My stomach growls, giving me away—just one more humiliation to tack on to my day.

"Uh-huh. Well, I can't have you starving while you wait for that jackass boyfriend of yours to come back now, can I?"

"Thank you." I give a small, appreciative smile.

She surprises me by wrapping an arm around my waist and leading me to a diner-style counter. "Come on. Sit down. I'll get you a menu. When you're done eating, you can call your parents and let them know what's going on." I take a seat on a stool while she reaches over to the cash register and grabs a menu.

"My parents are gone."

She puts a hand to her mouth in horror. "Oh, honey. I'm so sorry."

"No!" I rush to explain. "It's not like that. They're in Europe on business for a month or so. I don't want to worry them over nothing."

She eyes me like a concerned parent. "I'll accept that for now. How old are you?"

"Eighteen."

"Alright then. I just wanted to make sure you weren't a runaway." She hands me a menu. "You order whatever looks good. I'll get you some water, or maybe a milkshake?" She raises her eyebrows in question.

"Water would be great." I notice she doesn't have the same Southern drawl as the rest of her family, and wonder where she's from.

"I'll get it," Colten says, coming from the back with clean hands, Josie trailing behind him.

"Fine," Twyla says. "Josie? Do you want to get her order?"

"I can do that." She looks happy at being asked, which surprises me. I would think most kids her age would have rolled their eyes, irritated at a request to do *anything*.

"Tess, it was nice meeting you. I have some things I need to get done before the dinner rush. Sorry again for being insensitive and rude. I'm not normally like this. I promise." Her smile is sweet and a little remorseful.

"It's okay. I understand."

"How could you not have your boyfriend's number memorized?" Colten asks me as he loads ice into a tall glass and fills it with water.

"I don't need to. It's all programmed into the phone."

"Unless you're stranded somewhere without it," he jokes, walking in my direction.

"Yeah, but when does that happen? It's a one in a million possibility."

He sets the glass by my hand and sits next to me with a smile that tilts on his full lips. "Well, your one in a million just happened, sweetheart."

A sudden adrenaline rush at the endearment has my cheeks firing up red.

Is he flirting? With lightning speed, I pick up my glass, hiding my face as I take a drink.

Now is not the time to be getting riled by a tall, sweet, good-looking, muscular, sexy human being.

Have I met one of those before?

Maybe in separate parts, but never all in one package, that's for sure.

Over the rim of my glass, I notice Josie behind the counter giving her brother a look like, *you're such a dork.* I set my glass down, feeling that most of the rush has left my face and find her assessing me.

"You're pretty," she declares.

"Oh, uh . . . Thank you." The kid's not afraid to speak her mind, that's for sure. Like mother, like daughter, I guess.

"What can I get ya?" she says, all business now, which seems odd given she looks around nine.

The shift in focus is the distraction I need to pull myself together. I set the glass down, pick up the menu, and arrange my face into an expression of intense contemplation. "What do you suggest?"

"Definitely the hamburger and onion rings."

I hand the menu back to her. "Then that's what I'll have."

"I'll be right back," Colten says. "I need to finish that oil change."

"Sure. No problem," I say, trying to sound casual, but breathe a sigh of relief when he is gone. He's wreaking havoc on my already stretched emotional state.

With Colten gone and Josie busy with other things, I take the details of my surroundings. The theme from the gift shop is extended here into the restaurant, which, now that I consider it, is more like a diner. Same clean white walls and natural wood, but there's also stainless steel, light-blue laminate countertops, and accents of wrought iron. I count seven stools at the counter, and five booths that line a wall of large windows that look out onto the main road. I wonder if Twyla has help. That's a lot to take on by yourself.

I look at Twyla's framed artwork again. Her paintings remind me of snapshots in time, scenic images captured by a camera, interpreted on canvas. She leans toward an impressionistic style—acrylic, I think, but hard to say from this distance. She likes the bright, bold colors. I watch as she waits on new customers, and wonder when she finds the time to paint. I like that she visits with everyone. Hard to say if they're regulars or just passing through. Either way, she smiles a lot.

I hear a car pull up and quickly swivel my stool around to look out the window, but it isn't Dax. I've done that a few times now, and it's pissing me off.

Where the hell is he? I circle back to face the counter.

"You look like you're ready to kill someone." Earl sets a plate of food in front of me, then holds out his large, meaty hand with a bright, warm smile. "I'm Earl. Just thought I'd make it polite and official."

"Sorry." I shake his hand and say, "It's nice to meet you."

"Nice to meet you, too. And don't be sorry. That jackass that left you here is the one who should be sorry," he says, his expression thoughtful. "So, I guess you're in a bit of a pickle, huh?"

"Momentarily, yeah." I appreciate the hospitality, but I'd feel better if I could pay the debt that's adding up.

He nods his head as if processing a thought, then says, "Alrighty then. I'll leave you be. Enjoy." He turns and goes back to the kitchen.

"Thank you," I say as he retreats. He must not be one for conversation, I guess.

His name doesn't suit him. Earl conjures up images of beer-bellied men with skinny legs who like to scratch their butts in public. This man looks like he takes exercise seriously and is too respectful to degrade himself around another living soul.

I take a bite of the burger and moan out of sheer pleasure while licking juice off my lips. Okay. My day just got a whole lot better. This isn't your ordinary greasy burger you'd expect at a diner on the side of the road. The beef is lean with a unique seasoning combination I can't quite place. The cheese is aged and sharp. The onions are caramelized. And all of it is topped with garlic dill aioli.

I'm in heaven.

I take my time savoring each bite until the sad moment when I'm faced with an empty plate and the reality at hand. "Earl. That was outstanding," I say loud enough for him to hear through the expo window—his only view of what's happening out in the diner. "Thank you."

He doesn't take his eyes off his task, but manages a thumbs up.

"I told you," Josie says in passing.

"You did." I wipe my mouth with a napkin.

Josie refills my water glass, then takes my plate. "Do you want some dessert?"

She's confident in her actions. Maybe she helps her mother when she's not in school, but she seems too young for that. "No, thanks." I rub my full belly. "No room."

"What are you gonna do now?" She takes away my plate and sets it under the counter. I picture a bin, holding all the dirty dishes.

"Wait, I guess."

And do what?

I've forgotten what it's like occupying my time without social media.

Josie shrugs a shoulder and goes into the back, returning with an open book of crossword puzzles, which she sets in front of me along with a pencil. "I usually have it done by now, but it's been a crazy day."

"Thanks. You sure you don't want to keep it for later?" I say mostly joking, because why would someone her age be doing crossword puzzles?

"No, that's okay. I think you're going to need it more than I will."

Sadly, she might be right.

CHAPTER 3

THE TRIP with Dax *was* a disaster, but for him to abandon me the way he did was a shitty thing to do.

The asshole is not coming back, and I'm so angry at him right now. I look down at the puzzle in front of me, but I can't concentrate. How can he do that? Just leave me here?

Should I call the police?

He didn't steal my car in the typical sense. Dax has a brand-new truck at home. He's just being a dick. And as much as I'd love to make him pay, it would mean telling my parents what happened—giving them one more thing to be disappointed in.

No—no police. I need to handle this myself somehow.

Twyla's speed has increased as more customers arrive. She doesn't look flustered, just efficient, and still manages to be talkative and pleasant to customers. While waiting to collect her order, I catch Twyla winking at Earl after he smiles adoringly at her. They're so cute.

Josie has been helping settle customers' bills and taking payments for gas. All three of them move with practiced ease, smiling and joking along the way. I catch myself smiling as well. The entire scene is endearing and makes me feel a little lighter.

I turn my head as the door at the opposite end of the diner opens and Colten walks through. My stomach gives an excited leap when his eyes lock with mine and a slow, easy smile spreads across his face.

You just got dumped and you're going all gooey-eyed over the first good-looking guy you come across? Get a grip.

"No boyfriend?" Colten asks, sitting on the stool next to me.

"Ex-boyfriend. And no. Not yet," I say on a slightly frustrated exhale. I'm not sure if the irritation is at Dax or at my reaction to Colten—both, I guess.

"Are you gettin' worried?"

"I'll figure something out."

I'm going to have to call my father. I could make up some bullshit story that has nothing to do with the car—tell him my purse was stolen and ask him to send money and hope Dax brings my car back home. Which I'm almost positive he will. Then I could pay these nice people back and find a way home.

I watch Twyla hurry behind the counter, fill a couple of glasses with ice and something from the fountain drink machine, then rush away again.

"Doesn't your mom have any other help?" I ask Colten.

"I help her all the time," Josie says indignantly, springing up next to her brother out of thin air.

I want to add "The adult kind," but I doubt that'd go over too well. "I'm sure you do," I say in response. "Maybe I could lend a hand. You know, to pay for the gas and food. It'll give me something to do while I wait."

Wait for what?

I need to just call my father, feed him the lie, and get it over with.

"Where will you stay if that boy of yours doesn't come back?" Earl asks from his window. I didn't realize he was listening.

"I haven't thought that far ahead." Even if I make the call, my father might not answer right away, and even if he did, I'd have to find a bank—

"There's a living space over this here building," Earl breaks me from my thoughts.

That would work.

"Earl!" Twyla snaps, catching his offer on the way past. "She said her parents are in Europe. She can easily call them."

"*Shhh*, woman." He grins, looking so much like Colten. "She needs a place to stay tonight. Chances are nothing will get resolved before tomorrow." He directs his attention back to me. "Twyla and I lived there until we saved enough money to build a house. We've been usin' it for storage. I'm sure it's dusty, but you and Colten could give it a good cleaning."

"I'll help," Josie says excitedly.

"I heard you asking to lend a hand," Earl continues. "You ever waitress before?"

"Earl!" Twyla shouts.

I turn to see her standing behind me, arms full, glaring at him like he's lost his mind.

"Maybe she needs a summer job?" he responds with a shrug.

"No, I haven't waitressed before," I say. But hey, this could be exactly what I need. I'd make a bit of money. I wouldn't have to call my father for help. He's offering me a place to live. I sit up taller. "I got into Harvard. I'm sure I can figure it out."

Twyla huffs out a breath before disappearing into the back.

"You got into Harvard?" Josie yells, startling me.

"That's Josie's dream school," Colten says, cocking his head in her direction.

"Really?" She's so young. Why would she be thinking about college?

Twyla bristles. "Well, waitressing takes a different kind of smarts."

Damn. I pissed her off again. "Sorry, I didn't mean it that way. I just didn't want you thinking I was brainless and would be more of a hassle than help."

"Harvard, huh?" Colten looks impressed.

Twyla walks behind the counter to the expo window. She picks up several plates and gives Earl a dirty look. He grins after her, looking pleased with himself as she walks away.

"Yeah, but I'm not going. I decided on NYU instead."

Colten reaches over and covers Josie's ears. "*Shhh.* Don't let her hear you, she'll freak."

She swats his hands away. "I can still hear, moron."

Colten turns to me, grinning at Josie's response, his blue eyes shining bright. I thought they were green. Nope, definitely blue—crystalized blue. "What's wrong with Harvard?"

Stop staring at his eyes!

"Uh . . ." What was the question again? Oh, right. "I like New York. With all its galleries and art museums, I couldn't imagine leaving."

"What do you think, Twyla?" Earl asks, when she's in

hearing distance again. "A little help this summer might be nice."

"I can handle things just fine," she snaps, hurrying past us with another armload of dirty dishes.

I like his idea, but Twyla obviously isn't thrilled with it. "It's fine, Earl," I say, but he raises a hand in a *just wait, give it time* kind of gesture. This really would be the perfect solution if she would go for it. I'd tell my father I found a summer job and that I'll be back before school starts. He'll be impressed with my initiative—maybe, hard to say—and I wouldn't have to tell him what happened with Dax. Although he might wonder why my car shows up randomly without me.

But . . . he won't know unless the doorman tells him. I could talk to Chester and say a friend will drop the car off, then my parents won't know anything is amiss. My parking stall isn't anywhere near theirs, so they won't wonder why my car is there without me.

I'm liking this idea more and more.

Tonight's meal is shrimp stir-fry over rice, or I should say *was*. Josie and Colten hoovered it. While I've been waiting for my ex-boyfriend to *not* show up, I got Josie to let me help around the diner. I can now stack the dishwasher and run it. I know where all the dishes and glassware go and how to roll cutlery. I even got a smile out of Twyla for my efforts. Speaking of, she's just appeared in front of us with three plates of coconut-cream pie. Each slice is an insane five inches tall.

"When you're done here," she says, "you all better get upstairs if you want that place livable before midnight." She regards me with a sympathetic look. "I don't think that boy of yours is coming back."

I laugh at Dax's new title. "That boy of yours." *Not anymore, he's not.* "No. Doesn't look like it." The mad has mostly worn off, and I almost don't mind being here anymore. I like it here. I like these people.

"I'll bring up the cleaning supplies when the dinner rush is over. Just load all our stuff in one of the back rooms, okay, Colten?"

"Yes, ma'am, but I can get the cleaning stuff."

"It's okay. I want to come up and check things out."

I wonder why Earl didn't offer to let me stay the night at their house. It seems like it'd be easier. Maybe he's thinking if I'm already living in the apartment, Twyla might be more receptive to me working over the summer. Smart man.

"Let's go," Josie says, sounding resigned to a dreaded task. I notice her dessert plate is already empty. When I don't move right away, she takes my hand and pulls me off my seat. I give Colten a questioning look.

He smiles, stands up with his dish, also empty, and stacks it on top of Josie's. "Just go with it. I'll be right behind you."

"I'm not done," I whine slightly. The pie is heavenly good, and I don't want to waste any of it.

Colten waits while I shovel in the last few remaining bites, laughing when I'm done. "Dad makes the best pie, doesn't he?" He stacks my plate on top of the others. "I'll take these to the back and grab the key. Meet y'all up there."

Ugh. My stomach's going to explode.

CHAPTER 4

A SET of stairs behind the building leads up to the second floor. Josie and I wait for Colten at the top. The sun is low in the sky, but it's still crazy hot, and I'm soaked in sweat by the time he runs up the stairs two at a time and unlocks the door. Josie enters first. Colten places a hand on my lower back, prompting me to go in next. The touch, a simple gesture with no more meaning than to direct, sets my nerves humming. I stare up at him as I pass and wonder why he has such a powerful effect on me. His hand falls away to shut the door behind us.

He quirks a smile. "What?"

I drop my eyes. "Nothing."

"It's so hot," Josie complains.

"And stuffy." I wipe sweat off my brow with the back of my hand.

"On it." Colten moves further into the apartment. "I just have to switch on the air conditioner, but we should open the windows and air the place out for a couple of minutes while it gets goin'."

Josie opens the window in the living room. I move to the one over the kitchen sink. As soon as it's open, a cross-breeze moves through the apartment. Colten must have opened the ones in the back. It's still boiling in here, but the movement of air helps big time.

With the blinds and windows open, I get a better look at the place. The walls are painted an off-white with a warm touch of yellow, the floors a rustic-plank laminate. Twyla wasn't kidding. There's a lot that needs to be done—boxes, furniture, and random stuff are everywhere.

"So this is the kitchen slash living room area." Colten motions to the main open area, then waves me forward to follow him down the hallway. He points to the left. "Bathroom." I poke my head in. Sink, toilet, tub. Nothing fancy, but functional. "Then there are two bedrooms across from each other."

I poke my head into each one. The smaller bedroom faces a grassy field, and the larger one, the street. The place is tiny, but cute in an outdated, homey sort of way.

"It makes more sense to load all the extra junk into the bigger bedroom," Colten says, "but we could cram everything into the smaller one if you want."

"It's fine. I'll take the smaller bedroom." I'd rather have a view of a green field than of the road out front with all the comings and goings, which I imagine would be noisier. I may not be here long enough for it to matter. My stomach clenches at the idea of having to go back home.

We start in on the boxes. The moving process is taking longer than it should. Josie wants to look through every one, which turns into a show and tell. The girl can talk. At least the place is cooling down now that the windows are closed and the air-conditioning is doing its job.

Twyla steps through the door with an armload of cleaning supplies. "How's it going?"

Colten rushes forward to help. "Perfect timing. It's goin' good." He takes a bucket full of cleaning sprays from her hand, then the mop and broom she has tucked precariously under her arm.

"Thanks, honey." She eyes him lovingly. I would have given anything to have my mother look at me like that. "I better get back downstairs."

"I'm sorry to be putting you to all this trouble," I say.

"No trouble at all. The place needed to be organized and could use a good cleaning. I was thinking . . . don't you want to call the police? That boy stole your car."

"I know." The anger washes over me again. "I'd like to handle it without getting them involved. I'm almost positive he'll take the car back and leave it with our doorman when he's done." Twyla's brow creases, looking displeased with my choice. "I don't want to involve my parents." *Please, just leave it at that.* "I want to deal with it on my own." This whole thing is humiliating enough without adding their disdain for my choices on top of it.

Her expression softens. "What about your wallet? Don't you have a credit or debit card?" she asks.

"Yes, but my father disengaged the tap functions on both— only a pin number will work, and Dax doesn't know it. He wouldn't use them, anyway. He has his own money."

"How will you get home?" she asks.

My heart sinks. She must have decided that she didn't want the help after all. "A bus?"

"There aren't any buses," Colten interjects. His mom gives him a funny look. "Well, none that run through town."

"How small is this place?"

"Small enough not to have buses, obviously," he jokes.

"Don't be a smartass." Twyla nudges him, teasing. He kisses her cheek. "I know you don't want to tell your parents what happened, but won't they worry when they can't reach you?" she asks me.

"They won't call, and I doubt they'll even notice I'm gone."

"Well, that's just silly. I'd be out of my mind if I didn't know where my children were."

And that's the difference in a nutshell. Colten's parents are caring, whereas mine are cold and heartless. "They're very busy people."

"Well, you're welcome to stay here as long as you want."

I'm confused. So can I stay and work, or is she just offering to be polite?

If I make myself useful somehow—show her I'd be an asset . . . "Thank you again for letting me stay." How do I bring it up, though?

"You're a sweet girl. I'm sorry this happened to you." She surprises me with a quick hug before heading to the door. "Josie, come on. I need your help." I stand in awe at the easy affection between this mother and daughter.

"You just said you didn't need any," she whines. "Can't I stay here? There's still lots to do."

"Colten and Tess can handle it. I'm sure you've been babbling their ears off. They could probably use a break."

"I have an IQ of one-thirty-two," Josie retorts, her nose lifted in the air. "I *don't* babble."

Twyla rolls her eyes. "So you keep reminding me. Let's go, Einstein."

"Yes, ma'am." Her head droops as she walks toward the door.

It feels like a now or never moment. "Um, Earl mentioned you could use some help in the diner," I say, treading carefully. If she would just give me a chance . . .

She looks at the floor, her brow furrowed. "Well, I—"

"I can show her what to do," Josie jumps in, her face lit up and excited. "Then I wouldn't feel guilty about going to my friends' places all the time."

"Oh, honey." Twyla's face falls. "You should never feel that way. I can handle it. I always do."

"Only because you refuse to hire any help," Josie says.

"Well, I've tried—"

"Mom. Why not?" Colten adds. "What have you got to lose?"

I briefly wonder if the whole family is secretly intervening on Twyla's behalf, by seeing an opportunity in me and seizing it.

"My sanity?" she says, looking exhausted. I hold my breath while I watch her process the idea. She looks from Colten to Josie to me. "Okay. Fine. We'll see how it goes."

"Yay!" Josie bounces.

"Thank you," I say, feeling overwhelming gratitude.

She waves me off. "You may not be thanking me tomorrow. Oh, I almost forgot." She pulls a key chain from her pocket. It has a molded starlike compass and a strip of metal with words on it. "For the front door."

"I have a key for her," Colten says.

"That one stays on the bulletin board. This one she can use while she's here."

"Thank you." I take it and read the inscription. *Wherever you go . . . come back to me.*

"Good luck, you two." Twyla smiles, kisses Colten on the cheek, and follows Josie out, shutting the door behind her.

"You're really lucky to have her," I tell Colten.

"Who, Josie?" Colten grabs hold of a high-top kitchen table and eyes me, indicating he wants me to take the other end. "She's a pain in the butt."

We move it under the window that overlooks the field and the stairs below. "I meant your mom, but Josie, too. And your dad. They're so nice." I set the key chain on the kitchen counter.

"I take it you don't have a good relationship with your parents?"

"Not really. No." We each pick up a box and bring it to the bedroom.

"Is that why you don't want to contact them?"

We head back to the living room for another load. It's mostly odds and ends now. This should be our last trip.

"I just need some time to figure things out."

"Are your parents alcoholics? Abusive? They must be bad if you don't want to call 'em."

"No. My father's okay, I guess. He's just never around. My mother . . . well, let's just say she hasn't ever let me forget I was a mistake and messed up her entire life."

Colten's horrified expression makes me like him even more.

I pick up the multipurpose cleaning spray and rummage through a bucket to find a sponge or cloth. "Yeah, well." I shrug a shoulder. "I was raised by a nanny—Maria. She was the closest thing I had to family. She was tough, but loved me like I was one of her own. If it wasn't for her, I don't know how I would have turned out."

"You seem okay to me." His expression is honest, thoughtful, but the compliment has my cheeks turning pink and a goofy laugh coming out of my mouth.

I cringe at the sound as I spray the kitchen counters and wipe. *Ugh.* It's all his—I flail imaginary arms around in my head—male energy or whatever. It's overflowing and making me crazy.

"Do you have brothers or sisters?" he asks, stopping my internal craze.

"No. I think my father would have liked a boy, but no way was my mother going through the whole pregnancy thing again. She complained enough times to know it would never happen. And yes, she's extremely vain—if you didn't get that already—and loves her plastic surgeon."

"Is she still around, your nanny?"

I stare out the window. "Maria was dismissed as soon as I could drive. My mother said we had no reason to employ her anymore." My eyes sting, threatening tears. I can't believe it still hurts this much. "She called immigration." I glance at Colten over my shoulder. "Can you believe that?" He looks up from sweeping debris in the dustpan. "So instead of just telling Maria her services were no longer needed, she does the most heinous thing possible to the woman who has mothered me since birth." I shake my head while rinsing my cleaning cloth.

His hand suddenly lays heavy on my shoulder. "I'm sorry," he says.

The sudden contact has me looking over my shoulder. The compassion in those striking blue eyes has me choking a "thank you" past the knot tightening in my throat. He drops his hand as I turn away and begin wiping the stove. I don't want him to see the tears that are about to fall.

CHAPTER 5

I'VE NEVER SHARED personal details of my life with a stranger —or anyone, really. My experiences have taught me that people rarely care about anything other than themselves. Colten is different. He seems genuinely interested. And because of it, my words tumble out effortlessly. I'm not sure if that's a good thing. I feel vulnerable.

"Did you talk to your dad about Maria? Couldn't he have sponsored her or whatever it's called?"

Dad. Dear old Dad. He's anything but. It sounds weird even calling him that. He's my father—intimidating, high powered, and too busy for little ol' me.

"I suggested it to him, but he said he couldn't afford a black mark on his reputation." I open the fridge, which looks clean, as Colten fills a bucket of water in the sink. "Apparently, he didn't know she was in the country illegally." My mother probably held the immigration status over Maria's head the entire time. "I begged and pleaded with him to help her, but he said it was out of his hands. After that, I rebelled. I was angry and wanted to get back at my parents any way I could, especially my mother. And since reputation was everything, I continually hit her where it hurt."

Dating Dax was an extension of that. He had that sexy, misunderstood, bad-boy thing going on.

Really? And I was surprised when he turned out to be a jackass and left me here?

I'm an idiot.

"How did that rebellion work out for you?" he asks, while scrubbing the floors with a mop.

"Eh." I shrug a shoulder. "I think the incident four months ago is why I'm not in Europe with them right now." I *really* wanted to see that Picasso exhibition. "My mother hosted a charity benefit to raise money for a women's shelter. All of New York's high society was there. One family had a son who my mother was dead set on becoming a son-in-law. I wore the dress she laid out for me but added a rainbow wig styled in a massive updo, went a little overboard on the makeup, and topped it off with black platform combat boots. I was *very* social." I laugh. "Introduced myself to everyone. Even flirted shamelessly with her pick, James Harrington the third, along with many others."

Colten dunks the mop and wrings it out. "Huh . . ." He doesn't look impressed by my cleverness. "The event was for a good cause, though."

He's judging me.

I guess I can't blame him. "You have to know my mother. And if she really wanted to raise money, she wouldn't have hired the most expensive party planner, who hired the most expensive everything else. It was all to raise her social standing.

The party swag alone was a thousand dollars a guest. It was disgusting."

His eyes go wide. "Wow. Okay." He looks like he's getting it now.

"If she would have hired small businesses, it would have been different. You know, like a local band, or maybe a smaller caterer—help the community, you know?"

"That would have been better." He picks up his broom and dustpan. "I'm going to sweep that way." He points down the hall.

"Sounds good." Okay, maybe that wasn't the right way to get back at them. It *was* a charity event, but my mother was relentless in her instructions of what she expected of me. And it wasn't just that. She insulted, degraded, and belittled me in the process. I'd had enough.

I take my cleaning spray and rag and head to the bathroom. Lucky for me, it isn't dirty, just dusty. After dealing with the tub, toilet, and sink, I get down on my hands and knees and start wiping down the floor. I don't enjoy cleaning, but it isn't completely foreign to me. Maria made sure I knew how. She said she didn't want me turning out as useless as my mother.

"Here, let me get that," Colten says, coming through the door with his mop.

He's enormous in the small space. We dance around each other for a second, trying not to touch as we shift positions, but somehow manage to brush up against each other. My hand shoots up, landing against his chest. I don't know why, it just happens.

He stiffens instantly, so I drop it with a "sorry" and rush out the door mumbling, "I'll just go clean . . ." without finishing the sentence.

"Why don't you grab the bedding?" he says when I'm halfway down the hall. "I think we left it sittin' on top of a box in the big bedroom."

"On it," I holler back.

When I get to the bedroom, I bend over with my hands on my knees to catch my breath. He barely touches me, and my body fires up like dry kindling. I plant a hand on his chest, and he turns to ice. I'm not sure my ego can handle any more hits today.

I wish we were done and I had the place to myself. It was easier when Josie was here—I had someone else to focus on, a buffer.

I gather up all the bedding in my arms and take it to the other room. They stored the mattress in plastic, so I don't have to worry about it being inundated with dust mites, which is good.

I'm struggling to get the plastic off when Colten walks in.

"Here. Let me help."

Nooo. I want to scream. Small space—too much Colten. "Thanks," I reply, because what else can I say? No?

I glance at him while he helps me pull the plastic off. He's not even that good-looking, if you dissect his features. His eyes are . . . his nose is . . . *perfect.* I groan to myself. "So, have you always lived here?" I ask, wanting to distract myself from my thoughts.

"Yep."

"Did you always want to be a mechanic?"

"As soon as I knew what one was, yeah. I started tinkering

with machines when I was little. Totally pissed my parents off 'cause I was takin' everything apart to see how it worked."

I lift and throw open the fitted sheet.

"When I was around eleven, I started hoverin' over the mechanic that worked at our garage, a nice ol' man named John. He didn't mind me watching and started explaining everything as he worked." The flat sheet is next. "Over time, he let me do oil changes, replace spark plugs—the straightforward stuff. By the time I graduated, I could fix anything wrong with a vehicle. Then when he retired a year later, I took over the business."

We settle the comforter in place, and throw the pillows on top. "When did you graduate high school?" I ask.

"Couple of years back."

"Did your parents make a big fuss with photos and parties?"

"All of it. It was a hell of a good time. I'm sure yours rented out the country club."

I bark out a laugh. "Yeah . . . imagine my surprise when the ceremony was over, all the parents were congratulating their kids, and mine were MIA. I hadn't seen them earlier in the day, but assumed they were busy and would meet me there. I mean, what kind of parents forget about their child's graduation?"

"Oh." His face falls. There's sympathy there. "That sucks."

I'm sick of how pathetic I sound. Poor little rich girl. "It's fine." I flick a hand in the air, like I'm over it. "When I called my father, they were already on their way to Europe. I could tell he felt horrible. Obviously, the slight was all my mother's doing. She's vicious like that. Anyway, he asked what he could do to make it up to me. As a joke, I said he could buy me an Audi TT." I pause for effect, knowing his love of cars. "It was delivered to our building the next evening."

"Your boyfriend stole an Audi TT and you're not freakin' out?" His voice raises several octaves, making me laugh.

"It was a gift given out of guilt—a materialistic *thing* given to me with no more feeling than a stapler. It meant nothing."

"I know, but it's worth like sixty grand!"

"Closer to seventy-five. The dealer sticker was still on it when it was dropped off. It's not *my* money."

He runs a hand through his hair, looking slightly disgusted. "We come from different worlds, Tess."

He keeps reminding me of that. I understand, though. People have mixed attitudes about the wealthy. "I'm not being bratty or ungrateful. You need to understand what it's like growing up the way I did. Money was in abundance. It didn't have value. I would have traded all of it to have a loving family like yours."

"Still. I'd be shittin' bricks—a car like that, just gone."

I shrug, for lack of a better response. It's hard for him to grasp, since, as he said, "his life is very different from mine."

We pack up all the supplies by the front door, then I follow Colten's lead as he flops down on the couch. It feels good to let my body melt into the comfort. I've been tense since Dax left. I hear myself sigh.

"So, what do you plan on studying at that fancy school of yours?" he asks.

"It's not fancy."

"It's expensive."

I roll my eyes. "Not everything is about money," I say. He shrugs a shoulder and makes a face like, *If you say so.* "I'm getting my degree in business management."

"But you said you love art. Shouldn't you be majoring in that?"

"My father wants me in business. Since I'm an only child, he expects me to move up in his company and take over one day —as if I'd ever want to be the CEO of Van Buren Incorporated."

"It's your life, Tess, not his. You're the one who has to live with your choice. You should do what makes you happy."

"He's paying for college."

"It's your life," he repeats.

"He'd say an art degree is useless, that with my intelligence I should be something that's a bit more . . . profitable."

"You said, 'He'd say it was useless,' not, 'He says.' You've never talked to him about it?"

"He's made his intentions clear and I don't like confrontation."

Wait a minute. But I've been confrontational since . . . My mind whirls and suddenly reality hits.

For the longest time, I was afraid if I defied him, he wouldn't love me anymore. The truth is, nothing changed when I rebelled. Defiant or obedient, it didn't matter. He was indifferent. So why am I still trying to please him?

Because you never know? Maybe I've misjudged him? There might still be hope?

Yeah right. Still, if I don't do what he wants, he might not pay for school.

"Why not double major in business *and* art? Wouldn't the management component be useful if you want to own your own gallery?"

"Oh." I blink, a little dazed by the suggestion. My father

would never know if I added the extra major. If he ever asked about my classes, I could just tell him about the business ones. My insides are jumping at the possibility. *I could kiss you!* "That's brilliant."

"There. Problem solved." His smile is big and bright. "You should talk to my mom. She has a degree in fine arts from Berkeley."

My eyes go wide. "How did she end up *here*?"

"Don't look so surprised. It's not like we're back-country inbreds."

"That's *not* what I meant. It's just . . . *Berkeley*. I mean, wow!"

He narrows his eyes slightly. "And now she's living in some podunk town in North Carolina workin' as a waitress in a gas station and displaying her wares on a gift shop shelf?"

I can't tell if he's offended or just being sarcastic. "Quit making me sound like a snob." I guess I've been doing it to myself all night.

He laughs and says, "I'm just givin' you a hard time. They claim it was love at first sight. My dad was going to culinary school to become a chef and had big aspirations, but his father became terminally ill and he had to come back to take care of him—help run the gas station and all. After he passed away, my dad didn't feel right abandoning somethin' that's been in the family for generations, so he renovated the building and opened the diner. Mom grew up in California, but when she came here to visit—as she tells it—she never wanted to leave."

"Sounds like it worked out for them."

"Yeah." We stare at each other for an awkward silence. Well, maybe just awkward for me. I've always hated lulls in conversations, and the fact that he turns my brain to mush, well . . .

"Is Tess your full name, or is it short for something?"

"Contessa."

"*Hmmm.* Contessa Van Buren. Sounds regal."

"Yeah. My mother's a social piranha. To her, it was befitting to someone of our 'class.' For obvious reasons, I shortened it. It pissed her off, so the change was a double positive."

Colten looks around. "We did a damn good job."

I smile, following his gaze. "We did."

"Not exactly what you're used to."

"It's perfect."

And it is. Every nook and cranny, because it's mine—well, temporarily. And this family that jokes around, respects and loves each other . . . is loyal. I feel like I've walked into another dimension. It's something I've never experienced before, and I'd like to be a part of.

We turn toward the sound of steps coming up the stairs.

"Josie?" Colten looks perplexed.

We both stand when the door opens and his mother walks in.

"Hi." She hands me a little bag. "Toothbrush, toothpaste, floss, and a little bottle of shampoo. We have a small necessities area in the gift shop."

"Awesome. Thank you." I hadn't thought of the things I would need.

"No problem. I'm going to get back down there so we can get home before ten."

"Thanks, Twyla. For everything. You and your family have gone above and beyond."

"I'm glad we could help. Are you about done here, Colten? Josie is itching to leave."

"We're done. I'll get the cleaning stuff and be down in five."

"Okay. I'll let her know. See you tomorrow, Tess. Just come down in the morning and I'll show you what's what."

"Sounds good."

After she leaves, I help Colten gather up the supplies.

"Well, if you don't need anythin' else, I think I'll grab Josie and get on home."

"No. I'm good." I walk him to the door. "Thanks for all your help. And for the conversation." Even feeling exposed, I enjoyed talking to him.

He turns in the open doorway, hand on the knob. "No problem. And as bad as it sounds, I'm glad you were abandoned here."

My mood brightens at the compliment. I laugh. "Thanks."

He nods. "Have a good sleep. See you tomorrow. Make sure you lock the door behind me."

"I will. Goodnight."

"Night." He shuts the door behind him, and I turn the deadbolt.

I look at my cute little apartment. Yep, all mine. I head to the bathroom with my toothbrush and toothpaste. I'm going to need some other necessities. I can't wash my face with that bar of soap that looks like it's been here since Twyla and Earl moved out. I brush and floss, wash out my underwear with the hopes it will be dry by morning, then fall into the comfy bed and listen as rain begins to tap against the window. There's a sudden crack of thunder followed by a long, drawn-out rumble.

Talk about your crazy days. It started out being the worst,

and then not so bad. And Colten . . . It would be nice if I could stick around and get to know him better *and* give him more time to know me. I didn't exactly show off my best self today.

I turn on my side and scrunch the pillow under my head. Well, we'll see how things work out at the diner. At least we have tomorrow—and one day can change everything.

CHAPTER 6

BETWEEN THE HUMIDITY, the poor-quality shampoo, no conditioner, and the ancient-looking hair dryer I dug out of a box, my usually silky-smooth waves now look like yarn—or worse, twine. I put on my clothes from yesterday. I can't imagine shorts and a T-shirt with flip-flops are appropriate to waitress in, but what other choice do I have?

I look at my reflection in the mirror. I've always been told I was cute, or attractive, even pretty. Though I've never felt that way, and without makeup, even less so. When you've been passively insulted by your mother your whole life, your self-esteem takes a nosedive. Whatever—time to get going. I pull my hair back into a ponytail and head down to the diner.

The humidity is stifling as I open the door.

"Well, look who finally woke up," Twyla says, standing next to the cash register with a hand mounted on her hip and a twitchy grin. Josie's giggling from behind the counter.

I feel a slight rise in panic. "What time is it? There wasn't a clock, but I've never been a late sleeper."

"Close to one," Twyla says.

"*Crap!* I'm so sorry," I rush out. My first day on the job and I'm ridiculously late.

"It's fine, honey. I'm just giving you a hard time. Yesterday was an eventful day. I'm sure you were worn out. Let's get you some food."

"No, it's okay. I'm late. I should get started."

"Food first." She points to an empty stool. "Sit."

Several customers at the counter are watching our interaction. I give them a shy smile as I climb onto the stool.

"Do you want breakfast or lunch?" Earl asks, leaning his head out through the expo window, smiling.

"Hey, Earl. Just some scrambled eggs and toast would be great."

He raises his spatula. "On it."

"Do you want coffee?" Josie asks.

"Please."

She fills a mug and places it in front of me. I sigh at the heavenly aroma. "I know," she says. "Wait until you taste it. Dad roasts the beans himself. Do you want cream?"

"Aren't you a little young to be drinking coffee?"

"Who says I'm drinking it?"

"How else would you know how it tastes?"

"Inductive reasoning. People order coffee and get lots of refills. Sometimes they *only* order coffee. If the people drink the coffee, then come back and order more coffee, they must be coming here for the coffee."

I look over at Twyla, who rolls her eyes. "They could be coming for the food and really need a caffeine hit." *Smarty pants*.

"That's why it's inductive reasoning, not deductive—make an observation, discern a pattern, make a generalization, and infer an explanation or theory."

I say, "Uh, yeah. I'll take the cream." How old is this girl again?

"*And* it smells amazing. Sugar's right in front of you."

"Thanks. How old are you?"

"Twelve. Well, almost."

Her answer surprises me. I really thought she was around nine.

"I know. I'm small for my age." She taps a spot over her heart. "I was born with a congenital heart defect, so I didn't grow like I should have. I had surgery when I was four, so I'm good now." She walks the length of the counter, then back again, setting a dish filled with tiny containers of half and half in front of me. "And if you start lookin' at me like I'm gonna break or something . . ." She fists a hand on her hip, looking so much like her mother. "Then you and I are going to have words."

My eyebrows shoot up. "Yes, ma'am."

I take a sip of my coffee.

Heaven.

When I'm done eating, Twyla takes me to the back room. "I know you don't have any clothes but the ones you came in, so . . ." She lifts a bulging black garbage bag. "I reached out to a friend of mine whose daughter is about your size. I remembered they were cleaning out her closet last weekend. She just graduated college and is moving to Charlotte to start her new job."

"You work fast." This is great. I hope something will fit.

"I knew you needed clothes to work in, so I called her this morning, and she happily dropped them off. Saved her a trip to the Salvation Army in Raleigh."

"That was extremely generous. Tell her thank you."

"I'll do that. You go ahead and change, then come find me."

"Is it okay if I use the bathroom here? It'll save me time not having to go all the way upstairs again."

"You bet."

I open the bag, rummage through, and pull out a plain green T-shirt. There are three pairs of jeans. I take all three in case one doesn't fit. Then I see the Converse sneakers. I look at the inside of the tongue to check the size. They're a little big, but they'll work.

"Are you ready?" Twyla is behind the counter, filling a glass with water, when I come out dressed in my new clothes.

"Yep. The coffee is kicking in and my brain is ready to learn. I could use a belt, though." I pull out the waist of the jeans, demonstrating how big they are.

"I brought one."

"You think of everything, don't you?"

"Parent of two and a full-time job? You get so you think in advance. Be right back."

She disappears into the office, then comes back, handing me a black belt. I loop the belt through, tuck in my shirt, and cinch the belt tight. The shirt is clingy, and the jeans are high-waisted, so it works.

"I decided there's no reason to fully train you in case you want to head back home after today. So if you could just fill water and coffee, clear tables, wipe them down and reset them, that should square things up for us with the gas and food from yesterday. I saw you got a crash course on the essentials last night from Josie."

"I did."

"Let me show you how the coffee machine works. Around here, we change the pot every twenty minutes. I hate stale coffee." She taps the stainless-steel counter of the expo window. "If you see food up here, take it to the table right away. We want to get it out hot. Earl can tell you what table it is supposed to go to if I'm not around. Any questions?"

"No. I think I got it."

I survived my first shift—barely. Twyla was right; it's way harder than it looks.

It started slow and easy, but when the dinner rush hit, I felt like I was spinning in circles. People who say tipping a waitress is excessive are full of shit. I'd like to see them try to do this job. I feel like I got my ass kicked and my feet are killing me.

Colten passed through at some point in the day and made a sarcastic comment about my hair. I had no idea what he was talking about until I finally made it to the bathroom—my reflection was horrifying, my hair sprouting every which way. After my hair tie broke an hour into my shift, I used a rubber band I found in the cash register, which obviously wasn't strong enough to hold my hair. I wish someone would have mentioned something earlier.

Colten and I sit side by side eating a late dinner. I must be dead tired if his nearness doesn't faze me. "Where did Josie go?" I ask. "I haven't seen her since this afternoon."

"Went to a friend's house. She'll stay the night, which is

good. I won't have to drive her home and I can catch up on some things, plus an emergency came in."

"A car emergency?" I laugh as though it's the funniest thing I've ever heard. Colten stares at me with an amused grin, like I've lost my mind. I think my brain's gone squirrely.

"Yeah. Sally-Anne drove up in a frenzy about an hour ago. The van she uses for her mobile dog grooming business started makin' a loud clunkin' noise. Sounds like the suspension needs work from what she was explaining. I told her I'd get it fixed tonight so she can pick it up for work first thing in the morning."

"That's nice of you."

"No biggie. She's a nice lady. Well, I better get at it." He stands up with his already empty plate. "See you in a bit."

I give him a thumbs up and take another bite of tonight's gourmet mac and cheese special.

The rest of the evening is easy, mostly catch-up stuff—dishes, filling salt and pepper shakers, rolling silverware, stuff like that. By around nine, I can barely keep my eyes open.

"We're all good here," Twyla says to me, handing over a small wad of cash pinned with a paperclip.

I leave the rag I was cleaning with on the table and take it. "What's this for?"

"Your tip money."

"Oh, but I—"

"Earned every penny. Between helping yesterday and today, you more than paid off the gas and food." She taps the bills with her fingers. "That's what you earned over and above."

I stare at the money clutched in my hand. "Wow. Thank you." I feel somewhere between elation and tears—elation at having paid them back, and tears because, though it isn't much, the money is mine, not my parents'—my first step in releasing myself from their hold. If it was up to me, I would never want to see either of them again. Other than financial support, they serve no purpose other than to make me feel shitty about myself.

"So. What do you think? You want to work here for the summer?"

"If you're offering me the job, then yes." I almost don't care that Dax took off with my car. I'm making money, and I get to spend more time with this family.

"Just one question. Colten says you come from money. Why not go home and enjoy the summer?"

"I like it here." Is the short answer. I don't want to get into the details about my mother, the loneliness, or how the few semi-friends I have are already gone, traveling. Here I feel like I'm part of something bright, happy, and unique. Well, unique to me, anyway.

"All right then. Tomorrow, I'll teach you the rest of what you need to know. In the meantime, I'll talk to Earl and figure out compensation details."

"Thank you." I feel lighter than I have in forever—exhausted, but lighter.

"Well. You look dead on your feet. Why don't you call it a day?"

I yawn openly, then cover my mouth when I realize it's gaping open. "Okay. What time do you want me tomorrow?"

"Ten works. I'll take you through the rest of what you need

to know before it gets too crazy. Come get breakfast whenever you want, okay?"

"Perfect." I yawn again.

"Oh, and hold on a minute." She goes into the back and comes out with an alarm clock. "I found it under a bunch of stuff in the bottom drawer of the desk. It works. I checked."

I thank her and head outside. Now I'm standing at the bottom of the stairs, staring at all the steps that lead up to my place. I'm not sure what there is to contemplate. I need to go up. Simple.

But there are so many of them. I whine to myself.

Deciding I'm too tired to make the climb just yet, I sit on the bottom step and set the alarm clock by my side. It's dark out. I look up at the stars twinkling overhead and sigh, content to be sitting down. I fold my arms on top of my knees and rest my forehead against them. I just need a minute.

"Hey." I feel someone nudging me. "Hey, wake up, sleepyhead."

"Go away," I grumble, briefly registering Colten's voice and wondering why he's in my room.

I feel myself being lifted, then cradled against a broad chest. That's weird. I snuggle in, deciding I like this dream.

A warm feeling of safety and contentment washes over me. I'm not sure I want to wake up—ever.

CHAPTER 7

I STARTLE at the bright sunlight shining on my face and sit up quickly, confused by my surroundings. When I finally clue in, I groan, still exhausted, and flop back on the pillow. I ache everywhere.

An alarm goes off. I look over at the clock that's making a horrid rhythmic sound on the nightstand. Nine-thirty. Crap! I jump out of bed. I've only got thirty minutes to shower and eat before my shift starts.

Why am I dressed?

I try to remember on my way to the bathroom. My bladder is going to explode. When I finish in the bathroom, I get a glass of water from the kitchen.

I don't remember getting into bed last night or setting up the alarm clock. After chugging the water on my way back to my room, I rummage through the bag of clothes. I must have been drained to the point of being brain dead.

I jump in the shower but can't wash my hair because it's all tangled in the rubber band I fell asleep in. I do my best to rearrange it, grab my key, and run down the stairs.

"I'm so sorry," I say, entering the diner in a frenzy.

"Whoa, take a breath," Twyla says. "And you're right on time. Hey, Colten told me he had to carry you up to bed last night. Honey, you fell asleep at the base of the stairs. This town is safe, but still . . ."

A memory floats through my mind until it becomes solid. "*Ugh.*" I hang my head. "I thought it was a dream. How embarrassing." Colten must have set up the alarm clock. I can't believe I slept through all that.

"*Pfff.*" She waves me off. "Don't worry about it. You were spent. Let's get you something to eat, and then we'll go through the rest of what you need to know."

I'm about to argue that I don't have time to eat, but I know she won't accept it, so I sit at the counter. I'll just get something quick.

"Mornin', sunshine," Earl says from his usual location. "What'll you have?"

"Just some toast, please."

"Come on, kiddo. Give me something more challenging. Belgian waffles with a drizzle of blueberry compote, a dollop of whip cream."

My eyes narrow as the corner of my mouth lifts in a playful smile. "That's not on the menu."

"No, but someday it could be. I need to keep my skills sharp." He winks.

"Sorry. Can't help you. I prefer to keep it simple in the morning. Besides, I need time to savor something that delectable."

"Delectable. I like that. Okay, fine." He waves his spatula over his head. "Another boring breakfast comin' up. But not just toast. You need sustenance for energy."

"What the heck happened to your hair?" Josie comes up next to me with a horrified expression.

"*Josie*," Twyla admonishes, rushing past with an armload of plates. How does she balance that many at once?

I reach up and feel my hair. "I fell asleep with the rubber band in and couldn't get it out, so I did the best I could. It's the first-ever messier messy bun."

Josie looks skeptical. "Uh-huh."

"Come here, baby." Twyla gives me a *tsk, tsk* on her way back from delivering the food. "Let me get the scissors."

"No way." I hold on to my hair protectively.

Her loud laugh is quick. "I'm not going to cut your hair, just the rubber band. Let me just take this water out and I'll take care of it."

When she comes back, Josie and I follow her to the office and I watch warily as she opens a desk drawer and pulls out the largest pair of scissors I've ever seen.

My eyes go wide. "*O-kay?*"

"Don't worry. I've had to do this plenty of times for Josie. Speaking of . . ." She turns to her daughter. "Will you keep an eye on things for a second?"

"On it." And she's gone in a flurry of energy.

"I'm not sure if I've *ever* been that energetic," I say.

"I know what you mean. She keeps us going, that's for sure."

With a couple of snips, my hair releases and falls to the middle of my back. I run my fingers through it as best I can, finishing with a heavenly scrub on the scalp. It's been pulling uncomfortably since I woke up.

"Here, let me get my brush." Twyla reaches for her purse.

She starts from the bottom, slowly getting rid of the knots in my hair. Every stroke is a gentle pull, followed by her hand sliding down my hair. I feel like a stray dog—grateful for the simple affection. I try to imagine my mother doing this, but I can't. Not in a million years would this happen.

Twyla finishes by pulling my hair back into a ponytail, my head tugging back slightly with each twist of the tie. "I found one of Josie's hair ties in with the brush."

"Thank you." I'm sure my hair is a frizzy mess, but oh well. Better than it was.

"I'll bring you some better hair products tomorrow."

"It's okay. I'll get some stuff in town after work." I'm sure they have a salon. How much is that stuff, anyway? Maybe I should stick with a decent grocery-store brand.

She puts the brush back and stows her purse in the desk drawer.

"Twyla?"

"*Hmm?*" She turns, facing me.

"How do you do this all by yourself? The waitressing, I mean. It's . . . hectic."

"I don't know. I just do. And Josie helps when she's around."

"Did you have help when the kids were little?"

She laughs. "Nope. I carried Colten in a front pack, later a backpack, and did the same when Josie came along."

"My hero."

She laughs. "Hardly. I'm not the first woman to do it all, and

I won't be the last. So, Tess . . . Earl and I had a talk last night. How about your hourly wage going toward food and rent? You can keep your tips, obviously. Lunch shifts are when I need the most help, and a couple of dinner shifts would be great."

"I'll work whatever you want. I've got nothing else to do."

"All right. We'll start with that and see how it goes. If Earl and I feel you're working more than your living expenses, we'll pay you in cash. Sound fair?"

"More than fair."

"Don't tell anyone I said this, but I'm grateful for the help. I don't have the energy the way I used to. I'm tired."

"Why haven't you hired someone?"

"Most people want full-time work, and it would be costly for us. You being here this way works out perfectly."

The simple praise has me beaming.

Today, Twyla has me working the counter, which is fine with me. It's easier to juggle five people individually than the possible six per booth. I do okay and by the end, I'm feeling more confident than yesterday.

After the lunch rush subsides, Twyla hands me two plates of food. "Here. Take this to Colten. I haven't seen him yet. He's got to be starving. You two can eat together."

I give her a look like, *Come on. Don't make me do this.*

"Oh, go ahead. So he carried you up and put you to bed . . . big deal." She turns me around and gives me a push in the garage's direction.

I carefully balance the two plates in one hand while I turn the doorknob, then push the door open with my hip. A country song plays in the background. I've never been a fan of country, but it seems to be the music of choice around here.

The garage is nothing like I expected. The walls are covered with vertical planks of aged barn wood. Old-fashioned metal signs are hanging all over, advertising everything from Coke to cigarettes to oil. A red and white antique gas pump sits in a corner. Next to it is a round high-top table with black vinyl and chrome stools. The cement floor is clean and painted red.

Colten hasn't heard me come in. He's in his coveralls, his face hidden as he stands under a car hoisted on a lift.

"Hey." The word sounds bashful and foreign coming out of my mouth. I stopped being shy around fifteen, when I realized I couldn't change what people thought of me and stopped caring.

Thanks Mom.

Well, I *do* care. I just don't have the energy to change it, even if I could.

He ducks his head out from under the car and says, "Hey." He pulls the rag out of his back pocket and wipes his hands while eyeing the food.

"Your mom had me bring lunch for you." An alt-rock song begins to play. Thankfully, he has a more diverse taste in music than I thought.

"I don't think I'm hungry enough for two platefuls."

I smile and laugh. "One's for me."

"Glad for the company. I'll clear a spot." He moves stacks of catalogues off the high-top and points to one of the two stools. "Have a seat."

I should just get the embarrassment of what happened last night out of the way. "Thanks for getting me up to the apartment last night."

He chuckles as he takes his seat across from me. "You were so cute, folded into a tiny ball at the bottom of the stairs."

The compliment has my stomach fluttering and my adrenaline pumping.

He called me cute. He thinks I'm cute.

You've been called that before.

But not by him!

"I'm glad I found you," Colten continues. "The wind kicked up and trash blew out of the can at the end of the building. I was picking it all up when I saw you." He smiles, lifting the tinfoil off his plate. "*Mmm*, it smells good. I'm starving. Thanks for bringing this over."

"Sure." I stare at the plate in front of me. "No problem." I'm not sure I can eat. My mouth has gone dry. "I'm going to run and get us water." I jump off the stool.

"No need. There are water bottles in the mini fridge over there." He points to a red, vintage-looking refrigerator with a Coca-Cola logo on the front.

I grab two bottles, sit back down, and quickly forget my nervousness when I see what's for lunch and my mouth waters. Chicken wraps with avocado, bean sprouts, and . . . cream cheese? I think there are cranberries in there as well. Next to my wrap is potato salad, kettle-cooked chips, and slices of garlic pickles.

"How are you not overweight, eating like this all the time?" I ask him.

"I'm a busy guy. Plus, I work out and run most mornings before work."

"I miss running." I'd get up at the crack of dawn and run in

Central Park. "Flip-flops and Converse will not cut it for footwear."

"Maybe Mom has some you could use. You should ask her."

"Yeah. I could do that, but I have small feet."

Colten looks down. "Oh, yeah. No, that won't work."

"How did Sally-Anne's car go? Did you get it fixed?"

He holds up a finger, chews, and swallows. "Finished last night, right before I found you."

My cheeks flush at the vague memory of snuggling against his chest. *Damn.* I look away and let my eyes roam around the room. "Your mom did a great job with this space."

"I'm glad you like it, but this was all me. Hey, you know, if Mom is working you too hard, just let her know."

Why would she be working me too hard?

Oh, because I'm not used to working.

I open my mouth to respond to the insult, then snap it shut. "Whatever." I bite down hard on a pickle and focus on my plate while I chew.

"Hey. I didn't mean anything."

I shoot him a blank stare. "The insinuation was there."

"And what would that be?" He crosses his arms over his chest and tilts his head, regarding me.

"That I'm lazy, spoiled, and have nothing to add to society."

"Wow, you got all that from one little comment?" The corner of his mouth edges up slightly as he picks up his fork.

Crunch. I take another bite of my pickle, his smile pissing me off. There's nothing amusing about this.

"Tess, what's going on?" His easy smile disappears. "You're far from lazy. If you were, Mom wouldn't consider keeping you on. Spoiled—from what I've seen—no way. And as far as adding nothing to society, where the hell did you get *that* from?"

My first night here when you were judging me. My mother's constant reminder.

"Never mind. Just forget it."

"No. You seem to be accusing me of something."

"Sorry. It's just you throw my upbringing in my face whenever you get the opportunity. I don't appreciate people assuming that because my family has money that I'm a rich, spoiled brat."

"I don't think that, and if I made you feel that way, then I'm the one that's sorry. All I meant was that my mother has one speed and not many can keep up with her, and if it's too much, let her know."

Crap. I'm cranky from not getting enough sleep and overreacted. "I should go." I start to cover up my unfinished food with the tinfoil.

"No. Stay and finish." He grips my hand and squeezes. "It's fine. You've had an intense couple of days. You're allowed to be on edge."

I give a little smile. "Thanks." I appreciate the understanding, but I still think I should go before I make things worse.

"Mom said you're not working the dinner shift today. Do you wanna come into town with me in a bit? You haven't seen it yet."

"Oh, uh, sure. That'd be great. I need to grab a few things." Like underwear, if I can find some. "But don't you have to work?"

"I can take a break. I'm the boss." He shoots me a grin.

"Josie's at a friend's, so I don't need to worry about getting her home."

"Right. She left shortly after I got here. It's nice that you look after her the way you do."

"We do what we need to do." He shakes his head. "That came out wrong. I meant that we all pitch in."

His family is an enigma to me, but then again, I've never had good role models. Well, other than Maria. "Did you ever mind?"

He frowns. "Why would I?"

"I think a lot of teenagers would be resentful of having to pitch in so much."

"Not me."

"Huh." I sit back on my stool.

He looks amused. "What?"

"I'm impressed. Do any of you ever argue, get angry, fight? Your family just seems so . . . perfect."

"No one's perfect. Josie can get moody at times, and she's a know-it-all. She'd probably say I was a slob and on the stubborn side. We're not robots, Tess. We have flaws."

"Good," I joke. "I was beginning to wonder."

He rolls his eyes.

"Do you live nearby?" I take another bite of my wrap.

"We have a house on the other side of town. I'm sure Mom or Dad will invite you to dinner at some point. We close up shop on Sundays around two and Dad really goes all out on the menu."

"So, you still live with your parents?"

"Now who's judging?"

"I'm not." Isn't he like twenty?

"Yes, you are. I live at home because it's easier for me to get Josie where she needs to go. My parents are at the diner at an ungodly hour and work late. Their house isn't super close to town, and I couldn't afford a place on the lake. It's convenient for both of us. We've talked about building an extra garage with an apartment over top, but none of us have had the time. I suppose we could hire someone to build it, but it's hard to pay someone when we can do a lot of it ourselves."

"You're all multi-talented."

"I suppose we all are."

I take my last bite, gather all the debris from lunch, and stack the lunch plates. "Well, I better let you get back to work."

"Yeah. I need another hour here. Does that work for you?"

"*Mmm-hmm.* That'll give me a chance to shower and change." I feel kind of gross after work. You wouldn't expect to get a sweat on, but you do. I stand up with the plates. "What are you working on?"

"Exhaust system has some big-ass holes. I'm replacing a few parts."

He grabs some things off his workbench and works his way under the car again while I make my way to the door.

"I'll see you in an hour? At your place?" Colten's voice is muffled, the sounds insulated by the car.

"Sounds good," I answer to nothing but legs and hips.

At my place. What a novelty.

I set the dishes on the dishwasher rack, help Twyla for another thirty minutes to kill time, then head upstairs to rinse my body and change into some shorts and a tank top from my goody-bag of clothes.

I wonder if Dax made it back home yet. I'll have to ask

Twyla if I can use her phone. I don't want our doorman calling my father when the car shows up without me. Would he even worry, or just think I was being irresponsible and ignore it? Twyla lets me use her cell phone with only a brief explanation, which I appreciate. I Google the name of our building and eventually get connected with the doorman. Chester tells me the car isn't back. I explain I will be out of town for the summer and ask if he could get the car to my parking stall when it's dropped off. He says it'll be no problem and tells me to enjoy my summer. That should keep any suspicions from being aroused.

CHAPTER 8

COLTEN WALKS in front of me on a well-worn path of gravel and weeds. He's in shorts and a light-blue T-shirt that pulls tight against his back and shoulders, his long legs making it hard to keep up.

"You okay back there?" he says over his shoulder.

"Yeah." It was pointless to shower. The heated humidity had my clothes sticking almost the moment I walked out the door, and trying to keep up with daddy-long-legs isn't helping.

I can see the town off in the distance. It's not far, but with this heat, taking a car with air-conditioning would have been nice.

"You don't have to walk behind me." He slows his step so I can catch up.

To the left of the path is a cornfield, and on the right is the main road. Even with our bodies pushed to the edges of the walkway, his arm is close to my shoulder when I come up alongside him. The nearness makes me self-conscious, or nervous. I don't know, maybe both—not that it's anything new when it comes to him.

"I've been thinking a lot about our conversation that first night," he says.

"Okay." *Eesh. Which one?*

"Does your dad know your mother is abusive?"

That wasn't what I was expecting. I thought he'd fish for the details about our opulent lifestyle. "She's not abusive. She's just a bitch."

He stops, halting me along with him. "No, Tess. She's abusive—verbally, anyway, and neglectful. It's not right."

I stare into heated eyes. I'm nobody to him and he cares anyway. "Thank you."

He looks confused. "For what?"

"Getting angry at the unfairness." I take him in, the serious expression, the defensive stance. "It's in the past, but . . . thank you."

"Is it in the past?"

I shrug. "Mostly." I avoid her as much as I'm able.

"Why doesn't your dad do anything? Have you talked to him about it?"

"My father is oblivious—always working, half listening. I tried talking to him several times when I was younger, but he'd say things like, 'I'm sure you just misunderstood,' or, 'Are you sure you heard that right? I'm sure she didn't mean it that way.' I discovered it was easier to stay out of my mother's way." I laugh, thinking back to when I was little, glued to her side. "I was the neediest child alive."

"You weren't needy. You were deprived."

It's weird to hear someone I barely know articulate my life

so accurately. Colten walks again. As I move with him, I watch the waist-high field of green ripple in waves as a gentle wind blows. "I was daddy's little girl in the beginning." A memory floats through my mind of me crawling onto his lap, him holding me tight.

"As I got older, he got busier and didn't know how to communicate when I started having thoughts and opinions of my own. He grew distant. So I tried harder. I was polite and engaging. I kept my grades up, stayed out of trouble. It's amazing what a kid will do for a few crumbs of affection." It's sad, really. "Then when everything happened with Maria, I stopped caring, mostly."

He stops, takes my hand, and tugs me into his arms. There's a moment of shock before my hands slide around his waist, gripping them at his back and holding on tight. It's been so long since I've been held for comfort. Dax wasn't an affectionate person.

"Seemed like you needed a hug," he says, as if I'm questioning his gesture.

I laugh against his chest, my heart pounding at the nearness. "Always." I'm in awe of this guy I met only days ago. With a simple gesture he's made me feel lighter, hopeful—for what, I don't know—happy. Maybe, someday, we can be more than friends.

He clears his throat, releasing me. I reluctantly follow his lead and let my arms drop. We begin walking again, the gravel crunching loudly beneath our feet in the silence.

"I've always had affectionate, caring parents. I took it for granted," he says, sounding contemplative.

"*Most* people take what they have for granted. It's human

nature." I think back to what Josie said about her heart, and I wonder if her health issues created their family bond, or if it was always there. "There's a big age difference between you and your sister."

"Yeah. It took that long for my mother to get pregnant again. I think she'd resigned herself to only having one child and then, surprise! I'm not sure they wanted to start over so late in life, but how do you resent such a gift?"

I would have liked to have had a sibling. At the same time, I wouldn't want another person to be hurt the way I was. Who knows, maybe my mother would have treated a boy differently.

"What are your plans?" I ask. "Will you stay here for the rest of your life?"

"You make it sound like a death sentence."

"I didn't mean to. You could be a mechanic anywhere. I was just curious."

"I enjoy working for myself and being close to family. I wouldn't mind doing some traveling if it was feasible, which it isn't, especially when I've got the only garage in town."

Soon, we reach the edge of the main street that runs through town. A quick scan shows several businesses with quaint storefronts—a cross between a resort and a hometown vibe.

"So how many people live here? How does such a small town support itself?"

"Tourists. There's a big lake nearby—camping, boating, all that kind of stuff. It gets crazy busy this time of year."

I look around at the handful of people milling about, then send him a questioning look.

"It's a Tuesday, and early for people out on the lake to come into town for dinner."

"I just realized. I don't even know the name of the town."

"Jasper Creek."

We walk past an everything-kind-of-store. "Can you wait outside?" I ask. "I need to grab a few things."

"Why do I have to wait outside? It's hot."

"Girl stuff." No way I'm letting him hang around while I pick out underwear and other personal essentials.

"Got it." He fidgets like I've threatened him with cooties. "How about some ice cream?"

"*Ooh*, yeah! That sounds amazing."

"What kind should I get you?"

"I don't know. What do they have?"

"It's all homemade. They have the basics and some creative combinations. Give me a ballpark flavor."

"As long as the word 'chocolate' is involved, I'm happy."

"That's easy enough. It's just a couple of doors down—Bell's."

"Give me around ten minutes before you order, so it's not all melted when I get there."

"Will do."

A bell rings on the door as I enter the store, alerting a lady behind the counter. She says hello as I pick up a shopping basket and asks if there is anything she can help me find. I tell her thanks, but I'll just walk the aisles to find what I need.

I carefully add up the items I put into the basket as I go. I don't want to run short on cash at the register. I'm not a big spender, but I've also always had a credit card, paid for without question by my father.

The only underwear available in my size is a package of

high-waisted briefs—granny panties. *Eesh.* Oh well, it's not like anyone is going to be seeing them.

I'll have to stick with the bra I have for now. Between that and the sports bra I found in the Salvation Army bag, I should be good.

With a shopping bag in each hand, I pass a couple of cute boutiques—all out of my price range. I could call my dad and tell him I got my purse stolen, like I had originally planned. He'd have one mailed to me, but that's family money, and I want to make it on my own—at least until school starts.

CHAPTER 9

BELL'S IS SUPER CUTE—PINK-AND-WHITE-STRIPED wallpaper, black wrought-iron chairs around white marble-top tables. Colten's sitting on one of the chrome stools at a high countertop talking to a tall, husky redhead with corkscrew curls piled on top of her head.

"Here comes trouble," she jokes.

I chuckle half-heartedly, not thrilled at being teased by someone I've never met.

"Tess, this is Naomi. She was our neighborhood bully who kicked my ass regularly growing up."

Naomi leans over the counter and drills Colten in the arm. "Don't tell her that! I was *not* a bully."

"Ow! Really?" He rubs the sore spot, glaring at her. "You only stopped 'cause I got bigger than you."

She winks at me as I sit on the stool next to Colten. "Big or not, I can still take 'em. I just wouldn't want to insult his *manhood.*"

Uh, okay? I set my bags on the floor.

"Hit me again and see what happens," he challenges with a cocky grin.

Naomi smirks in return, then walks over to the frozen display case. She slides the door open, reaches in, then comes back, setting an already prepared bowl of chocolate ice cream in front of me, followed by a spoon. "So, I hear your boyfriend left you at the gas station." She crosses her arms over her chest, waiting for my response.

Damn, she's blunt. And I don't appreciate Colten gossiping about me. I fake a polite smile. "Yeah."

"That sucks."

"I guess."

"You're not very talkative," she says.

I struggle with aggressive people. They're unpredictable.

"She talks my ear off just fine," Colten says. "Quit scaring her," he adds, the words muffled around a mouthful.

"I'm fine." Although, I wish I could be anywhere else right now.

She leans forward and briefly touches my arm while sporting a big, toothy grin. "Don't mind me. My bark is a hell of a lot louder than my bite."

Colten scoffs. "Your bark is loud as shit."

Naomi gives Colten a tightlipped glare before she turns back to me. "What will you do now?"

"I'm working at Earl's Diner."

"Twyla hired you?" She looks taken aback. Colten must not have told her everything.

I nod my head. "I am." What's with this girl? I'm not roadkill.

"Good for her," she says. "She needs the help." Oh . . . okay.

"It's funny, though." She eyes me curiously. "Most people in your situation would be figuring out how to get home, and you've figured out a way to stay."

She's fishing for information, and I'm not about to give her any. I shrug a shoulder as I pick up my spoon. "*Mmmm*," I say as the flavor hits my tongue. "This is amazing." Truly. As in next level, fucking amazing. "What's in it?"

Naomi's face lights up at the compliment. "Thanks! I design the combinations myself. This one is chocolate ice cream with pecans, graham crackers, peanut butter chips, and toffee pieces."

I take another bite, shielding my mouth as I talk. "So good. What did you get, Colten?"

"Vanilla." The word rolls off Naomi's tongue with bitter distaste.

I look at him, dumbfounded. "Seriously? Vanilla?"

"What's wrong with vanilla?" His whiney tone says he's been hassled about it before.

"It's *boring*," Naomi and I say together. She laughs at our timing, whereas I only give a small smile.

"No, it's not," Colten says, looking insulted. "Taste." I barely have time to open my mouth before he shoves in a heaping spoonful.

"Cold." I wave a hand in front of my mouth. "Too cold." I roll the icy creaminess around my mouth, swallowing while fighting a brain freeze. "Okay fine. That's good too." I lick the excess ice cream off my lips.

"Real vanilla beans make *all* the difference." Colten's eyes linger on my lips as he speaks.

"Uh . . ." I stall out, lost in him watching me.

The pause has him shifting his eyes up to mine, then immediately to his bowl. "Yeah, it makes all the difference," he repeats and scoops another bite into his mouth, not taking his eyes from his ice cream.

Uh, yeah. It's uh . . . My brain stutters and trips over itself until I turn my focus back to the hunky chocolaty goodness in front of me.

"You know . . ." Naomi says, pausing until our attention shifts to her. "A person's taste in ice cream says a lot about them."

"You trying to say I'm plain and boring?" Colten gives her a stony glare.

Both her shoulders and eyebrows raise and lower. "I'm just saying."

"Man. All a guy wants is some ice cream and *shee-it*, I get psychoanalyzed."

Naomi leans over and back-hands him in the chest. "Don't be such a baby."

Colten jumps off the stool and bolts around the counter. Naomi squeals and takes off running in a fit of laughter to the back room.

These two are crazy. I lean over, trying to get a glimpse of the commotion, but I can't see anything. Loud crashes and bangs have me jumping off my stool, thinking that I better see what's going on.

I'm almost to the entrance when Naomi comes out laughing hysterically, her beautiful hair now a frizzed explosion, followed by Colten, sporting several red marks on his arms. She must have slapped the crap out of him.

"It looks like Naomi won," I say, laughing on the way back to my stool.

"It's all a matter of perspective." Colten lifts his chin and puffs his chest out as he walks toward me.

"Uh-huh." I turn to regard my ice cream intently. "Did I mention how good this ice cream is?"

"Perspective my ass," Naomi retorts, repositioning herself behind the counter. "I'd say you sustained more of the damage, as per usual."

He slides back onto his stool. "Yeah, well. I refuse to hit a girl."

"*Pfff.* You puss—"

Naomi's words are cut off when the door opens and a young couple comes in with a little girl.

"Hey, y'all." Naomi soothes her hair back, switching gears. "What can I get you?"

"Miss Nomi, I want chockwit." The little one bounces excitedly.

"Do you want a happy face on it?" Naomi gushes with affection.

"Can I, Mom, can I?" Her eyes lift, pleading.

"Sure, baby. Thanks, Naomi. She sure loves coming here."

"I'm glad to hear it," she replies. The little girl has her nose pressed to the glass as Naomi scoops the chocolate. "This enough?" she asks the little girl.

"More!" She claps.

"How 'bout this?"

"More, more, more!" She jumps up and down.

"I think that's enough," her dad says, putting his big hand on top of his daughter's head and messing up her hair.

"*Daaad,*" she drags out the word with exasperation.

I catch Naomi as she winks at the girl and adds the extra scoop. She turns her back on the family while she doctors the treat, then comes out from behind the counter and squats down to the child's level.

With adoring eyes, the little one looks up at Naomi, then at her treat. "It's so pwitty. Look, Mommy and Daddy, look." She holds it up so they can see.

I lean over so I can see as well. There's a small sugar cone for a hat, multicolored sprinkles for hair, blue gumdrops for eyes, a red candy for the nose, and chocolate chips arranged in a smile. Cool.

"That's super special, Maisie," the mom says.

The little one stares at it in awe while Naomi gets the parents' order and takes their money.

On their way out, Naomi says, "Y'all come back soon, ya hear?"

"Bye, Miss Nomi," the little girl calls back as she waves. "Thanu fo my happy face."

"You betcha, sweet thing." She waves back. "Next time I'll make you a dinosaur."

The little girl's eyes light up as she takes her dad's hand and starts squealing out words of excitement.

Naomi is not who I thought she was. I'm still not sure if I like her, but even with all her rudeness and rough edges, she seems to have a heart the size of Texas.

"Cutest little thing," she says when the door shuts behind them. "Hey, are y'all coming to the beach Friday night for the Fourth of July?"

"I guess," Colten says. "I hadn't given it much thought yet."

"You never make plans," she admonishes, then turns to me. "Most everyone is back from college and we're having us a BBQ and a bonfire before the fireworks. It's fun. You should come."

I didn't realize we were that close to the fourth. Dax and I left New York on a whim, and without my phone, I don't have a clue what day it is. I look at Colten, who's busy texting someone, so I tell her, "I don't know." I don't want him to feel obligated.

"I can pick you up if you need a ride," she offers.

"I can take her," Colten says before I can respond.

"It's okay," I say. "You don't have to." I'm sure he'd rather be with his friends.

He leans over, nudging me with his shoulder. "No trouble at all. Naomi, delicious as ever, but I need to get back to work."

We fight over who will pay. Naomi wins when she tells us to "fuck off," declaring it's on the house.

I sneak a five-dollar tip under my bowl while Colten talks to her about the party, then slide off the stool and pick up my bags.

"I'll see y'all on Friday then?" She smiles at us.

I nod and Colten gives her a thumbs-up.

I still find her intimidating, but I like her relationship with Colten. It's weirdly cool how they interact—two people who have grown up so close together—more like brother and sister than just friends.

A blast of hot, humid heat blasts me as we leave Bell's. "I swear it's even hotter than when we went in," I complain.

"Yeah. It's unusually hot for this time of year."

I walk next to him as we head back. "So, about this lake—how big is it?"

"About ten miles wide, thirty long."

"Does your family have a boat?"

"Yes, but we don't get out on it as much as we would like." He moves to take my bags.

"It's okay. I can carry them."

"I was raised better than that." He extends a hand, and I pass them over. What can I say? I appreciate the thoughtfulness. "So, where is your favorite place to travel? You mentioned trips with your parents."

We continue our walk, discussing my cherished locations and other random things. Then, before I know it, we're at the steps to my apartment and he's handing me my bags.

"Is there a grocery store nearby?" I need a few things like milk and snacks. I didn't want to get it at the general store and have the dairy sit out too long.

"Yeah. Not far. I can take you whenever. Just let me know."

"Thank you." I set my foot on the bottom step. "See you at dinner?"

"Yeah. If I'm not there when you're ready to eat, come find me."

He wants me to find him. "Okay." My smile is huge, I know, but I don't care. I climb a couple of steps.

"Tess?"

I turn at his voice, hoping for what? I don't know. "Yeah?" I look down at him. He doesn't have sunglasses on. His eyes— more green than blue today—stare up at me with an unreadable expression.

He grips the back of his neck and gives it a rub before dropping his hand and says, "Nothing. I'll see you later." He turns and disappears around the building before I have a chance to respond.

The cool air in the apartment smacks me with relief. I want to drop on the couch and let my body cool, but I'm thirsty. I fill a big glass with water and chug it while staring out the kitchen window.

What was Colten going to say?

Probably something about the BBQ, or maybe something about getting groceries? *Or*, that he wants us to have a burn-us-to-the-ground fling?

Yeah, right. I wish. I chuckle to myself.

Ugh! I feel like I'm twelve years old with my first crush. But I'm not, this is reality, and my life is a mess.

I turn and lean against the counter. There's no TV and I don't have my phone or computer. I need to find something to keep myself occupied between work and sleep. Walking to the back bedroom, I search through boxes, looking for books. I need something to take my mind from going where it wants to go and shouldn't. I find a book that looks interesting and curl up on the couch to read.

My stomach wakes me up sometime later, rumbling with hunger. I swing my legs over the edge of the couch and pick up the book I dropped when I drifted off. Looks as though the sun is close to setting. Wow, I slept a long time.

I check the clock in my bedroom. It's already seven. The dinner rush will be over. I feel bad bugging them for food, but they did say it was part of my wage. Maybe Twyla could use some help finishing up for the night.

I lock the door behind me and take in the warm breeze and the clean, earthy scents. The temperature has gone down a bit, which is a relief.

There are only two cars parked in front of the diner when I open the door.

"So shopping was a success?" Twyla passes me with a coffeepot in hand and tops up a customer's cup at the counter. "Were you able to get everything you needed?"

"I did. Thank you."

"You have a seat at the bar and tell Earl what you want. You must be starving."

"I am," I say, excited for Earl's cooking.

"You just missed Colten."

Disappointment sweeps over me as I sit down and wait for Earl to notice me. Twyla goes behind the counter and taps the metal ledge of the expo window as she passes.

Earl looks up suddenly, looking at Twyla, who nods her head in my direction. "Oh, hey there. What'll you have?"

"Surprise me." Anything he makes will border on ecstasy. He waves his spatula in the air like a call to arms and disappears.

"Did Colten take Josie home?" I ask Twyla. I'm curious. Maybe he had a date.

"Yeah, about thirty minutes ago. She had stuff to do for brain camp."

I'm pretty sure I give her a *what the fuck* look. "What's brain camp?"

Twyla leans against the counter, rag fisted at her hip. "Simple answer? Summer camp for exceptionally bright kids. It was her idea. She researched it online and presented it to us.

This will be her first year. I'm a little nervous about it. She's never been away from home this long."

"You all are so close. It's nice to see."

"Speaking of family, Colten told me a little about yours. I'm sorry, honey. It's not right. You deserve better."

"Thank you." My heart hurts and lifts all at once.

She squeezes my wrist affectionately. "Your parents? Don't know what they're missing, you hear me?"

I nod, tears burning the backs of my eyes when Earl says, "Order up!"

"Thanks, baby," Twyla says, reaching for the plate, then sets it in front of me. "I need to get back to it. Enjoy your meal."

I swallow hard, nod my head, and stare at my plate. "Thank you. I'm sure I will." I honestly didn't know people could be this nice.

In my periphery, I see Twyla shuffle through order tickets in her apron. She finds the one she wants and walks off. A customer must have looked like they were ready to leave.

I take a deep, shuddering breath, pick up my fork, and turn my attention to the grilled steak in front of me. If the world was filled with people like the Reed family, civilization would have a better chance of survival.

CHAPTER 10

COLTEN PICKS me up for the Fourth of July BBQ around five in an old, beat-up red truck. "I expected more from a mechanic," I tease, climbing in and buckling up.

"Sorry, princess. I left the Porsche at home."

Yeah, right. "Call me princess again and I'll smack you into next week." I hate being stereotyped. *Oh shit.* I can't believe I just told him I'd smack him.

"Little one, you couldn't hurt a flea," he says, looking over his shoulder as he backs out of the parking spot.

"Well, big things come in small packages." Well, that was a lame comeback.

"I suppose they do." He shoots me a quick grin, making my skin tingle, as he straightens out the wheel and drives out of the parking lot.

"I'm excited to see the lake. We used to stay at our cottage in the Hamptons on weekends when I was little. I've always loved the water."

That didn't sound conceited at all.

"Our lake isn't as grand as an ocean, but it's great on a hot summer day."

I'm surprised he didn't tease me about the extravagance. "What was it like growing up here?" I ask.

"The same as growing up anywhere, I guess."

"I grew up in a penthouse in one of the most densely populated cities in the world and went to a private school."

Just shut up, I scream at myself.

What is wrong with you?

I don't seem to have a filter today. Or maybe this is how I've always been, and I never noticed before.

He flashes me a smile. "Point taken. Well, everyone here knows everyone, so you couldn't get away with much. Having the lake so close meant doing lots of outdoor activities. I've had the same friends since kindergarten. We've never been rich, but always had everything we needed." He turns left at the end of town and we're now following a two-lane road with forest on either side.

"It's beautiful out here—so lush."

"We get lots of rain, and the humidity helps keep the green through the long hot summer."

I reach out the open window, letting my hand glide in waves through the wind. I'm grateful for the breeze. He doesn't have the air-conditioning on for some reason; either that, or it doesn't have it.

Five minutes later, Colten turns off the road at a sign that reads "Jumpin' Jack's Beach." The dirt road is bumpy with a continuation of the tall pine trees on either side.

"That's an interesting name," I say.

"What?"

"The name of the beach. There was a sign."

He looks in the rearview mirror. "Huh. Didn't notice it. Someone musta made it official."

A bump in the road sends us flying up out of our seats and has me grasping the door handle. "Bumpy," I say, laughing at the adrenaline pounding in my throat. "Is there a story behind the name?"

"Always. Stories are huge in the South." He flashes me a quick grin. "Apparently this guy, Jackson Wells—not the brightest bulb in the box—found some fool's gold at the edge of the lake and went a little crazy until someone clued him in. The name stuck. Not many tourists know about this beach. With a sign, that might change."

The road ends at a large open space. Colten pulls in next to several other vehicles and has my door open before I get my seatbelt off. I'm not used to the chivalrous behavior, but I don't mind it.

At the back of the truck, he lowers the tailgate as he slides on a ball cap. "Here." He hands me a pile of blankets and towels, then pulls out a cooler. "Follow me." He jerks his head toward a path with a hint of water sparkling in the distance.

As soon as we reach the sand, I kick off my flip-flops and lean down to pick them up, losing a couple of towels in the process. I gather them up and chase after Colten.

I'm surprised at how fine the sand is. I was expecting it to be rocky, more like dirt. Oh, *wow*. The water looks amazing—a refreshing cobalt blue. It's another hot day. I wish I had a bathing suit, but I had to settle on a fitted pink tank top and cutoff shorts.

Several people are milling around—I'd say close to forty of

them—and everyone looks to be around our age. Off to the left, there's an intense-looking volleyball game going on. To the right, a stocky guy with a long spatula is flipping burgers over a fire pit with a metal grate balanced on a border of rocks.

Colten picks a spot a little way back from all the people and sets the cooler down. "Perfect day," he says. "Mom made sure I packed the sunscreen for you." He hands it to me from his back pocket. "I know it's late afternoon, but your skin's light as an egg. You're bound to burn." He sets his sunglasses on top of his hat.

"An egg?" I set the load I'm carrying down and take the bottle from him, laughing. "That's what you think of when you look at my skin?" I laugh.

His eyes fall to the exposed area above my chest, then scroll up and over my face. I can feel my skin flush under his gaze. He seems to catch himself and looks down, reaching for a blanket. "That was the first white thing I could think of," he says.

Did we just have a moment?

"Here." I extend a hand. "Let me help with that."

I shake my head at myself. Just stop it. No moments, no more complications. Just friends.

"It's okay. I've got it. Just need one for now." He whips it up in the air and lets it billow down. "The others are for you if you get cold later. It can get chilly this early in the season after the sun sets." He still isn't looking at me.

Someone yells his name. We both turn to where the volleyball game is being played. "I'm getting my ass handed to me," one of the players says. "Get your gargantuan self over here!"

Colten holds up a finger, telling him to hold on a minute. "Do you mind?" he asks, still avoiding my eyes.

"Go. I'm good. You don't need to babysit me." But I sure appreciate him asking.

"You can bring a towel and sit on the sideline and watch, if you want."

I hold up the bottle still in my hand. "Maybe in a bit. I think I'll get this sunscreen on first." *And get my mind on something other than you.*

"Suit yourself." He takes off his beat-up, faded black ball cap that says Forza Motorsport on it and plunks it down on my head. "Extra protection. It's my favorite hat, so don't lose it."

I hand him the sunglasses still attached to his hat and work on adjusting it to fit. "I'll protect it with my life. What's Forza Motorsport?"

"Uh." He looks down, rubbing the back of his neck, looking embarrassed and cute as hell. "A video game. I used to play it a lot when I was a kid. My parents got me the hat for Christmas when I was twelve."

"Colten!" the guy yells again. "You comin' or what?"

"Yeah, just hold on a sec," he fires back, then says to me, "You're good?"

I settle his hat on my head, pulling my ponytail through the back slot. "Never better."

"Looks good on you." He grins. "All right. See you in a bit." He whips his shirt over his head and jogs over to the game while I sit here with my mouth hanging open.

Holy shit! His torso is bronzed like his legs—no farmer tan there—his abs are ripped, his chest built to perfection.

Sunscreen! Yep. Time to put on the sunscreen. Anything to distract me from my thoughts.

I sit on the blanket and begin lathering up my body. When I finish with my legs, I stretch them out in front of me and lean back on my hands while taking in the view of the lake. Dense forest surrounds the water with cutout sections for houses. Several boats dot the lake, making use of the beautiful day. It's beautiful out here.

Colten dives for the ball, keeping it in the air. Cheers erupt all around. I watch as people interact. Everyone is at ease with each other—the camaraderie forged at a young age seems so natural. It's organic, fluid. Another difference between Colten's upbringing and mine—the friendships. Mine are surface at best.

When I was young, I had scheduled playdates with hand-picked children deemed acceptable by my mother. Extracurricular activities were jammed into every vacant space of my time. By the time I got to high school, the friendships I had were borne from a shared dislike of our manicured rigidity —our bonds cemented by the need to break free. With Maria gone, and no one to monitor my actions, I did pretty much whatever I wanted. Not all my friends were in the same situation—their parents were protective and overbearing. The necessity for deception only added to the revelry. Weekends were usually spent at a house party or in any of Manhattan's many nightclubs—all of us had fake IDs.

I can't say I was ever close to any of those high school friends, not really. We were all damaged in one way or another and when our senior year ended, so did most of the friendships. There were many reasons—trust issues, jealousy, depression, drugs, alcohol addiction. I still talk to a couple of them, but those relationships are tenuous at best.

This isn't my town, and these aren't my people, but I feel more comfortable here than at any other time in my life. I feel I could easily belong. No one is looking over and judging me, wondering who I am or why I'm here.

"Hi," a soft voice says from above me.

I look up at a petite girl with long, straight, black hair pulled into a ponytail and eyes the color of coal. "Hey."

"You must be Tess. I saw you come with Colten. I'm Sri. I was so sorry to hear what happened to you." A similar sentiment to Naomi's, but with a completely different delivery. It makes all the difference.

I guess word gets around. "Thanks. Did you want to sit down?"

"Sure, thanks." Sri kicks off her flip-flops and sits on the blanket next to me, pulling her knees up to her chest. "Naomi said you are working at Earl's?"

"Yeah. I enjoy it there."

She nods. "They're nice people. And you're staying upstairs?"

There's a loud cheer, and I look over to see Colten high-fiving his teammate. "I am."

"That's awesome. I'm glad Twyla finally has some help."

"She works hard," I say. "I'm incredibly grateful for the job." *And Colten and his family saved my ass.*

We sit in silence for a bit and watch the game. She must know Colten well. I wonder what questions I could ask that wouldn't alert her to the fact that I'm into him.

Even though I shouldn't be.

"So, how long are you staying?"

"Hopefully for the summer."

She smiles at me. "You're a lot stronger than me. I'd be freaking out, calling the police, the feds, the National Guard. What did your parents say?"

I laugh. "It's a long story. And I think if I hadn't traveled as much as I have and been mostly on my own since I was sixteen, I would have been more freaked out. And Colten and his family have been great." I look over at him. He runs out of bounds, hitting the ball back to his teammate, who volleys it in time for Colten to run back and spike it down on the other side.

"Fair enough. I guess sometimes we find ourselves right where we need to be."

"Exactly!" I turn to her, smiling at her perspective. "They took me in without a second thought. Who does that these days? And Josie is adorable. She's like a thirty-year-old woman in a little girl's body."

"I know. I used to babysit her sometimes."

I wonder if Sri and Colten ever dated. "Are you in school?" I ask.

"Yeah. I just got back. Second year at Duke."

"Oh, yeah? What are you studying?"

"Pharmacy."

"How's it going, ladies?"

A scrawny-looking kid with bad acne parks himself next to me, holds out his hand, and says, "Chaz."

I have to stop myself from laughing as he gives me the *I'm-making-a-play-for-you* grin. "Tess." I shake his hand. Then he extends it to Sri, who takes it cautiously. He's obviously not a local.

"So, do you ladies live around—"

Naomi shoves him out of the way and takes his spot.

"Hey! Was that called for?" He stands up, brushing himself off.

"Yes," Naomi says. "It was." Chaz slinks off.

"That wasn't nice," Sri says.

It was awful. I feel bad for the kid.

"Trust me. He's been hassling every girl around here. He's relentless. I did you a favor." Naomi looks toward the fire pit. "Y'all hungry? I hear the burgers and hotdogs are ready. I'd get them now before they're all eaten or the gulls get 'em." She stands up and holds out a hand, pulling us up one at a time, never giving us a chance to respond.

I'm still not sure about Naomi. She's so—everything. Abrasive, loud, blunt, rude. I guess I'll have to wait and see.

We walk as a group toward a picnic table loaded with food.

"You can't leave in the middle of a game!" I hear someone shout.

I turn to see Colten running toward our blanket. "Food first," he yells over his shoulder. He stops in front of the cooler he brought and opens the lid. Taking out a large bowl, he heads our way. "Hey Sri. Glad to be done with school?" He sets the bowl on the table with the other food, peels off the wrapping and sticks a large spoon into the macaroni salad.

"Exceedingly glad. My brain was ready for a break."

"I find that hard to believe, coming from the smartest girl in school."

"We only had twenty-two kids in our graduating class. That's not saying much."

"That's it?" I pick up a paper plate and a hot dog bun. "Wow, such a small class."

Sri adds a hamburger to her bun and drops a hotdog into mine. "That was a record-high year, right, Colten?"

"Coulda been broken since we graduated. I haven't kept track."

I scoop macaroni salad onto my plate, then gesture at the bowl to Naomi, silently asking if she wants some.

"Sure," she says. Her plate dips slightly as I plop it on. "Thanks."

"Colten, who made the salad?" I ask.

"Dad. They're at their own party, visiting with friends. He made extra for me."

"Lucky us," Sri says. "His food is the best."

I nod in agreement and continue to load my plate. "I wish I had my running shoes so I could work off all this extra food I've been eating." I load my hotdog with onions, sauerkraut, ketchup, and mustard.

"What size shoe do you wear?" Naomi asks.

"Seven."

"I wear the same size," Sri says. "I have an extra pair you can use. I'll drop them by the diner."

"Really? That'd be great." Getting up early before the heat becomes unbearable isn't a problem. I used to do it all the time. I'm so excited I get to run again.

Our little group heads back to the blanket. Colten has me hold his plate while he lays out a second blanket. I'm ecstatic that he sits next to me, although it makes it hard to focus on eating.

"So, Dawson's missing another Fourth of July BBQ?" he asks Sri, leaning over me.

"Yeah." She blushes.

Who's Dawson? I wonder, but the conversation moves on.

I can feel the heat radiating from Colten's body, as if it isn't hot enough already. I glance over at his bare shoulder, then follow the line of muscle to his forearm, then to his hands. He has strong hands.

My study of his anatomy is interrupted when he lifts a forkful of food. I pick up my water bottle, needing something cold against my dry throat.

He jumps up. "I'm off to play."

I shield my eyes up at him. "You're done already?" I don't know why that's a surprise. He eats faster than anyone I've ever seen.

Colten gives me a playful smile. "I was hungry. Hey, y'all come over and cheer for me."

"Still eating." Naomi holds up her plate that's still half full. "We'll be over when we're done."

He gives a thumbs up and runs to the net.

"Colten's good," she says to me. "He could have easily played at a Division One college, but he had no interest in going."

"Uh-huh," I say, staring off in his direction, noticing the way his back tapers down to a narrow waist, and how his shorts hang just right over his perfect—

"Mechanics was—is—his thing," Naomi continues, "and there ain't nothin' school could've taught him he didn't know or couldn't have learned on his own."

"Uh-huh." I watch as Colten joins the game. He bunts the ball to his teammate, setting him up for the spike.

"So, you two seem to have gotten close in a short time." Naomi nudges me with her shoulder, getting my attention.

There's an insinuation in her tone that has me not wanting to meet her eyes. "We see each other a lot throughout the day." Is she jealous? Maybe she has a crush on him. "He's nice."

"He is." She picks up her fork and moves the food around on her now mostly empty plate. "I like you, Tess, but you won't be around long. I don't want my boy getting his heart broken."

I can add protective to the list of Naomi's traits. But I don't mind this one so much. "It's not like that. We're just friends."

"You sure about that?" She glances at me sideways.

"Sooo," Sri says, interrupting the interrogation. "Tess. What's your story? Are you in college? Just starting?"

"Just starting. Going to NYU in the fall."

Naomi whistles. "That's a good school. Big bucks, too. Did you get a scholarship like Sri?"

"No." I wish. "My grades were good enough to get in, but not high enough for an academic scholarship, and I've never played sports."

"So, your parents are loaded?"

I nod and bite into a carrot. Why does it always come to this?

"*That's* why you weren't freaked out about your car." Sri points her celery at me.

Colten jumps to serve, slamming the ball to the other side for a point.

"Hey, are you all ready to go watch the game?" I stand, wanting to avoid where this conversation is going. I'm not completely done with my food, but close enough. They can meet me over by the net when they're finished.

"Here it's pronounced 'y'all,'" Naomi teases.

"My mistake." I laugh, surprised by the friendly barb.

Naomi stands up. "Sri, are you done?"

"Yes, I'm beyond stuffed."

We gather up the garbage, dump it in a big bag someone set up and find a spot on the sidelines to watch. Sri introduces me to everyone around us, but they already know who I am. *Ugh.*

Colten's height gives him an advantage. Naomi's right. He's good.

I catch sight of Chaz again. He's working some of the girls on the other side of the court. The poor kid needs some social mentoring.

With two-on-two teams, the competition is fierce, the cheers and taunts boisterous. It's obvious they've grown up playing together regularly.

When the game finishes, Colten lifts his sunglasses on top of his head and walks toward me, eyes fixed on mine in a way that makes my breath catch in my throat. He reaches down and grabs my hand—*oh my*—and yanks me up. "Come on. Naomi, Sri—grab two more and we can be a team."

Oh. I feel a little silly where my thoughts were going. But in my defense, when a guy looks at a girl that way, he isn't thinking about volleyball.

"Colten?" I move to his side. "I have to warn you, I almost failed my gym class."

He laughs. "Nobody fails gym class."

I give him a sympathetic look. Volleyball was my worst sport.

CHAPTER 11

I BUMBLE, fumble, and smack the ball all over the place—mostly everywhere it isn't supposed to go—but I can't remember the last time I laughed so hard. *Oh crap.* I've just kicked sand in Colten's face. I didn't realize he was diving for the ball and instinctively kicked at it.

"I'm so sorry! Are you okay?"

He looks up at me sideways from his stomach. "You weren't kidding. You really do suck." He pushes himself up onto his knees and wipes his mouth on the back of his forearm. Everyone is laughing around us. Thankfully, he was wearing eye protection.

Grinning, I offer a hand up. "Told you."

He grips my hand, and before I realize what he's doing, he yanks me forward until I'm tumbling down beside him. "I'm not sure you've played hard enough." He grabs fistfuls of sand and throws it at my chest, stomach, and legs while I laugh, shove, and squeal at him to stop.

"Oh, no you don't." Naomi tackles him off me. "You leave my girl alone."

"How is she 'your girl'?" he laughs, pushing her off. "You *just* met her."

"*Someone's* got to look out for her." The intuitiveness of her words catches me off guard, filling my heart with a new respect. She lunges at Colten again, but this time he's ready and grips her under a leg, flipping her to her back.

"Oh, it's like that huh?" With lightning speed, she rolls away, comes up behind him and grips his wrists. In a blink of an eye, he's on the ground and she's twisting her legs up with his into a funky-looking pretzel.

These two have a bizarre relationship. First their roughhousing at the ice cream shop and now this. No, Naomi's never had a crush on him. They're like siblings habitually trying to best each other.

"See. I can still take you," she says, then hollers up at me, "Quit smiling like an idiot and pin him."

I know what she's talking about. I've seen WWF before. I look at everyone standing around watching the melee. But I can't do that!

"Hurry!" Naomi yells, making me jump.

"Okay, okay." I sound panicked as my feet rush forward. But when I throw myself across his chest, I'm full-on laughing my head off. And the countdown begins. This is crazy!

His sweat-licked, sandy body writhes underneath me as he pushes back, trying to buck us off. Is he mad, being taken down by a girl? A quick glance shows he's enjoying every moment.

"Five, four . . ." Naomi continues the countdown.

Colten smacks the side of my leg three times and calls out, laughing, "You win!"

"He's done," I tell her, and sit back on my heels, out of breath. That's harder than I thought.

"That's right, sissy boy. Tap out," she continues to goad him. Using his body as a brace, she pushes herself up.

He's grinning. "Fine. Whatever. Help me up." Colten holds a hand up to her. She claps it and hauls him to his feet. "You should have kept on wrestling. You could have gone pro."

"Eh. Got better things to do." She dusts herself off, unfazed by the compliment.

"How'd you learn to do that?" I ask her, in awe. She's big, but Colten's taller and a hell of a lot thicker.

"Took some martial arts growing up and was on the guys' wrestling team in high school."

"That's allowed?"

She smirks. "I didn't give them a choice."

"Y'all done playing?" someone from the other team asks.

"I think so." Colten walks over to him with a hand out. "Great game."

The guy returns the sentiment, and everyone disperses. Sri waves at me from the sidelines as she drinks from her water bottle. Naomi walks over to her and dusts herself off with a towel.

"You wanna come and rinse off in the lake?" Colten picks up his hat, which I lost during the wrestling match, and smacks it against his legs to get the sand off.

"I don't have a bathing suit."

"You don't need one."

My eyes go as round as quarters. *I'm not skinny dipping in front of all these people!*

It takes him a moment before awareness sets in. "Oh. No. I meant you could go in with your clothes on, you know . . . instead."

Of course that's what he meant, you idiot.

"No. It's okay. Clothes take forever to dry, and in this humidity . . ."

"You'd rather spend the rest of the day covered in sand?"

"No. I guess not." I do feel like a walking piece of sandpaper. Even cleaning my legs off would help.

"Hold on." Colten runs up to our blanket, throws his hat down, then walks quickly back. "Ready?"

"Okay. Sure."

The water is a lot warmer than I expected it to be. The small rocks hurt my feet. I step carefully, not wanting to lose my balance and fall in. I work my way in to just past my knees and try to shake as much sand out of my shorts as I can, then begin the seemingly impossible task of washing the grit off my legs. When I believe I've done a fair job, I start on my arms.

"That's slow and painful to watch," Colten says.

"What?" I look up. He shakes his head at the way I'm cleaning myself. "Oh." I laugh, then continue my task. I hear him coming toward me, but don't think anything of it until he's scooping me up. "What are you doing?" I squeal.

Before I have a chance to grab on, Colten sends me flying, limbs flailing, a good three feet into the air before *splash*. I hit the water, fighting not to sink below the surface, but it happens anyway. I kick to the top, coughing and sputtering.

"What the hell!" When I attempt to touch the bottom, I sink

again, but keep my face lifted toward the sky, treading water. "You're lucky I can swim," I gripe, not appreciating the dunking.

"Can't everybody?"

His expression is smug, the shit. "*No*," I say indignantly.

He dives under and comes up in front of me, whipping his hair out of his eyes, then wipes the water from his face. As soon as he's done, I douse him. "That was unnecessary. You nearly drowned me," I say.

He stands up. The water reaches just below his shoulders, proving I wasn't in any danger. "I didn't take you for the dramatic type."

I splash him again. "You're a lot taller than I am."

"It would've taken you the rest of the night to get the sand off the way you were goin' at it. And you're not getting in my truck covered the way you were."

"Your truck is already filthy."

"*No* it's not. It's just old." He lies back, his torso and legs bobbing at the surface as he floats closer to shore. I see him scrub his scalp, then dips under again, rising with his hair slicked back and water droplets gliding lazily down his pecs.

I swallow hard. It doesn't hurt to just look.

He has no idea how ridiculously sexy he is. I paddle closer and splash him again—I hate that he has this effect on me.

He turns away at the last second. "What was that for?"

"Because . . . just because." I swim away from him. When the water is just below my chest, I unzip my shorts, wiggle out of them, and swish them in the water to get all the sand out. I do the same with my underwear, then put them back on. Next, I squat deeper in the water and pull my tank over my head, then remove my bra. I notice Colten staring at me as I clean them out.

"What?" I look down. "I'm covered."

"Not in my imagination, you aren't," he snaps back.

I smile to myself. It's nice to know I'm not the only one affected. I turn away from him and put my clothes back on, then stand up. "Better?"

He looks at my chest, then walks toward me. "I better get you a towel before you get out."

I look down. "Why? I'm covered."

"Your top is see-through."

"I'm not sure what the big deal is. My bathing suit, if I had it, would cover a lot less."

"Lord, help me," he mumbles as he passes on his way to the shore. "Sorry I threw you in. Seemed like a good idea at the time."

"No." I beam a smile after him, thoroughly enjoying his discomfort. "You were right. All that sand would have been uncomfortable." I follow him out of the water.

He hands me a towel when I get to the blanket. "I don't want you catching a chill."

The sun is low in the sky, but it's still hot out. "A chill?" Instead of wrapping the towel around me, I bend over and wrap it around my hair, twisting it, then flipping it over.

"Oh, uh." He hands me his towel.

"I'm good." I'm being bad, I know.

"Oh, okay. Sure." He focuses on the lake. "So, um, the fireworks here are awesome—better than you might expect. There is a collection box, and all the campers and people who live here chip in."

"Is that so?" I unwind my hair from the towel, give it an extra pat-down, then throw it onto the blanket.

"Uh-huh."

"Should we head over to the fire with everyone else?" I ask, finger-combing my hair.

His eyes dart to my body and away, as if he can't stand to look at me. "You sure you don't want to cover up?"

My face falls with instant mortification. I misread him. "Are you ashamed to be seen with me?"

I said that out loud? Oh, crap. I never—

"*Hell* no. It's just your clothes are clinging to you and—" Looking irritated, he picks up the towel I dropped. "Guys will be staring."

Relief washes over me. The familiar fear of not being enough dissipates. "Seriously?" I give a small smile. "What's the difference between my clothes clinging to my body and a bathing suit that covers almost nothing?"

"Bathing suits aren't lacy." He shoves the towel into my hands and storms off.

His attraction to me makes him angry? I don't get it. I wrap the towel around my body and run after him. "Hold up," I holler. When he looks back, I swear I see relief in his eyes.

The fire is huge, crackling high into the sky. The grate had been removed and layers of wood stacked vertically against each other. Stories are told, memories shared, as the sky turns slowly from a cobalt blue to an inky black.

Boom. An explosion detonates over the water, getting everyone's attention, followed by an impressive display of colors that crackle into oblivion.

The fire is left behind as we all move down the beach to the water's edge to watch the show. Colten drapes a blanket over my shoulders. He must have run back to get it. I motion with my index finger for him to come closer, then closer still. I stretch up on my toes and kiss his cheek. "Thank you." The kiss was a bold move, but he does so many unexpected, thoughtful things that mean a lot. It felt warranted.

"Uh . . . You're welcome." His eyes meet mine as he touches his cheek. There is a flash of something in his expression before another loud explosion has him turning his face to the sky.

Whatever he was thinking instantly charged my body with adrenaline, and as I stare at his profile a little longer, I wonder how I could be so affected by this person I've known for only a few days. And I'm starting to think it isn't just physical. He touches something within me I didn't know existed. And yes, the timing is all off. The last thing I need is a summer fling. *Boom.* I flinch, then look up to the sparkling beauty that lights up the sky, then flickers into oblivion. Whatever becomes of our time together, I'm glad I met him.

As promised, the fireworks are outstanding, with lots of *oohs* and *aahs* from the crowd. When they're finished, most people walk to their vehicles, while a few stragglers stay behind by the fire. I say goodbye to Naomi and Sri, making plans for the three of us to get together in a couple of days, then climb into Colten's truck.

"That was fun," I say as we turn onto the asphalt and head toward town. "I had a good time."

"I'm glad. You fit in easily enough." He sends a quick smile in my direction, his face tinted red by the dashboard lights.

"It's easy to do when everyone is so nice."

"Yeah. It's a good group of people."

On the drive, I ask follow-up questions about the stories told around the campfire. It was fun to hear the memories, but without context, some made little sense. Like something going wrong with Mentos frozen in ice cubes, a teacher and a foghorn under a chair, car parts as decorations at a dance. It was funny with the bits and pieces and everyone laughing around the fire, but now, getting the full background has me laughing so hard my belly hurts.

He pulls the truck to a stop at the base of my steps. I wipe my eyes and take my first full breath since the stories began. "I needed that." And I did. The tension he causes within me needed to be released.

"Nothin' like a good laugh to loosen the spirit. That's what my granny always used to say."

"She sounds like a smart woman."

"She was something, all right. One of a kind, that's for sure."

We stare at each other silently for a moment, the dash lights illuminating our features, a tension building under the surface between us. "Well, I should get going," I say, deciding not to linger in the uneasy silence any longer. "I'll see you Monday? You don't work on weekends, right?" The thought depresses me. I've gotten used to seeing him several times a day.

"No. But you never know. I might pop in."

I climb out of the truck, made happier at the possibility. "Sounds good. Thanks again."

"No problem." I start to shut the truck door. "Tess?"

"Hmm?"

A pause has anticipation swirling in my stomach.

"Um . . . you be careful goin' up those stairs. Your porch light must be out. The truck shoulda triggered it—it's motion sensor. I'll get Dad to change out the lightbulb when he comes in tomorrow."

Disappointment washes over me. "Okay." My emotions are all over the place today.

"I'll wait until you're inside."

"Thanks."

At the door, it's difficult to see the slot for the key. I hear him back up and light suddenly shines up the stair with just enough brightness for me to slide the key in. With the door open, I wave at him before stepping inside and locking it behind me. I haven't heard him drive away, so I look out the window, curious. His truck sits idling. I wonder what he's doing.

Maybe thinking of me the way I'm thinking of him?

I can only hope.

After a couple of minutes, he backs out and turns, disappearing around the side of the building.

I guess I'll never know.

CHAPTER 12

MONDAYS HAVEN'T CHANGED for me since I left school. They still suck. This man is being . . . *Oh my god*. I know he's old and everything, but does he have to be so rude?

"Don't let him get to you," Twyla says as she waits for her order. "That's just how he is."

"Who?" Earl sets her food under the warmers of the expo window.

"Jeb." Twyla nods her head in the old man's direction.

"Oh." He rolls his eyes before turning away.

"Why is he *like* that?" I ask. "And why do you let him get away with it?" Of all the people who wouldn't tolerate bad behavior, it would be Twyla.

"He's not always that way. The man has had a rough time of it. I know it's no excuse. I guess I've just learned to ignore it."

"Girl!" Jeb shouts at me. "This coffee gets any colder, I'll be needin' a blowtorch to defrost it. And where the *hell's* my pie?"

I grab the coffeepot off the warmer. Twyla takes my arm and

holds the other hand out for the pot. "Give it to me. I'll go. He's in rare form today."

"No. Your food's ready to go out. I can do it." My stomach twists in knots as soon as I say it.

"Sorry about that," I say, setting his dessert in front of him. I even hit him with one of my *I'm-young-and-cute-and-you-should-be-nice-to-me* smiles, hoping to charm him.

No such luck. His scowl etches deeper into his wrinkled skin. "You forgot the ice cream," he barks at me.

"Sorry. Hold on a sec." I run behind the counter, drop a scoop of vanilla into a small bowl, and hurry back, placing it next to the pie.

He stares at me, his frown growing bigger—if that's even possible—sending a prickly heat of fear up my back and under my arms. I'm in a full-out sweat now. "Was there something else you needed?"

"Are you *stupid?*"

"Excuse me?" His words are like a slap in the face. My cheeks burn from embarrassment.

He smacks his hand on the table, making everything on it jump—and me with it. "You're supposed to *heat* the pie, *then* put the ice cream on *top*. Why would Twyla let someone so incompetent work here?"

Something inside me snaps, draining all the fear from my body.

"Jeb!" Twyla shouts at him. "Cut the crap!"

"No worries," I tell him, tight-lipped. "I'll take it back and fix it the way you want it." The anger that vibrates through me as I hurry away quickly replaces the horror and embarrassment his words and actions sliced into me.

Twyla sidles up next to me behind the counter. "Sorry about that. I knew I should have taken him. He's never been this bad." She takes a step back, looking me over. "Are you okay?"

"Never better," I say through clenched teeth. Then it hits me. He's nothing to me. His words are irrelevant. He's the one with the problem, not me. A nervy self-assuredness washes over me, and suddenly I'm in control. "Don't worry." I feel the wicked smile as it curls the corners of my lips. "I've got this."

"Now I'm worried for Jeb," she mutters under her breath, before getting what she needs and heading off.

I heat the pie in the microwave and dump the ice cream on top, march over to his table with renewed purpose, and set the plate in front of him. He narrows his eyes at me as if he's about to snap out another vicious comment. All the years with my mother, and this one man can snap me from my passive tendencies into an assertive, fearless tower of strength.

"*Don't*," I say, my voice low and controlled, "say another word unless you want this pie dumped on your head." I glare down at him.

He has the nerve to smile up at me. "I like her, Twyla!" he shouts over his shoulder. "She's got grit!"

Twyla looks stunned.

Me, I snap my mouth closed, a little stunned myself. "And —and if you talk to me like that again, you can get your coffee elsewhere. Got it?"

His smile widens. "Yes, ma'am. Got it."

I turn on my heels as everyone in the diner claps. I give several grand curtsies before moving behind the counter, where I face away from everyone and slap a hand over my heart. It's beating fast, but *damn* I feel good.

"Way to go," Earl says. "Who knew that's all it took? Twyla's been puttin' up with his crap for years."

"I feel like I just tamed a dragon."

"Pretty much did."

Colten comes in after the lunch rush and sits at the counter. Hair going every which way, greasy coveralls on, smudges of dirt on his face, and he still gets me riled.

"Colten, get your grimy butt off my stool!" Twyla shouts, without an ounce of real anger behind it.

"I just want a piece of pie before I finish with Barney's ol' clunker. That hunk of junk shoulda been laid to rest *long* ago."

"Give the man a break," Earl calls out. "He and his wife christened that car in high school. It's sentimental."

"Ah, Dad. You could have kept that to yourself."

"Facts of life, son. And the pie's all gone." Earl nods in my direction. "The dragon slayer sold the last piece."

Colten regards me quizzically.

I give an indifferent shrug. "No big deal, just taking care of business." Inside, I puff up with pride and revel in the nickname Earl's given me.

Colten looks between his dad and me. "What'd I miss?"

"What's going on?" Josie enters the room just as Colten asks his question. She must have been at a friend's house again.

"This one," he says, pointing at me with a long wooden spoon, "took on Jeb. *And won!* You shoulda heard her." His proud smile makes my heart trip. I can't remember ever being praised by either of my parents—nothing was ever good enough. But this simple little feat has won me a heap of admiration from a man who barely knows me.

"Way to go, slugger." Colten gives me a playful punch in the arm. "I'm impressed. That man's been a thorn in Mom's side forever."

"So they tell me," I say, grinning.

"He's scary," Josie adds.

"Josie, he's not scary, just . . . angry sometimes." Twyla comes up beside me and drapes an arm around my shoulder. "And *you* made a new friend today," she says to me. "I guarantee he'll only let you wait on him from now on."

I groan at the prospect.

Colten jumps down from his stool. "Well, since the pie's all gone, I better go and get that sorry excuse for a car fixed." He walks toward the garage door, but then turns, eyeing me. "Wanna come help?" His grin makes my legs feel a little unsteady.

"As if. I can barely figure out how to open that gas thingy."

"The what?" he asks.

"You know. The thing on the side of your car you open to put the gas in."

"That's not a thingy. It's a thingamajig."

"Oh, well, thanks for clarifying." My smile widens.

"No problem. Come keep me company when you're done."

"All right." I'm giddy at the invite. "Be there in about twenty."

I finish with the last customer, refill the salt and pepper shakers, napkin dispensers, and then wipe down the counters.

"Do you need help with anything else?" I ask Twyla.

She's cleaning out the coffee pot using ice and salt with a little water. She swirls the mixture around for a bit, then dumps it out in the sink. "No. I think that's about it. Great job today."

The compliment feels great. "Thanks. I'll see you later for dinner." She's got me working a double today.

Twyla gives a nod as she continues her chore. "Oh, I forgot to tell you. Sri came by early this morning on her way to work and dropped off some running shoes."

"*Eeee!*" I squeal. "That's awesome."

Twyla's eyebrows arch. "I don't think I've ever seen anyone so excited about shoes."

"Running is my thing." Rain or shine, I'm lost in my music, breathing hard while my feet hit the pavement. It's the only time I've ever felt free . . . that is until I came here.

CHAPTER 13

WITH THE RUNNING shoes in hand, I hurry up the back steps to my place, plop down on the couch, and try them on. They fit perfectly. I can't wait for tomorrow morning. I'll set my alarm for eight and get a run in before work. *This is awesome!*

After changing into shorts and a tank top, I count my tips—forty dollars—then shove the money into the Mason jar I found the other day. I use the bathroom, fix my hair, and head to the garage.

There's an alt pop song playing on his Bluetooth speaker this time—Halsey, I think.

Colten pokes his head out from under the hoisted car when he hears me. "Hey, dragon slayer."

"Ha, ha. What are you working on?"

"Come and look."

I climb under the car with him. "You see this hose?" He pushes on it. "How it's startin' to crack?" I squint, trying to see the tiny imperfections, then nod. "It's part of the braking system. If it gets a leak and loses enough fluid, the system can't build up enough pressure for the brakes to work. It's a good thing I caught it." He removes the hose and picks up my hand. "Here, hold this." Then places my finger over one of the holes it was clamped to.

He walks over to his tool bench and looks through his drawers, takes a drink of water, wipes his forehead, looks through his tools again. He's taking forever.

"Hey. My arm's getting kind of tired here."

"Oh, right," he says, pushing away from the counter with a goofy grin.

Colten ducks under the car. With his chest flattened against my back, he reaches up to re-clasp the new hose. His hands stop in mid-air. The closeness triggers a sweet ache, and I'm tempted to look over my shoulder to see if his feelings match my own, but he swiftly clamps the hose and steps back. When I turn to look at him, his mouth is set in a hard line. He doesn't look happy. Maybe it was the wrong size hose?

"You can let go now," he tells me.

He continues his task and doesn't say another word. I stand to the side, shifting uncomfortably from one foot to the other. Something's changed and I don't know what it is.

"I'll just, ah, go sit," I offer.

"Sure." The word sounds clipped.

As I slide onto the stool and question if I should go, I notice a "Private Property. Do Not Enter" sign over his tool chest. I wonder what the story is behind it. It's well-worn and obviously taken from somewhere. Looks like someone took some shots at it with a BB gun or something similar.

"Ah, hell. Here's another one," he mutters.

"Do you need me to plug the hole again?"

"No. It's fine," he snaps.

"Did I do something wrong?" I'm not usually one to pipe up and ask, but, hey . . . this is the new me, right?

"*No.*"

"You sound pissed." My confidence is dwindling rapidly.

"Not at you." He forces an exhale.

"Is it the car?"

He steps out and faces me. "No, it's me. I had already drained the brake fluid. I was—it was a joke. I thought it would be funny to see you under the car, gettin' your hands dirty and all."

"Oh." Instant embarrassment.

"It was stupid. I didn't expect . . . I shouldn't have . . ." He looks at his feet.

"You were making fun of me? Because of how I was brought up?" I feel ridiculous for enjoying the intimate moment when he was just goofing around.

"No. I—"

"Ha, ha. Yeah. I get it." I cut him off, not wanting to hear his excuses. "You won't be laughing next time I bring food and you're wondering if there's something unsavory about it." A pathetic attempt at covering my humiliation. His expression tells me that my deception failed.

He takes a step in my direction, wiping his hands on a rag he pulled from his back pocket. "Sorry. I've been known to have a warped sense of humor. Sometimes it backfires."

"Don't worry about it." I slide off the stool. "I think I'll go and see if your mom needs any more help."

He reaches out and touches my arm. "Hey—"

"It's fine." My hand is on the doorknob.

"It had nothing to do with your family's money. Honest." I turn and face him. "I would never intentionally hurt you. This is how me and my friends are—we joke, tease, harass, prank."

The concern on his face speaks truer than any words, and I know he's being honest. I take a deep breath and try to remind myself that he's not my mother beating me down—he's just teasing me in a familiar way. I should feel honored that he considers me in the ranks of his closest friends, right?

"Forgive me?" he begs, looking miserably uncomfortable.

"Yeah, sure. Your food's safe, for now."

"*Phew!*" He wipes a hand across his brow. "I like when you bring me lunch. I'd hate to worry that my food's been tainted." He waits a beat, twisting the rag in his hand. "Can you hang out a little longer?"

"Sure." *I guess.* Besides, if I leave now, things will continue to be awkward. I need to accept the joke as it was intended. He wasn't trying to be malicious.

I sit on the stool as he dips back under the car. He moves from front to back. I imagine him checking every hose. One of my favorite songs comes on—"Twenty," by Laur Elle. I wonder if this is on his personal playlist. I'm impressed if it is.

"Damn. This car should just be put out of its misery."

"Found another one?"

"It needs a ridiculous amount of work." He searches through a five-foot-high tool chest, finds what he needs, then disappears under the car again. "So why the passion for art? Was it somethin' in particular that sparked your interest?"

"Actually, yeah. When I was about ten, we were in Paris. My father was busy with work and my mother wanted to shop. Since she didn't want me tagging along, she hired a college student who sidelined as a nanny to hang out with me for the day. Turns out she was majoring in art. When she asked me what I wanted to do and I didn't know, she brought me to the Louvre, the National Museum of Modern art, and the Musée d'Orsay—her favorite places.

"The way she talked about the art . . ." I look for the words to describe it appropriately. "She gave them life—every color, shape, and texture had meaning and purpose. She articulated visuals into words, beyond the basic first impressions, and captivated me with her explanations of creative styles and the artists themselves." My spirits lift at the memory. "When we returned home, I had to battle my mother to take art classes— she was opposed to the idea. Eventually I got what I wanted, but found out after a few years that I didn't have the eye, or talent, or gift—whatever you want to call it. So I studied everything I could instead. The internet became my playground, with endless sources of material. And Maria was kind enough to take me to the museums, then to galleries when I was a little older. I loved watching the artists' careers develop. It was fascinating."

"Maybe you gave up too easily."

"Possibly. But I could never create what was in my mind. It wasn't natural—it didn't feel good, not in the way observing it did. It's similar to me taking dance. I could do it, but without talent, hard work can only take you so far."

He laughs. "The idea of a little you in a tutu . . ."

"The tutu was cute, but my lack of coordination wasn't. My mother pulled me out after my first recital. She told me I was an embarrassment."

He ducks down. His angry eyes find mine. "That's awful!"

"Yeah, well. I didn't really enjoy it anyway."

He disappears into the car again. "Did you go to Paris a lot?"

"Usually once a year. We would follow my father when he would spend a month overseas. Not because he wanted us with him—my mother just wanted to shop, and had no problem pawning me off on whoever she could. We both got what we wanted." I watch his movements a little longer, then say, "You mentioned that you'd want to travel if you could. If you could go anywhere, where would it be?"

"Australia, then probably New Zealand."

"How come?"

"I've always wanted to surf."

"Couldn't you do that in California? It's a lot closer."

"I could. But it's not the same and there's so much to explore there."

My eyes catch the beat-up sign again. "Where did the 'Private Property' sign come from?"

He laughs. "Me and my best friend Dawson stole it."

"Was there a specific reason, or were you two just being deviants?"

"A little of both. We have a drive-in theater just outside of town. They closed it down for a bit. It was a favorite childhood location—lots of great memories there. The sign pissed us off."

I jump off the stool. "What about these old license plates?" The embossed states read Michigan, Indiana, North Dakota, California, Texas, and many more.

I hear him sifting through his tool chest again, and then he's looking over my shoulder. "John left those behind." His breath caresses my neck as he speaks, sending chills up my spine.

"I've always liked them, so after the remodel, I put them back up."

He's so close. This time I don't hesitate. I look over my shoulder. His square jaw is dotted with coarse stubble, his long, dark lashes fan over crystalline eyes of an indeterminate color. I'm transfixed, and when his eyes lock with mine, I can barely breathe.

A blink and the connection severs. His eyes drift to his hand, hovering so near my face. He looks surprised that it's there and quickly drops it. Turning away, he moves toward the car.

When I find my voice, I tell him I'm just going to get some air. I don't hear his response as the door to the outside closes behind me. I lean over and put my hands on my knees.

Holy shit, that was intense.

That kind of energy could either light up a city or burn it to the ground. As much as I want us to be more than friends, I should steer clear, because every time I'm with him, I need more—want more.

This isn't good. It was cool at first, a novelty, but shit, this is becoming a whole lot more. And like Naomi said, I won't be in Jasper Creek long. Either way, I'm bound to get hurt. I don't have the kind of luck not to.

I watch as the corn stalks across the road blow in a gentle rhythm with the breeze, back and forth in waves of liquid green. It's peaceful, simple. Something my life is not.

"Hey." He sticks his head out the door. I stand up so fast I get lightheaded and take a step back. "Are you okay?" he asks.

I try my best not to look flustered. "Yeah, fine. What's up?"

"I was going to grab something to drink. Do you want anything?"

He seems so unaffected by what just happened. It's kind of pissing me off. "No. I'm good. I think I'll go for a walk. That field across the street is calling my name." I need to do something away from him, and I've seen people walk through cornfields in movies. I always thought it looked cool.

"You wanna walk in Stanker's cornfield?" He says it like it's the most ludicrous idea he's ever heard.

"Yes." I bristle slightly. "Do you think they'd mind?"

"I doubt they'd ever find out, unless you were in the field while they were harvesting. They own over three thousand acres. Their house is over on the lake. Maybe I should go with you."

"No. That's okay, I—"

"Let me just get a drink and wash up and let Mom know in case someone needs me."

"No." I hold up a hand, palm facing him. "It's okay, really."

He rips open the snaps on his coveralls, already pulling out of his sleeves. "I'll just be a minute." *Frick*. I wish he'd stop doing that. It is so friggin' . . . distracting. "Maybe you should come in out of the heat until we leave."

"It's okay. You won't be long." He nods in response and goes back inside, and I lean against the wall to wait. He may pretend that nothing happened between us, but that was a hell of a lot more than nothing.

CHAPTER 14

IT'S NOT long before he comes out in a T-shirt and shorts. "Ready?" he asks.

I push off the wall. "Uh-huh."

When we reach the road, I stop and look both ways while he continues across without a care in the world. He stops and turns midway and looks at me. "Not much traffic here," he says, chuckling.

"Still . . . a car could be coming."

"You'd hear it before you saw it."

Which is true. The sound a car makes would stand out in a silence broken only by crickets or grasshoppers—whatever's making all that noise.

Are crickets and grasshoppers the same thing?

After crossing the road, we come to a three-tier wire fence. "Here," Colten says. "Let me just . . ." He lifts the top strand, then steps on the lower two so that I can crawl through.

"Thanks."

"No problem."

I copy his action, but his body is a lot bigger than mine, and pulling those wires apart is not as easy as it looks. Once he's through, he reaches down, picks a long blade of grass with a fluffy end and chews on the base. I look over at him and laugh.

"What?"

"I've never seen anyone do that in real life. In the movies, maybe."

"Do what in real life?"

"Chew on a weed."

"It's wild wheat."

"Okay," I laugh. It's still a weird thing to do.

The corn is tall enough that I can glide my palms over the tops. I see Colten watching me out of the corner of my eye, probably confused by anyone finding this interesting.

"There's a stream nearby. It cuts right through the property."

He tags my arm and takes off running. "Come on."

The rows run opposite to the way we're traveling and running isn't an easy task—my legs keep getting tangled. I look up to get my bearings, but I'm alone.

"Colten?" I call out.

He doesn't answer, so I yell louder and move forward cautiously. Something grabs my ankle. I scream and kick out my foot like, *get it off, get it off*, then brush off my ankle frantically.

Colten jumps up. "Gotcha!"

I perform a full body shiver of revulsion. I'd thought for sure it was a snake or, *eesh*, a big-ass spider. I hate anything that slithers or crawls. Damn him! My heart feels like it's going to pound right out of my chest. I give him a shove. "Don't do that! I'm a New Yorker, you idiot. I've taken the best self-defense classes money can buy. You're lucky I didn't hurt you."

He's roaring with laughter, his hands raised in defense. "Yeah, you looked lethal. That squeal was terrifying."

I whack his chest with the back of my hand. "Asshole! I thought something bit me."

"Nope. Just me." He grabs my hand and leads me forward. "We're almost there."

My free hand moves to my stomach where my nerves are jumping from the connection. The feeling reminds me of a roller coaster. The free-fall drop, but also that moment before you descend, and you know you're going to be terrified and possibly puke, but it's such a rush, you don't care.

I am so screwed.

He lets go of my hand when we reach the edge of a small cliff. The stream is down a deep bank of dirt and grass that's dotted with pretty wildflowers. It's about fifteen feet across to the other bank, maybe more. It must make harvesting tricky.

Colten works his way to the bottom of the ravine, then holds out his hand to me. Always the gentleman. I take small steps down the bank, but momentum has my feet moving too fast. He lets out a loud *oof* when I crash into him at the bottom.

I fumble, trying to right myself. "Sorry."

"No problem," he says as I take a clumsy step to the left, then back up the bank. He grips my arms to steady me. "Hold still." He laughs.

The sand is deep and uneven. "I'm trying," I grind out before finding my balance. "Okay. I'm good."

"Are you sure?" He makes a show of releasing my arms with slow, careful exaggeration.

I roll my eyes up at him, my expression flat. "I'm fine."

It's a good thing he stopped me from running and took my hand. The corn runs almost to the edge—I could easily have tumbled over and seriously injured something.

I follow him downstream to a widened-out area, where the slow-moving water has pooled.

"Where does the river go?" Is it a river or a stream? I don't have much experience in this area.

"It feeds into the lake."

I squat at the water's edge, swirling the tips of my fingers in the coolness, then look up at the high banks. We're out of sight down here. It's like a secret hideaway.

He smiles carefree and asks, "Wanna go for a dip?"

"Really?"

"Why not? It's hot, and the current isn't strong. It'll feel good. Me and Josie used to swim here all the time."

"We don't have bathing suits or towels."

"Didn't stop us at the lake." He laughs.

"That's because you didn't give me a choice."

He lifts his shirt over his head and pulls off his shorts, leaving nothing on but tight, black boxer briefs. I stare, my brain instantly lobotomized. "You can leave your clothes on if you want," he says with a cocky grin as he wades in.

Is this payback for the Fourth of July BBQ?

"You comin' in or what?"

"I'm coming," I say, my voice sounding clipped.

I'd say two can play at that game, but I'm wearing granny panties and a sports bra. I opt to leave my shorts on, obviously, and pull my T-shirt over my head, laying it on top of my shoes.

He's already in the water up to his waist.

My feet sink into a squishy, slimy bottom. "There aren't any leeches in here, are there?" Add slimy things to my Things I Hate list. My cautious steps have taken me up to my knees.

"No leeches. Maybe some gators, though."

I freeze, looking around.

"*Kidding.*"

"You really do have a dickish sense of humor."

He raises his hands. "I couldn't resist."

And alligators. Add those to the list.

I roll my eyes and take another step forward. The water goes up to my stomach. One more step and the bottom drops away. "I didn't expect it to be this deep."

"Dad and I dredged out this section. Well, mostly Dad. I was around five when we did it. It's where he taught me to swim— this and the lake. When Josie came along, I'd bring her out here to keep her out of everyone's way."

"This feels *so* good."

Colten dunks under, then comes up in front of me. I cup my hands and squirt water into his face, payback for the alligator remark. He swipes at his eyes, clearing them, and gives me a look like, *it's on*, then douses me in a massive wave of water.

I turn my head, laughing at the last second, then lay both my hands on his shoulders and push myself high above him, intending to dunk him under. But he doesn't move, just stares up at me grinning, his feet firmly planted on the bottom.

"Damn you for being so tall." One of my hands slips suddenly and my body crashes down onto his.

He jerks his head to the side, avoiding collision as his hands grip my waist. "You're kind of klutzy today." He lifts me up and throws me.

I let out a shriek of a laugh as I go flying. Damn him. He did it again. *Splash.* A heap of water goes up my nose and down my throat as I go under. *Kuck.* I'm coughing and choking when I surface. My eyes sting and I can't see. I'm still hacking up water when arms grip me around the waist.

"Sorry. It went down the wrong way," I gasp. I lock my legs around his waist for support. "How dirty is this water?" I blink hard a couple more times and I wipe under my eyes. "I've swallowed about a gallon of it."

When I can finally look at him clearly, he's staring at me with heat burning in his eyes, then something else—anger, hurt, worry—but I've moved on to his lips, wondering how they'd feel against mine. His hands grip my thighs and we're moving through the water. I tuck my head under his chin and rest it against his chest. I think I've died and gone to heaven.

"You can let go now," he says, his voice empty of emotion.

Okay, maybe not heaven.

My eyes move to his, confused by his tone. I look down and realize we're standing on the shore and I'm still clinging to him like a monkey.

"Oh, right. Sorry." I release my legs and slide down his body. A nervous giggle escapes my lips, a little embarrassed at where my mind was drifting—something about clothes going every which way, my hands gliding over heat and muscle.

His mouth remains in a fixed hard line. He's obviously not thrilled with what just happened. I don't understand why he gets so mad when something . . . um, happens between us. There must be something more to it. Then it hits me. I'm so stupid. "There's someone else, isn't there?" I say.

Wait, Naomi would have told me if he had a girlfriend or I would have met her by now.

"There's no one else."

Oh . . . Well, then I don't get it.

"But you feel it too, right?" I ask hopefully. I'm so confused by his reactions to me. He has to feel it. His responses . . . Maybe I got it all wrong.

"Doesn't matter. Tess, I don't do flings." He runs a hand through his hair. "It's not how I'm made."

"Neither do I," I bite back. Does he think I'm a slut? He's the one who wanted to strip down and go swimming.

"No, I didn't mean it that way. It's just, well . . . you could leave any day. Hell, you're goin' off to college in the fall." School seems so far away at this moment. "And you were just with someone. I'm not gonna be your rebound guy."

Seriously? His words are insulting.

He picks up his shorts and slides them on. "Look, you are amazing . . . stunning"—his eyes drift over my body—"and I feel things for you, but I got no business getting involved with someone who's just passin' through." He reaches for his shirt and pulls it over his head, sliding his arms in a little more forcefully than is necessary. "Christ, you haven't even been here a week."

"It's fine," I say, pulling my shirt on and trying not to look as crestfallen as I feel. "I get it. No problem." I slide my mucky feet into my shoes. "We're friends. I didn't mean to make you uncomfortable."

"You didn't make me uncomfortable," he says on a frustrated exhale, then starts pushing his way back through the corn. "Come on. I have work to finish."

I follow along in his wake, the sting of rejection crashing in waves over my fragile self-esteem.

When we reach the station, I tell him I'll see him tomorrow. He gives an absentminded wave that stings my pride further as he walks to the garage door.

"Tess?" he calls out, stopping me before I turn the corner.

"What!" I snap back, not meaning to.

"Sorry about how I reacted." He shifts his weight and runs a hand through his hair. "It's just . . . You understand, right?"

I give him a thumbs up and continue my way up to my apartment.

I rinse off in the shower—my second time today—and attempt to process what just happened. When I get past my ego, what he said is exactly what I've been telling myself. That I just got out of a crappy relationship. The last thing I need is a summer fling. It's just that when I'm around him, my mind throws logic out the window and I become a needy, sex-crazed lunatic.

I release a heavy sigh and check the clock in my room. It's almost time for me to get back at Earl's, but I still have thirty minutes to kill.

Nosing around in the extra bedroom, I come across a box of old photo albums and sit on the floor to look through them. Josie had brought them out when we were cleaning the apartment, but Colten redirected, and I didn't get to see many of the pictures. I flip through the pages. Colten was such a cute little kid. His hair was a lot lighter than it is now, almost white —and those big blue eyes.

Page after page I smile, living vicariously through images of a family I wish I'd had. All the happiness and fun they had together—the love evident in every image. I want that someday —joy, fun, happy memories, growing old with someone, children. Crazy thoughts for someone just eighteen, but still. With only my own dysfunctional family as an example, I didn't know that it could be like this. Now that I do, I want it more than anything.

Someday.

CHAPTER 15

THE UPSIDE of waitressing is the rush—the adrenaline high you get when you're crazy busy. Your mind goes a hundred miles an hour in all different directions and when you're done, you feel like you've accomplished something extraordinary, especially when you don't make any mistakes. Even if you do, it's not a big deal, usually, but still, there's something about a job well done. It feels incredible. Another upside of being busy is my brain doesn't have time to think about my day in the river with Colten.

It's past the dinner rush, and my stomach begins to growl. I should ask Earl sometime if I could cook with him—learn a few of his recipes.

Josie is at the counter already, eating. "Hey, kiddo," I say.

"Hey." She smiles up at me.

She spent the last part of her day in the gift shop reading and manning the pumps. When Josie isn't around, they lock that entrance, so people just come and go through the diner's entrance.

Tonight's family special is herbed, braised chicken with rosemary, parmesan-roasted potatoes, with grilled corn and brussels sprouts.

"You go ahead and eat," Twyla tells me. "I got it from here on."

"Are you sure?" There are only three booths of customers by now, but I never want to assume.

"Absolutely."

"When will *you* eat?"

"I eat as I go." She takes a potato off Josie's plate and pops it in her mouth, grinning at me.

Earl sees me through the expo window. "The special?"

"Yes, please." I follow Twyla behind the counter and fill a glass of water while she washes her hands. "Do you want a refill?" I ask Josie, nodding to her glass.

She pushes it forward. "Yes. Thank you."

"Regular or diet?"

"Regular."

I load the glass with ice, then press the dispenser to fill it.

"Order up," Earl calls from his window.

I set Josie's glass in front of her. "Thanks, Earl." I retrieve my plate and sit next to Josie at the counter. "Were you at a friend's earlier?"

"Yeah. Spent the night, but she and her mother had plans, so they dropped me off."

"You leave for your summer camp soon."

"Yeah. In a week and a half."

"Are you excited?" I take a bite of chicken. *Frick*, this is good.

"Very. I like my friends here, but I get bored easily. I'm looking forward to meeting new people, working on new challenges."

Someone nudges me. "I like the shirt." Colten sits down on the other side of me.

It's a faded blue T-shirt, with a rainbow on it, saying *Hilton Head, South Carolina*. "Thanks. Another hand-me-down." I guess things are back to normal between us. That's good. I don't want to mess up the friendship we have.

"It doesn't seem to bother you." He lifts the corner of my shirt and drops it.

"Why would it?"

"Don't rich people have an aversion to second-hand anything?"

I give him a look like, *Seriously, again with the money thing?* "Not this one." *Get over it!* I want to yell at him.

"She's rich?" Josie exclaims.

"My parents are," I say, scooping up another forkful of vegetables.

"Wait. I'm confused. You come from a wealthy family, and you're stuck here waitressing all summer? Why?"

"I enjoy working here." I take another bite.

Her eyes bug out. "Are you crazy? You've got museums and major cultural venues, events, Central Park . . . oh my god, the architecture, the history. The galleries—"

"Josie, chill," Colten says.

"It's fine," I tell him. "This is a nice change, Josie."

"You're crazy." She rolls her eyes to her plate.

"Not really. The city's crowded, dense with buildings, lots of pollution, horns blaring all the time. It can be more exciting to visit than actually live there."

"I guess. Hey, can I come visit you sometime?"

"Maybe." Showing her all the sights and seeing everything through her eyes would be fun.

Twyla sets a plate in front of Colten. "How's everyone doing?"

"*Mom*. Tess said I could go visit her in New York. She lives there."

"I know." Twyla looks at me.

"I said maybe," I clarify. "Obviously, it would be up to you," I say to Twyla. "You could both come."

"I would love that, but getting away from the business isn't possible."

"Maybe Colten could drive her up or you could send her on a plane." The thought of Colten visiting sets me buzzing with possibilities.

Enough already!

"Can I, Mom? Please?"

"We'll see, baby. Now eat your dinner," Twyla says, moving off in another direction.

"I hope I didn't create an issue," I whisper to Colten when Josie gets up to grab something.

"Only that we'll never hear the end of it."

I smile sheepishly. "Sorry."

"Don't be. Your heart was in the right place."

"Could you drive me over to the grocery store after dinner? Do you have time?"

Is it bad that I still want to spend time with him when I know I'll only be making it harder on myself?

Probably.

Nope.

Definitely.

"Sure. I'm done working for the day. We can go whenever."

As we eat, Josie goes on and on about New York. When we're done, we all clean up our mess, and then Colten tells his mom that he's taking me to get groceries and will be back shortly.

"Honey," she says to me, "I can give you a key to the diner and you can come down and get anything anytime you want."

"Thank you, but it's okay. I just want to pick up some snacks. Believe me, I eat plenty here."

She runs a hand up and down my upper arm affectionately. "Okay. Colten, Josie's itching to get out of here, so come right back."

"Yes, ma'am."

"She can come with us," I say.

"If you're sure she won't be a bother," Twyla says.

"I'm right here," Josie says, arms crossed over her chest. "I'm not a child."

"I know, sweetie." Twyla pats her arm, placating her.

"Come on, Josie." I take up her hand. "How good are you at picking out a watermelon?"

"Good, I guess."

"Excellent. I've been craving some. Maybe you and your brother could help me eat some of it when we're done shopping."

Josie's smile gets huge. "Yay!"

"You ready?" I ask Colten.

"Right behind you." He takes out his keys.

"I just need to go to the apartment first," I say on the way out the door.

"Sure. We'll wait for you in the truck."

I run up and pull my Mason jar out of the cupboard and shove most of my tip money in, keeping enough for what I need at the store, then lock my door and head back down.

I pick up a carton of milk, cereal, granola bars, some fruit, a watermelon, and a book that's a little more to my liking than the one I found in the apartment. Josie approves my choice, having read other books from the same author. I tell her I'll give it to her when I'm done. She's continually surprising me.

At the conveyor belt, Colten takes a divider and places it down for me as I unload my basket.

"You like mystery?" Colten comments on the novel as we stand, waiting our turn.

"I choose based on the descriptions. It can be any genre. Do you enjoy reading?"

Josie snorts.

"Don't be rude." He tweaks her nose. "Not a whole lot. If I do read, it's mechanically related. Movies are my favorite way to kill time."

"Do you have any change?" Josie holds out a hand to Colten.

"No. And you don't need any candy."

"I have some." I pull out a handful and dump it in her hand. "Get me some M&M's if they have any."

"Okay," she bubbles, and rushes off.

"The last thing she needs this late is sugar," Colten says.

"You only live once, right? And you act like she's five."

He smiles as we move up in the line. "I know. She's grown so fast, I forget sometimes."

The cashier gives me the total. I count out the bills and hand them to her, then shove the receipt and change in my pocket.

"Do you have Sri's number?" I ask Colten on the way to the door.

"Yeah. I can give it to you."

"I don't have a phone, remember? I was just wondering if you could text her and thank her for the shoes for me?"

"She gave you shoes?"

"She lent me an extra pair of running shoes."

He pulls out his phone. "You like to run?" he asks. I watch as he texts with his index finger. Texting obviously isn't his thing.

"I do."

"Maybe we can run together."

Before I can comment, Josie is back. "Here," she says, holding out cupped hands filled with M&M's.

I hold a hand out, and she dumps about half into them. "Thanks." They're a little sweaty, but I don't mind. I offer some to Colten, which he accepts, popping them into his mouth all at once. I eat mine one at a time, reasoning that the colors have different flavors, but knowing they really don't.

We pile into Colten's truck. Josie's on my lap, the two of us sharing a seatbelt, and the shopping bags are on the floor between my legs.

When we get to my place, Colten carries the watermelon up

to the apartment. It's huge. Not like the ones bought by our chef at home. Then again, we aren't exactly a watermelon-eating family—too messy.

In the apartment, I hunt through kitchen drawers, looking for a large knife while Colten puts the groceries away. It all feels oddly domestic, and sadly, I like it.

"Found it," I say. "Now, I need a cutting board."

Both Colten and I search through cupboards. We bump into each other and both mumble a sorry. The nearness reminding me of the awkwardness at the river today.

"Got it," he says when he finds it.

"Bring it over here." Josie's waiting at the high-top table. "That way, we can eat it as we cut it."

"How about we cut it in half in the kitchen?" Colten negotiates. "And I'll bring the other half to the table. Otherwise, we're going to have a huge mess, with that table being so small."

"Okay," Josie says. "That makes sense."

He wraps the one half in cellophane and puts it in the refrigerator. The other half is now on the table, dripping stickiness over the sides of the cutting board as he cuts it into wedges.

I take my first bite. "*Mmm*, this is good."

"You're in the right part of the country for the freshest watermelon. Florida, Georgia, and Texas are the main growers."

"Is this another one of your talents?" I ask, jumping up to get paper towels. "Food trivia?" *So lame*. He makes me nervous, and I wish he didn't.

"You pick this stuff up hanging around Dad. Thanks," he says, taking a paper towel from me.

"So, Josie." I set a paper towel next to her. "What's been going on in your world?"

Colten gives me a distressed look while shaking his head.

"Well, Amy likes this guy, James, but Sarah likes him too . . ."

And on and on goes the teenage drama in Jasper Creek.

CHAPTER 16

I GOT UP EARLY this morning to run and really pushed myself hard. It was the only way I can get the images of Colten's near naked body out of my head. They've been stuck there for days.

The runs have helped, but now I'm waiting for the lunch rush to start, slicing lemons, and it leaves too much time for my mind to wander. I've never felt so out of control. Relationships were just there, and when they were over, I dealt with it. I got hurt sometimes, but it wasn't anything I couldn't handle. Everything is so much more intense with Colten. In a way I'm glad he just wants to be friends, because I'm not sure how well I'd bounce back when things ended. And they *would* end. He has his life set here and mine is destined for big cities.

"Hey, *girl*," Jeb yells at me. "It's dead in here. Come take a load off."

"Hey, *old man*," I holler back on my way to his table. "You know my name. Use it."

Since our run-in three days ago, Jeb has been here every day for pie and coffee. That's all he ever gets. He comes between the breakfast and lunch rush, sits at a booth, and, as Twyla predicted, only wants me to wait on him. He's been polite in his own way, and for some bizarre reason, I look forward to seeing him—even though he tips like crap.

"Fine, *Tess*," he says as I sit down across from him. "What the hell kind of name is Tess, anyway?" he mumbles.

"It's the one my parents gave me. What the hell kind of name is Jeb?"

"Smart mouth on ya."

"Yeah, well, you bring out the best in me." I plant my elbows on the table, rest my chin in my hands, and grin at him.

"So I hear you're a Yank. How'd you end up down here?"

I drop my hands into my lap. "My boyfriend—sorry, ex-boyfriend—took off with my car and all my stuff, leaving me stranded here."

He snorts. "No shit?"

"Yup."

"Dumbass."

"You got that right." I lean back against the booth.

"How do you know I'm talking about him?"

"Because you secretly like me, and I'm sure you've realized by now that if you piss me off, I might spit in your coffee."

He stares at his steaming cup a moment, shakes his head, then takes a sip.

"What's *your* story?" I ask. "Why are you such an ornery old buzzard?"

A slow, crooked grin shows a couple of missing teeth toward the back of his mouth. "Not much of a story. Son died thirty years ago in a car accident. Wife died two years later from grief. I'm a retired vet who's seen too much, and for the most part hate the world and all the idiots in it."

Heartbreaking, but I nod, keeping my expression passive. "Makes sense." He wouldn't appreciate sympathy or pity.

He twists his mug in a circle, then says, "I'm sorry about the other day. I should have said something sooner. Couldn't get up the nerve, but the guilt's been eating at me." He looks up. "There, I said it. Now, don't you have some other people to attend to?"

"Okay." I assume his half-assed apology has to do with the first day we met. I move to stand up.

"It was the anniversary of my wife and son's death." He starts picking at his napkin. "Even after all these years, it still hits me hard."

I touch his gnarled hand as I sit back down. "I'm sorry."

The same day? Did she commit suicide—from grief?

"Thanks." The word sounds uncharacteristically soft, coming from him. "Look, I best not keep you."

I get up, smiling. "You want a refill?"

"When you have a minute." I cock an eyebrow at the nicety. "Fine. Get me a damn refill."

I walk away chuckling to myself just as Naomi walks in.

"How's it going?" she asks, sitting on a stool at the counter.

"Good. Just a sec." I hurry away to fill Jeb's cup, then return and set the pot on the warmer. "Can I get you something to eat? Maybe a dessert?"

"No, thanks. I had lunch. And I get enough dessert trying out different recipes at Bell's."

"I would be jealous except I have Earl's pies. Coconut cream is my recent favorite. So what's up?"

"I came by to see if you wanna come out for pizza tonight with Sri and me. Do you work the dinner shift tonight?"

"Hey, Naomi," Earl says, his head sticking out his window.

"Hey, Mr. Earl. How's it going?"

"Ah, you know, same ol'."

"Yeah, I hear ya."

And he disappears.

"No, I don't work tonight," I say.

"Meet us at Di Napoli's pizza at six. It's on Main Street across from Bell's, but down a few doors."

I laugh to myself. It's *actually* called Main Street? I've been calling it that all along and didn't know. "Sounds fun."

Twyla enters from the back. "It is so hot out there! Thanks for covering the rest of my shift," she says to me.

"No problem. Did you get your errands done?"

"I did. Hello, Naomi. How's your summer been?"

"Miss Twyla." She nods in greeting. "Like every other. Work, play, work, play. I'm fine with uncomplicated."

What's with the Mr. and Miss?

Twyla gives her shoulder a squeeze. "Nothing wrong with that. Is Tess taking care of you?"

"I just came by to invite her for pizza tonight with me and Sri."

"Fun." She beams. "When did Sri get back from school? She dropped something off for Tess, but didn't have time to talk."

"Last week, but she's back working over in Raleigh, so I haven't seen her much."

"Well, you tell her she needs to stop by for a longer visit."

"Yes, ma'am. I'll do that."

Twyla says, "I see Jeb is here. Is he behaving himself?"

"He is," I say with a smile.

"Glad to hear it. I need to go talk to Earl. I will talk to you all later. Naomi, it was nice seeing you."

"I'd like to settle up sometime today." Jeb's rudeness has Naomi's eyebrows rising.

"I spoke too soon," I tell Twyla, then holler at him. "Be there in a minute." She nods and heads to the kitchen.

"He always that way?" Naomi's face sours. "I could boot his ass outta here if you want."

"It's tempting, but no. He's okay. Just has a loud bark." I wink at her.

"Ha, ha. Whatever," she retorts, getting the barb. "I'll see you at six."

"Sounds good."

I lay Jeb's bill down in front of him. "What's her problem?" he asks, eyeing Naomi as she leaves.

"You and your cantankerous attitude. She's a friend of mine. I had to hold her back from tossing you out on your butt."

He hacks out a dry cough that almost sounds like a laugh and slaps a ten-dollar bill on the table. "Keep the change."

I stare at the generosity, wide-eyed.

"Don't get used to it. I ain't made of money, but seeing as you were stranded here and all, I think you could use a little help." He struggles to stand up, but I know better than to help him.

"You old softy." I kiss his cheek, surprising him. "But don't you worry. I'm doing fine."

"Then give me my change back." There's a twinkle in his eyes.

"No way." I grip the bill to my chest. "This is the most thoughtful gift anyone's ever given me." And that's the truth!

"Well, now." He looks choked up as he pats me on the shoulder. "I'll see you again soon."

"All right. Drive carefully."

With a slight wave over his head, he grumbles something as he limps his way out the door.

My lunch shift is over and I have four hours to kill before I meet my friends, so I decide to go bug Colten.

I know. I'm a glutton for punishment, what can I say?

"Okay. Time to teach me how to fix my car," I announce, entering the garage. "Well, should the need ever arise."

"I doubt that will ever happen." He ducks out from under the car. "You would just call a car service to pick you up and AMA to deal with your vehicle. Am I right?"

"Whatever." I wave him off. "I've got too much free time on my hands, so I might as well learn something useful."

"All right. Today, we are replacing brakes. Why don't you watch me do the first wheel and we can do the next one together?"

"Really?" I'm surprised. "I wasn't expecting you to take me seriously."

"Are you in or out?" he challenges.

"In," I say excitedly. *Cool.*

"Okay. I already have the tire off. So next we have to . . ."

I stand next to him listening to the instructions, but all I can think about is how good he smells. This is the first time I've noticed before. It isn't overpowering, but uniquely Colten.

Ugh! I've got it bad.

"Tess? You still with me?"

"Oh, yeah, sorry." I shake the thoughts from my head and focus on his instructions.

"What's on your mind?"

As if I could be honest. "Just tired. I'm going for pizza with Naomi and Sri tonight," I add quickly, realizing my excuse of being tired could have been a mistake. I don't want him to tell me I should go have a nap, being that I want to stay here with him.

"That'll be fun," he says.

"Yeah. So after we take the pads off, then what?"

"First, we have to grease these slide pins." He does it over his work bench with gloves on, then comes back up and slides the pins back in. He removes the gloves, flips them inside out, and shoves them in his back pocket. "You want to grab those new pads laid out on the table?"

His workspace is well organized. "These?" I hold them up.

"Yup." He continues working as he talks, making it look so easy. "Are you excited for school to start?" he asks.

"I guess so."

He gives me a questioning look over his shoulder.

"I mean, I am. I just . . . I like being here," I clarify.

"You'll be bored by the end of the summer—don't worry." The offhand joke has me tensing. "So next we set the calipers back in place, then tighten them back up and we're good to go."

"Why would I be bored?" I ask, feeling slightly annoyed and I'm not sure why.

He drops his hands to his sides and faces me. "Come on, Tess, this place can't hold you. It's got nothing on Manhattan with all its fancy trimmings. And NYU . . ." He smiles like, *Come on. There's no comparison.* "You get to start on your future, study what you're passionate about."

It can't hold me? What the hell does that mean?

"So it's okay for you to live here, but not me, because . . ."

"It would never be enough."

"Why not?" My skin prickles at the possible insinuations. This is about money. It always comes back to money with him.

"You have opportunities where you come from. This is just a stopping point. Something you can tell your kids about, how one summer you worked in a diner in the middle of nowhere."

"Are you serious?" I snap.

How can you think that?

Being here has been the best thing that's happened to me since *forever*, and now he's telling me I'm just slumming it for shits and giggles? "You don't think your family and what you have here has value?"

"Of course it does." He's sounds as irritated as I do. "What's that have to do with anything?"

"*Everything!* My mother never hugged me, touched me, said I love you." He has no idea—*no idea*—what he's got and how lucky he is. My jaw is clenched as I try to contain my anger. "My father? He might as well be on Mars for how far away and oblivious he is. So as far as this being enough? I'd say it's everything I've ever wanted. As far as opportunities, life is what you make it."

I turn abruptly, needing to get out of here.

Colten's hand snakes out and grabs my wrist. "Tess, I'm

sorry." He releases me when I freeze. "For your pathetic excuse of a mother and father, and for belittling your time here. I just meant that you're about to start, really start, your life—study something you've been passionate about since you were ten. This is a fun summer experience, nothing more."

"You're wrong. It's a lot more than that, but I don't expect you to understand. You can't." He starts to speak, but I stop him. "But it's okay," I rush out, feeling embarrassed by my outburst and needing to end this conversation. "I shouldn't have overreacted the way I did." I look down at the hands shoved into his pocket of his coveralls. "How did we get on this topic anyway?" I say with a weak laugh.

"I asked about school," he replies, with a look of confusion.

"Right. Totally excited. Pumped, actually." I'm walking backward toward the door. "Hey, thanks for the lesson. I think I'll go get cleaned up. I'm excited for pizza." My legs can't carry me out of here fast enough. I turn.

"Tess."

"Have you been to Di Napoli's?" I say over my shoulder, my hands on the doorknob. "Right, been here your whole life— of course you have." I quickly open the door and shut it behind me. I lean against it for a second, catching my breath.

Twyla's eyebrows are bunched when I notice her looking at me. I push away from the door and wave at her as I pass, not stopping until I'm in my apartment.

I can't fault him for having an easy life—that's not fair. It's unusual, though. Everyone seems to be dealing with *some* kind of trauma. But Colten and his family don't seem to be marred by the realities that plague most people. They don't have that look, a hardness behind the pristine exterior that hides severely scarred hearts and minds. And, really? It isn't fair for me to call his life easy. They all work hard. But they work together with love and laughter. I'm tired of feeling alone, and here, I don't.

CHAPTER 17

COLD AIR and fragrant pizzeria smells blast me when I open the door to Di Napoli's. Sri catches my eye from a nearby booth and waves me over as Naomi looks up.

"Are you okay?" Naomi says. "Your face is beet red."

I slide into the booth across from them. Sri hands me a glass of ice water. "Here, have a drink. It'll help."

I do as I'm told. It helps and so does the air conditioning. "Thanks. It's *so* hot out." Even with only a sundress on, I'm melting.

Naomi hands me a menu. "Welcome to the South, sugarplum. What do you want on your pizza?"

"I'm fine with whatever you all want—except anchovies."

Naomi scrunches up her face. "Fish do *not* belong on pizza, and anyone who says otherwise is messed in the head."

Just then, a short, robust waitress with an apron wrapped around her ample waist walks up. She's older, maybe in her fifties. Naomi says, "Rosa, this is Tess. Tess, Rosa."

"Nice to meet you," I say.

"I heard about your situation." She shakes her head in disgust.

I'm getting used to everyone knowing about my business. "Yeah, I know, but it's okay. Right now, I'd rather be here than anywhere else." Take *that*, Colten Reed.

She pats my shoulder. "Good for you, making the best of a bad situation. What are you having?"

Naomi hands her back the menu. "A large Di Napoli."

"Same, same. Always the same. You see my menu? There are lots of good things here. Tess? You don't want to try my manicotti? Maybe a big slice of the lasagna?"

"Sorry. I'm craving pizza."

"Fine. I will bring you the pizza and the others to try. You pay for the pizza. The other is on the house. You don't know if you don't try, eh? And I'll bring another water."

"Thanks, Rosa," Sri says. "I'd love to sample some of the other dishes."

"Always the peacemaker," Naomi teases her when Rosa leaves.

"What?" she complains. "That was thoughtful of her."

"I thought it was sweet," I agree. "So, what's on this pizza we're getting?"

"Almost everything you can—" Sri looks up. "Uh-oh."

I turn and see a stunning blonde walking in. "What?"

"That nightmare is Colten's ex," Naomi explains.

I gape at the six-foot tall, long-legged blonde walking through the door. Her hair is long and silky. She's thin— unnaturally so. And stunningly beautiful.

"What's she doing here? No way she'd eat Italian," Naomi grumbles. "Too many carbs."

"What is she doing back in *town*?" Sri says.

"Yeah. No kidding. The girl couldn't get outta here fast enough."

The leggy blonde catches sight of us and walks—no, glides —in our direction. I already dislike her—the fact that she was Colten's girlfriend at one time probably has a lot to do with it.

"Naomi, Sri. How y'all doing?" She leans into her hip, striking a pose.

"We're good," Sri says. "How are you?"

"What are you doing here?" Naomi's words are out before the girl can respond.

She returns the rudeness with a pleasant smile. "I'm picking up pizza for my dad."

"No, I mean back in town."

"My father hasn't been feeling all that well. I came to see him for a little bit, then I'm back to Europe."

"Delilah's a model," Sri tells me, as if that explains everything.

In a way, it does. "So do you mostly work in Europe?"

"I do." She smiles, looking pleased that I've asked.

"I wonder if I've seen you during Paris Fashion Week. I was there the last couple of years with my mother." It wasn't by choice. She basically dragged me there because she didn't want to show up alone.

"Oh, uh, really?" she stammers out in surprise. "I was. I modeled for Couture."

"That must have been an amazing experience."

She flips her hair over her shoulder. "It's exhausting, and everyone is *so* temperamental, but it's great for the career."

"Delilah," Rosa calls out. "Pizza's ready."

"Well, I best be movin' on. It was good to see y'all." She eyes Naomi and Sri before turning away and, I swear, catwalks her way to the counter.

"That's Colten's ex-girlfriend?" I'm a little in awe, despite my jealousy.

"Yeah, the bitch," Naomi says, not too softly. "She cheated on him at the end of senior year, then as soon as school was done, left as fast as her skinny little legs could carry her."

Colten's words from earlier today come back to me. *It will never be enough.* I wonder if he was thinking about Delilah when he said that to me. The reasons he doesn't want to get involved make more sense now.

The girl gives us a flippant wave as she leaves. Sri is the only one to return it.

"I don't know what that boy ever saw in her," Naomi says.

"Well, look at her," I retort. "She's gorgeous."

"Colten doesn't care about that," Naomi says protectively. "They started dating when they were fifteen. She'd barely gone through puberty and was tall and gangly—didn't look anything like she does now. Then her mother got a hold of her and took her to New York for the summer she turned sixteen. When she came back, she looked like that." She thumbs toward the door. "The shy, sweet girl was gone, and the stuck-up, self-absorbed, self-centered thing that you just saw took over."

"She didn't seem that bad," I counter, feeling a little guilty for judging her so quickly.

"She's not," Sri says, giving Naomi the evil eye.

"It's been a couple of years," Naomi says. "She could have changed some, but I doubt it."

"You know, life as a model is grueling, and there are lots of

pressures and expectations on them. It's not all glamorous."
Now I'm defending her? "I knew a couple of girls that were
with the Ford Agency in New York. It's a cutthroat business."

"Whatever. She broke my boy's heart."

Rosa is back. She sets the entrees between us, then reaches
behind her and takes a massive pizza from a pimply-faced kid
and sets it down. "You take whatever's left home with you, yes?
I don't like waste."

"Yes ma'am," Naomi says.

"Good girl." She nods in satisfaction, then turns to busy
herself elsewhere.

"There's so much food," Sri says with big eyes. "I'm stuffed
just looking at it."

"Well, there isn't much room in that tiny little body of
yours." Naomi inhales the scents and hands out the plates.
"Dig in."

The conversation is light. Their stories and easy banter fill me
with happiness and laughter. Naomi's funny in her sarcastic,
brute-force kind of way. Sri throws out these insightful power
balls that take a second to process, then *wham*. You're laughing
your head off.

Now I'm stuffed and ready to explode. I couldn't stop
eating. The food was incredible.

Another good reason for wearing a loose sundress, besides
the heat? It hides the food baby.

I'm grateful for the long walk back. It will help digest
dinner. Ugh. I'm so full.

I let Sri and Naomi keep the leftovers. It didn't seem right keeping them when I get so much free food at the diner.

The sun is close to setting. It's that time of day where all the colors pop—the golden hour—and thankfully it's cooled slightly. When I get back to the station, I'm surprised to see the door to Colten's garage propped open.

"What are you still doing here?" My words trail off when I see Colten stand up from his stool and Delilah stepping out from between his legs. I feel an inner growl starting. It's not my place to be upset, but seeing the two of them together feels like a betrayal somehow.

Colten moves to the side, distancing himself further. "Delilah, this is Tess. She's waitressing here this summer."

"We've met. Hi," I say. "I'm sorry. I didn't mean to barge in on anything." My voice sounds strained. Realizing this, I plaster on a smile. We're friends. He can see whomever he wants, even his cheating ex-girlfriend, if he's that much of a moron.

"You didn't." Colten's voice has a hard edge to it. "She was just leaving."

"I was?" she purrs, reaching up to touch his cheek, but he tilts his head out of her reach. "Well, I guess I am. I thought we could catch up, but maybe not."

"I have work to do."

"You always did. Your cars were always more important to you than I was."

"That wasn't the problem, Delilah."

"Wasn't it? You were never around." She pouts. "I got lonely."

It's as though I'm not even here. Maybe that's her angle. She wants me to know I'm irrelevant when it comes to them.

"Just leave." Colten walks toward me. "You know the way."

"That I do. You sent me on my way plenty of times."

I can see Colten's jaw working. He's holding back. I want to yell at him, *Let it out. Unleash on the bitch.*

"Good luck," I say when she's close to passing me. "It's a competitive field, and being that you're, what, twenty, and almost past your prime?" Her jaw drops. "It must be tough to maintain. Oh well, I'm sure you can work those few extra pounds off in no time." *Oh, yeah. I like the new me.*

With eyes bulging, she hustles past. Colten releases the doorstop and lets the door shut behind her.

"You didn't have to do that," he says.

"Yes, I did." And it felt damn good.

A cockeyed grin spreads across his face. "Never seen her tongue-tied before."

"Glad I could help. Are you okay?"

"Yeah." He walks back to the table and sits. "She slid up to me just as you came in. Nothing happened."

"Thanks. But you don't owe me an explanation."

"I guess not." He shrugs, opens a catalogue, and flips through the pages, but doesn't look as though he's focusing on anything in particular.

"Was she your first love?" I climb onto the stool across from him.

"First and last, but I'm not sure if it was really love. We were so young when it started, and things just kept going 'cause . . . well, they just did."

"Naomi told me she cheated on you."

"Yeah, well, Delilah was right. I didn't have much time for her." He shakes his head. "That's not true. I had the time, just not for her. I should have broken it off, but the fallout didn't appeal to me. She made it clear she was leavin' town as soon as she graduated." He drops his head back and stares at the ceiling for a beat. "I don't know. I figured it would be easier to let her leave than deal with the confrontation. Her cheatin' on me was her way of dealin' with it, I guess."

"There's no excuse. She could have just as easily broken up with you."

"True. I think she was trying to prove she was worth more than the attention I was givin' her. In a way, it was my fault— my indifference hurt her."

"You can justify it however you want, but what she did was shitty. And it hurt you."

"Yeah." He walks back toward the hoisted truck. "Probably more than I admitted to myself."

"Sometimes it's easier to bury the bad stuff than deal with it." I know. I've buried plenty. "Hey, um. I'm sorry about earlier. I didn't mean to get so heated."

"It's okay. You were right. Sometimes I forget how good I have it."

I smile in a way that I hope lets him know all's well. "I'll let you get back to it." I stand up.

"No. Stay." He grabs an extra pair of coveralls off a hook and hands them to me. "Lesson number two. Oil change."

Not only can I waitress, soon I'll know how to change my oil, and I can sort of replace my brakes. I wonder what lesson three will be?

CHAPTER 18

COLTEN CAME to see me after the dinner shift and asked if I wanted to go to the drive-in. Realizing it was still operational, I gave him an emphatic yes. I'd never been to one before.

We haven't seen much of each other since Delilah showed up at the garage two days ago. I figured it was because we've both been busy, but then I wasn't sure. So on top of being excited to experience an iconic tradition, I'm relieved that everything is fine between us.

"How does a drive-in survive in such a small town?" I ask as we pull out of the parking lot.

"The townies and vacationers go, and, well . . . there's a story behind it."

"Of course there is."

"Back in the fifties, there was a wealthy man named George Townsend who fell in love with the area and built a house on the lake. Apparently, he loved movies and didn't want to drive all the way to Raleigh to watch one, so he built the drive-in. It was never a financial goldmine with the town bein' so small, but the tourists loved it. When he died, he left money in his will to make sure it would continue. Thing is, it only plays old movies. Over time, he'd acquired a massive collection, and the projector hasn't been upgraded."

"But you said it was closed down for a while."

"His family contested the will. All said and done, it re-opened. Not sure what will happen when the money runs out, or if it makes enough to stay open on its own. Don't know the details, but it's been goin' for a long time. Maybe it always will."

Instead of turning right to go to the lake, Colten goes left, makes another right onto a dirt road, then stops at a ticket booth and pays for our tickets. We continue on past a large concession stand that looks straight out of the fifties, then drive up and down the rows to find a spot. It must be a regular thing to do on a Thursday night—there's a car parked at nearly every sound station.

There's a pleasant breeze as we watch the original *Frankenstein* and share popcorn. Our hands bump into each other occasionally as we dig in the bag, followed by an "Oops" or a "Sorry." I'm trying not to be affected, to just focus on the movie, but it isn't holding my attention the way I wish it would.

I need to think about something else. My parents. That's a *great* buzzkill. They'll be back in New York in a couple of weeks. Frick. I hope my father lets me stay. I should call him soon. I told Twyla that my parents won't notice I'm gone, and they probably won't, but if they did? I don't want them filing a missing person's report. Uh, could you imagine?

I take a drink from one of the water bottles Colten brought along. I'll tell my father I have a job and I'll be home in time for college. He shouldn't have a problem unless he had plans for me to intern for him this summer. He never mentioned anything. And now that I've talked to Chester, I'm confident he won't find out about the car.

At intermission, we walk to the concession stand. Some friends stopped Colten with a mechanical issue. So after using the bathroom, I stand in line by myself. He mentioned he wants Junior Mints and I'm craving Twizzlers.

The building is lit with yellow fluorescent lights, casting everyone in a warm glow. The line is long, but it seems to move fast.

"Hey, girl." Naomi hip-checked me, scaring the crap out of me. "I didn't know you were comin'."

"Neither did I," I laugh, catching my breath from the assault. "Colten asked me at the last minute. I had nothing else to do, and he had popcorn." My eyebrows pump up and down.

"That does it for you, huh?"

"That and the company." *Oops.* Didn't mean to say that.

"Hey," she warns. "I told you I don't wanna be moppin' up after another broken heart, ya hear?"

"Yeah, I know. Don't worry. We're just friends."

"Uh-huh. But you want it to be more, and he's being cautious." I give her a quizzical look like, *How the eff did you know?* "It's easy to put the pieces together when I know my boy so well."

I smile. "He's lucky to have you."

She gives a firm nod and says, "Damn right."

I tell the attendant my order, hand over the money, then pick up our treats. Naomi steps up to the counter as I step to the side. I notice no one questioned her cutting in line.

I catch sight of Chaz, the annoying kid from the beach, near the play equipment, pushing a little girl on a swing. She's laughing at the flying airplane sounds he's making. It's adorable.

I elbow Naomi and jerk my head in his direction. "Maybe we misjudged him?" The girl makes a flying leap off the swing and falls. A cry of pain reaches us as she holds onto her knee. Chaz instantly scoops her up and cradles her against his chest. He kisses her knee, then makes fart noises against her cheek, sending her into a fit of giggles.

She watches the exchange with me, then says, "Maybe."

As we wait for her order, the Junior Mints are tugged from under my arm. I hold on tighter, thinking someone's stealing them.

"You can release the death grip," Colten says from behind me.

I laugh. "Oh. Sorry." And hand them over.

He says hi to Naomi while opening his Junior Mints, dumps some into his hand, and pops them in his mouth. He leans the box in my direction. "Want some?"

"No thanks. It'll ruin the flavor of the Twizzlers." I tear open the pack and take one out, rip off a piece with my teeth. *Mmm.* The strawberry kind. I've never liked the cherry flavor.

"You told me you were an anything-as-long-as-it's-chocolate girl," Colten says to me as Naomi's order number is called.

"I am, but chocolate needs to be savored, and movies require focus, therefore . . ." I hold my treat up. "Twizzlers."

"That's very methodical of you," he teases.

I shrug. "Chocolate is serious business." I hold the long red ropes toward him. "Want one?"

He pulls one out and takes a bite, his face immediately puckering. "You're right. *Uck*. They taste horrible together."

"*See*. I've learned from experience." He quickly pops more Junior Mints into his mouth, like he's trying to relieve the bitter taste. I don't think it helps, because his face is still screwed up.

Naomi wanders back over, her hands full of french fries, M&M's, and a large drink. Colten immediately pulls out several fries and shoves them into his mouth.

"*Hey*," Naomi gripes.

"Clearing the palate," he says.

I laugh. He must have gotten that one from his dad.

"I don't give a damn *what* you're doing," Naomi barks out. "Stay out of my damn fries!"

"He had a flavor emergency," I say, still laughing.

"Y'all are weird."

Colten nods toward the rows of cars. "Who did you come with?"

"Justin, Sri, Kyler, Mason, and Rachael."

"Did someone bring a van?" I ask.

"Nope. Convertible. They charge by the vehicle, and everyone loves watching movies in Justin's car."

"Speaking of cars," Colten says. "When are *you* going to get one?"

"Somewhere between pigs flying and the sky opening up and raining frogs."

"You know I can fix up anything you get. I'll only charge you for parts."

"Where do I need to be goin'?" She pops a fry into her

mouth. "I live in town. I can walk anywhere I need to and catch a ride anyplace else."

"True enough."

"I better get back," she says. "The movie's about to start."

"It's not like we don't know what happens," Colten jokes.

"My fries are getting cold." She bumps him as she passes. "See ya. Bye, Tess."

"Bye," I shout after her. "Does Naomi leave for school in the fall?" I tear off another bite of my treat as we walk back.

"No. Her family has always been poor, and when her father got injured and couldn't work anymore, they needed her help. There are seven mouths to feed and her mother's income doesn't cut it. Her two older brothers help as well. They work as carpenters over in Raleigh, and are doing well, from what I hear. I'm sure she could figure something out with college if she wanted to, but she likes her job at Bell's, and basically runs it, since the owners are never around."

We climb into his truck. "Good for her." I point a Twizzler at him. "As long as it pays the bills, right?"

"That's something you'll never need worry about. You probably have a nice-sized trust fund."

"Why are you so obsessed with my parents' money?" I mean, *frick*. Every conversation we have seems to circle around to it.

He leans away, looking flustered. "I'm not."

"You are too! You're always making comments or teasing me. Colten. It's. Not. My. Money."

"I know. I'm sorry if it comes across like I'm hassling you. It's just different, and hard to relate to. I guess I'm curious. And maybe I'm still trying to wrap my head around why you want to stay here and work when you don't have to." He turns in his seat and faces me. "I get that things aren't good back home, but still, with all that money, you're free to do whatever you want."

"There's a difference between freedom and independence. I have the freedoms that money can buy, but I'm far from independent. Not when my parents have the control and my mother gets a twisted sense of enjoyment out of torturing me." Colten's face hardens. "So . . . can we be done with the money fixation now?"

"It's not right—what she's done—and I hate that you've had to deal with it. And yes. I won't bug you anymore. At least I'll try."

"Fair enough."

The movie starts, ending the conversation. I'm glad. I'd rather not think about my situation. That sounds bad. I'm lucky in that I'm not starving and I have a roof over my head. It's just, you get to a point where the other stuff makes you want to take your chances and fend for yourself.

Deep into the scene where Frankenstein comes back to the lab, I notice Colten looking my way. I turn to him. "What?"

"Nothing. I was just thinking that you look pretty."

My pulse kicks up a notch. "Oh, uh, thank you." That was random. Nice, but . . . random.

"You're welcome." He dumps the rest of the chocolate mints into his mouth and returns his focus to the movie.

I wonder what made him say that. Was he thinking of something in particular? Do friends say that kind of thing to each other? I didn't even make an effort with my appearance. I threw on the sundress from the other night—when I caught him with Delilah. My hair is knotted up at the back of my head, and I don't think I'm wearing any makeup.

He was probably just being thoughtful, but damn if he doesn't keep giving me mixed signals. I'm probably making more of it than it is. It was a few simple words. It's not like there was any heat behind it, you know? Like, his eyes weren't beaming subliminal sexual messages at me or anything.

Whatever his intention, the simple compliment leaves me feeling light and happy, but also a little edgy. Knowing his past with Delilah, I understand his concerns that Jasper Creek won't be enough and I'll leave, and he's not interested in flings. I'm not either, but doesn't he realize how unusual this attraction is?

Maybe it's only unique to me. I *really* want to kiss him— just once. I want to know what it feels like. I mean, what if it's just an attraction with no real chemistry? A kiss would help determine that. Maybe he's a horrible kisser—all slobbery and no finesse. That would end the torture instantly.

But what if it's amazing?

I take another bite of my chewy treat and try to focus on the movie, but all I can think about are his lips—the fullness in equal measure on top and bottom, how soft they seem.

I glance over at him to be sure I'm remembering right. Yep. He has such nice lips. And his profile is equally balanced— nothing too prominent, angled, or jagged.

Maybe I could just do it—kiss him. This is the new me, after all. I go for what I want—nothing stands in my way.

No, that wouldn't be right. I need to respect his feelings, and it would most likely piss him off since that seems to be his reaction every time we have a moment.

When he turns and gives me a quick smile, I wonder if he senses my thoughts.

No. If he did, he wouldn't be smiling.

Okay. Snap out of it. This is not happening. It would only complicate your life and piss him off.

CHAPTER 19

"ARE you up for a drive around the lake?" Colten asks. The movie has ended and the spotlights are just coming on. "The sky's clear and the humidity isn't too bad, so the stars should be incredible."

"Sure."

Alone with Colten, stargazing. Just kill me now!

We follow a line of cars out of the parking lot, then pull out onto the road that takes us toward the lake. It's incredibly dark out. Colten's headlights shine directly in front of us and on the bottom third of the woods. It reminds me of a scene in a horror movie. A truck driving along a lonely, dark road, when suddenly, a masked man with a bloody knife or maybe a zombie steps out in front of the headlights. The truck swerves and hits a tree.

I laugh to myself as I lean my head against the passenger window and look up at the sky. I'm sure I'm safe from—"Stop! Pull over."

"What? What's the matter?" As soon as the vehicle stops, I jump out. "Are you okay?" He sounds alarmed.

"Yeah. I just wanted to see." I gaze up at all the twinkling lights in wonder.

"You scared the crap out of me." He must understand my sudden fascination, because he shuts the headlights off. "Awesome, isn't it?"

"I've never seen anything like it." I stand mesmerized as he comes up beside me. "It's . . . wow."

"Being away from the lights in town helps." He grabs my hand and heads back to the truck. "Come on."

I hold my ground. "But it's so pretty. Can't we stay?"

He tugs me back toward the truck. "I know a better place. It's not safe to be parked on the side of the road in the dark."

"Oh, okay. You're right."

We climb back into the truck and continue down the road. He navigates the curves a little longer before he slows and pulls onto a rough dirt road. You could hardly call it a road. It's a singular lane closed in by dense trees. We hit bump after bump, knocking us close to the roof a couple of times. When it opens to a small clearing, I notice the reflection of his headlights on the water ahead of us.

He carefully maneuvers his truck until the truck bed faces the lake, then turns off the ignition. "Wait for me." He opens his door, rushes to my side, and holds out a hand to help me down. "It's dark, and the ground is uneven. I don't want you twisting an ankle."

His kindness continues to amaze me. "Thank you." Although he's probably remembering my klutzy moves at the ravine the other day.

He keeps my hand in his as he guides me to the back of the truck and drops the tailgate. I let out an unattractive squeal when he lifts me by the waist from behind and plunks me in the truck bed. "I could have managed on my own," I say.

Good thing it's dark or he would have seen my hideous underwear.

"This was easier." He laughs on his way back to the driver's side. When he comes back around, he's carrying an armful of blankets and towels. He throws them near my feet, then hauls himself up next to me. "I also brought a jacket in case you get cold."

"Thanks." I slide my arms into the sleeves. The jean jacket smells like him—musk and pine, and something uniquely Colten.

He begins to lay out the blankets, so I reach out to help. As soon as they're situated, he lies down, placing a towel behind his head, then rolls up another one and sets it down for me. "It might be a little sandy. I haven't shaken the blankets out since the beach."

"It's fine." I pause a moment, taking in the intimate scene as my heart twists with want, then quickly lie down next to him. I focus on the sky and try not to give too much attention to my thoughts, even though hope races through me like a freight train at full speed.

There could always be a tipping point. He could change his mind. And why are we out here, all alone, where one thing could easily lead to another?

Oh, right. Stargazing.

Well, you never know.

It is breathtaking and doesn't take long before I'm lost in the scene before me. "The Milky Way is . . . unbelievable," I say, my words delivered with reverence. "I saw a shooting star!" I whack his stomach with the back of my hand. "Did you see it?"

"*Oof*," he breathes out. "No, I missed it." He turns to me.

"Sorry," I laugh, facing him. "It's just . . ." Excitement pings against my insides. "I've never seen one before." I turn my gaze back to the sky, hoping to see another one. "That was . . . Wow!"

"You should see it in August during the Perseids meteor shower. The streaks of light are constant."

"I'm impressed you know the name of a meteor shower."

"I can Google as well as the next person. And they're not really stars, but meteors burning up as they enter the earth's atmosphere. You know that, right?"

"I suppose I do. I just never thought about it in technical terms."

He locks his hands together over his chest. "Do you know any of the constellations?"

"Some."

I search the sky, then point to the four stars that make up a warped square. "The Big Dipper."

"Yup."

I move my hand up to the left and find four more dots closer together. "Little Dipper. That's all I know."

"I don't know many either, but in between the two you mentioned is a long zig-zaggy trail of seventeen stars that makes up Draco."

"As in Malfoy? From *Harry Potter*?"

He laughs. "Same name—not sure about the relation."

"I see it. Cool. Are you and Delilah going to hang out while she's here?"

"That was random."

"Just curious." I'm not exactly sure why she popped into my head. Probably just wishing she hadn't hurt him and this moment could be a chance for more.

"She's gone."

His tone is clear—he's done with her. I tilt my head toward him. "Was it hard seeing her?"

When he faces me, our noses are less than a foot away. I weep internally, *So close, yet so far.*

"No. It's been years since we were together and even longer since we were really a couple. Things changed when she turned sixteen. She'd gone to New York and came back different. It got old, quick."

"But you stayed together."

"Yeah. Like I said before, I don't know why. We fought all the time. She was all about appearances, and mine wasn't ever good enough. She wanted out of here and this is where I want to stay, and the rest is history."

"Do you wish that it didn't end that way? Do you still have feelings for her?"

"I think you always hold a special place for your first, uh . . . love, but other than that, no."

My first boyfriend put so much pressure on me to have sex that when I finally relented, it was painful and over in like thirty seconds. I regretted giving in. My following experiences weren't a lot better.

"Are you cold?"

"A little." I wouldn't mind some of his body heat. The light jacket isn't quite enough and my legs are bare.

He fumbles around and pulls another blanket over me. I was hoping he was going to tell me to snuggle in closer, but the disappointment keeps racking up.

"How much longer before you contact your family?"

"Ready for me to leave now, huh?"

"*No.*" He pauses. "I was just wondering."

"Before they get back from Europe. I'm hoping my father lets me stay for the summer. I don't see why not."

"When are they back?"

"Another couple of weeks."

"So that's maybe all I've got, huh." It's more of a statement than a question.

I want to scream, *But I'm right here!* "I live in New York, not Siberia, and there's FaceTime, texting, emails—lots of ways to stay connected."

He doesn't respond, so we continue to stare at the stars in silence.

"Tess?" I feel a nudge. "We should go. You fell asleep."

"I did?" I open my eyes wide and stretch my arms out in front of me.

"Did you know you snore?"

"I do not!" I say, mortified.

He laughs. "No. You don't."

"You love to tease, don't you?"

"Only people I like."

"Thanks. I think."

He likes me?

Ugh! I'm pathetic.

Colten drives us back to town and parks at the base of my steps. "Here you go."

"Thanks for taking me stargazing and for the movie." I don't want the night to be over.

"Maybe we can go again next Thursday," he says. "*Swamp Thing* is playing."

"Oh, wow. I can't miss *that*," I say sarcastically.

He smiles. "See you tomorrow?"

My stomach jitters with excitement, as it always does at the thought of seeing him. "Absolutely." I take off his jacket and hand it to him, then open the door and climb down from the truck. I give a quick wave before I shut the door behind me.

The exterior light clicks on as soon as my foot hits the bottom step. He waits until I open the apartment door before gravel crunches and he backs out and drives away. I shut the door behind me and stare out the window where his truck was parked, willing him to come back. But he doesn't. Resolved at the way things are, I get ready for bed and prepare myself for a restless night's sleep.

CHAPTER 20

I RAN this morning and worked a double shift today, so I'm completely wiped out. With the day done, I flop on the couch, raise my feet on the armrests, and pull a throw pillow under my head. Every part of me is sore and heavy.

Someone is knocking on my door. I'm so out of it, I struggle to comprehend what's going on.

I must have drifted off without realizing.

I roll off the couch and stumble to the door, whipping it open at the incessant knocking.

Naomi pushes in past me. "What took you so long?"

"I'm sorry. Did we wake you?" Sri, my thoughtful and, at the moment, preferred friend, stands outside looking apologetic.

"It's okay." I rub my eyes, then open them wide, willing them to focus. "Come on in." I wave my hand lazily toward the living room.

"Why are you sleeping at nine o'clock on a Friday night?" Naomi makes it sound like it's the most ridiculous thing ever.

I walk to the sink and fill up a glass with water, knocking

it back, then turn to Naomi. "I worked an *extremely* busy double shift." Her hair is free from its usual binds—a stunning orange mane of corkscrew curls cascades over her shoulders and back. "You should leave your hair down more often. It's pretty."

She looks surprised by my compliment. "Thanks. It's a lot to deal with, that's why I usually keep it up."

"It's great to see you two, but why are you here?" I rub my sleepy eyes again.

"Go change," Naomi orders. "We came to take you with us."

"Where are we going?" My legs will barely allow me to stand. I can't imagine doing anything other than crawl into bed.

"To a house party."

"Maybe she's too tired," Sri says.

Naomi plants a fist on her hip. "It's Friday night. We're young, it's summer. And we need to celebrate life. Need another reason?"

"You don't have to come if you don't want to." Sri places a gentle hand on my shoulder. "We just thought we'd stop by and see if you were up for it."

I think for a moment, then decide I could get a second wind if I put my mind to it. "I need caffeine."

"They're still open downstairs," Naomi says. "I can get you something while you're gettin' ready." She heads to the door. "What do you want?"

"Oh, uh, an iced coffee, please."

"On it." She's out the door in three long strides.

"What should I wear?" It's not as though I have a lot of options, but still.

Sri looks down at her jean shorts and halter top. "Anything casual."

"Good, because that's all I have. Temperature?"

"Hot and sticky."

"Got it. I'll just be a minute." I throw on the jean cutoffs I came here in and a soft yellow T-shirt from my hand-me-down collection. "So, are you seeing anyone at school?" I call out from the bathroom as I reapply my eyeliner.

"Not really. I don't have time for relationships."

"School can't be *that* bad."

"It's worse." Sri comes to the door. "Don't get me wrong, I find it all interesting. If I didn't, I wouldn't be subjecting myself to the stress. It's just that there's so much to memorize. It can be overwhelming. And I need near perfect grades to get a scholarship for my master's degree. My parents saved up for my undergraduate—but anything past that, I'm on my own."

I turn off the light and follow Sri back to the living room. "That's a lot of pressure," I say.

"It is, but I'm doing it."

"Good for you. Have you always lived here? Your accent isn't as strong as the others."

"No. We moved here from Washington, D.C., when I was ten. My parents are both freelance graphic designers and can work from anywhere." She laughs. "I know. Weird that we would end up here, right? Mom and Dad came to visit a friend who has a house on the lake and fell in love with the place. Thought it would be better to raise me here than in a big city."

Naomi walks back through the door, holding out an iced coffee. "You ready?"

I take my first sip and sigh. *So good.* "Yep. Thanks for going and getting this." I hold up the clear plastic to-go cup.

"Sure. No problem," she replies.

I slip on my shoes, and after locking the door behind me, I follow my friends down the stairs. I'm surprised when we pass the car parked at the bottom. "We're not driving?"

"No," Sri says. "That way we can drink if we want. It's only a fifteen-minute walk."

"Smart." Are they planning on staying the night? I've never had friends sleep over before. At first my mother wouldn't allow it, then there was no way I wanted my friends to witness her insults and sudden tirades.

We all walk along the gravel path Colten and I took to go to town. "So," I say. "Both of you graduated with Colten?"

"Fishin' for the good stuff, huh?" Naomi teases.

"No." *Maybe. Why not?* Who better to get it from than his best friends?

Naomi shoots a thumb in my direction as she says, "This one has a thing for Colten."

"*No*, really?" Sri pretends mock-surprise.

"Ha, ha," I say. "I was just making conversation."

"Sure you were." Naomi elbows me in the ribs.

They fill me in on Colten-related stories—some embarrassing, some not—and then razz each other about their own cringeworthy situations. The comradery is intoxicating, while the laughter fills my heart and makes my sides ache.

As we take a left at the end of Stanker's cornfield and cross a bridge over the river, I'm reminded of my body wrapped around Colten's and the feel of his heated skin burning against mine.

It's pointless to go there.

Breathe. Let it go.

I tune back in to Sri and Naomi's conversation. There's a whisper of music on the breeze. It has an electronic beat and seems out of place on this dark country road. When we take another right turn down a narrow dirt road, it becomes more prominent.

There are tall, leafy crops on both sides of us. The road takes a slight curve, and there, way at the end, sits a large lit-up shed.

This is the party?

When we get closer, the shed starts to look more like a house, or a building converted into a house.

The music is loud now. It's a perfect location for a party. Who's going to complain way out here?

"What kind of crop is this?" I ask, shaking a pebble loose from my flip-flop.

Naomi answers. "Cotton."

"Really? Where are all the puffballs?"

She laughs. "That doesn't come until late in the fall."

Cotton stalks surround three sides of the house, with enough cleared away for a lawn. There are people spread out everywhere, talking, laughing, and having a good time.

I follow my friends into the house, which is a lot larger than I expected, probably because of the open concept and exposed vaulted ceiling. There are lots of people inside as well, but it doesn't feel crowded yet. The back of the house is made up of large windows with open patio doors that lead out to a huge wooden deck.

This is so cool.

"Nash, this is Tess." Naomi introduces me to a guy with dark mahogany skin, light amber eyes, and a broad smile.

"Hey," he says over the loud music. "I remember you. You got into that tussle with Naomi and Colten at the volleyball game."

I give an embarrassed smile and a thumbs up. "Yup. That was me."

"Come on in. Grab a beer or one of them coolers or whatever." He points to the kitchen. "The fancy stuff is in the fridge. Keg's outside. Where ya from?" he asks me.

"Manhattan."

"What the heck ya doin' here?"

I chuckle. "You haven't heard?"

His eyes give me a quick once-over. "Why would I know your business?"

"Sorry. I thought everyone did."

Naomi cuffs him playfully on the back of the shoulder. "She's the one that got left at the gas station."

"Oh, right. *Damn.*" His fist covers his mouth. "So, what do y'all want? Never mind. I know what Naomi is gonna have and Sri will be headin' to the fridge." He zeroes in on me. "What can I get you, big city?"

"Beer's fine."

"Follow me."

"I'll see y'all outside," Sri says, heading to the kitchen.

At the keg, Nash fills two red plastic cups and hands them to Naomi and me. I trash my coffee to-go in the garbage.

"Thanks," I say. "I like your place."

"Yeah? The parents thought I needed my own space. Besides helping them farm, I deejay. So, they put me as far from the main house as possible. The land and this structure have been in my family for a long time. They didn't want to tear this ol' outbuilding down, so we renovated it. It was a win-win."

"Nice. Is this music yours?" I wave into the air at the sound. Sri joins us.

"No. Zeds Dead."

"Will you be mixing later?"

"You bet." His head turns in the direction of a girl with a killer afro. "I'll catch up with y'all later. Macon just showed up."

"You ask that girl out yet?" Naomi asks.

His shoulders slump. "Not yet."

"You're a chickenshit," Naomi blasts him. "Tonight's the night. If you don't ask her, I'll wrestle you to the ground and bitch slap you until you're squealing like a stuck pig. Then she'll *never* give you the time of day, no matter *how* cute ya are."

His eyes narrow. "You wouldn't."

An eyebrow raises like, *You want to test me?*

"*Fine.*" He stalks off.

"You're riding on the side of excess as usual," Sri says.

Naomi shrugs, unconcerned. "Naw, he just needs a little push, is all."

CHAPTER 21

THE THREE OF us have been standing around talking over the music that continues to pump out of the outdoor speakers, when I'm suddenly elected to fill our beers.

Bulb lights square off the patio and lend a soft light to the many familiar faces as I weave my way through the crowd to get to the keg. The closer I get, the denser the people, until finally, I have to squeeze my way through the inner ring.

"Colten," I call out, surprised.

He looks over at me, wide-eyed. "Hey. How did you get here?"

One of the guys he was talking to taps him on the shoulder and says, "See ya." Colten nods and they disappear into the crowd.

"Naomi and Sri came by the apartment and dragged me out," I say, ecstatic to see him.

"Nice. I stopped by and knocked, but you didn't answer. I figured you were zonked out after such a long day at work."

He thought of me.

My insides do a little happy dance. "I *was* sleeping when they came by, but there's no stopping Naomi when she wants something. And she offered to get me coffee."

"Ah, that'll do it." An extremely tall, skinny guy comes over to the keg, shoulder checking Colten. "Have you met Dawson?" Colten asks.

The infamous Dawson. "No, I haven't. I'm Tess." I give a small wave.

"I've been hearing a lot about you from my friend here." Dawson slaps a hand on Colten's shoulder, gripping it firmly before releasing.

I grin up at Colten. "Oh, yeah?"

Colten gives his friend a shove. "Don't you have someone else to hassle?"

"Get out of my way so I can fill my beer, and *I will*."

Colten moves aside. "You missed another great Fourth of July party." He raises his water bottle to Dawson.

"Maybe, but I had a blast at Hilton Head with the family."

"Dawson's family rents a place there every Fourth," Colten clarifies for my benefit. "I've gone with him a couple of times." He turns to his friend. "The Kingsley twins still around?"

A sly grin spreads across Dawson's face as he fills his cup with beer. "They sure are." He finishes and takes a sip. "Well, I'll leave y'all be. I'm gonna make my rounds."

I hold up the three empty cups when Dawson is swallowed up by the crowd. "Do you mind filling while I hold?"

"Not at all," he says, picking up the tap.

I wish I could think of something to talk about, but my brain is blank. "Okay, well . . ." I start when the three cups are full. "I guess I'll see you around."

"Sure." He looks a little surprised that I'd just leave him there.

It feels weird too. Our daily lives are so closely stitched together and anytime I've been away from work, he's been with me.

Just as I enter the throng of people, I realize I should have invited him to come stand with us. I turn around, but some girl is leaning into him, giggling. *Ugh, gross.*

Navigating my way back is near impossible with my hands full. "Took ya long enough," Naomi says, taking two of the cups from my hands, giving one to Sri.

I raise an eyebrow. "Are you that desperate?"

"*Pfff*, not the way you mean. It's hot and I'm thirsty."

"I could have gotten you water," I tease.

"Shut up." She sips. "This tastes better."

"I met Dawson." I eye Sri, remembering her blush when his name came up at the BBQ.

"Really?" She perks up, looking around.

Naomi jerks her head in Sri's direction. "She's had a crush on him forever. Both have been dancin' around each other, too scared to say how they feel."

"And who have you put yourself out there to?" Sri crosses her arms over her chest.

Naomi gives an apathetic shrug of her shoulders.

"So, what's the deal?" I ask Sri.

"Dawson and I, well . . . we've always been good friends." Naomi snorts and Sri glares at her. "The timing was never right, then I was leaving for school. I have six years to get through. What's the point? Plus, I don't want to ruin our friendship by making things awkward if he doesn't feel the same way or if things don't work out."

"Seriously? Can you not see the way he looks at you?" Naomi grips her chin, turning her attention to where Dawson is standing.

There's a gaggle of girls all around him, but his eyes are only on Sri. He raises a tall red cup to us and smiles. Sri smiles and waves.

"Don't you owe it to each other to see if there's something there?" I ask, feeling the misery of wanting someone I can't have and hoping her story will end better than mine. "Besides, what's he doing for a living? Can he do it where you are?"

"He's been working for his father as an electrician since high school. I assume that hasn't changed."

"So you haven't talked to him since you've been back?" I ask.

"No. This is the first time I've seen him."

"Oh, for fuck's sake!" Naomi shoves Sri in Dawson's direction. "*Go.*"

"But I . . ." She stumbles forward, her beer spilling in front of her. Dawson sees her and is already walking in her direction.

The music changes and becomes fuller, louder. "Come on." Naomi tugs on my arm, pulling me toward the house. "Nash is starting."

"Farmer boy DJ," I tease.

"Hey, that's good."

People are already dancing when we step inside. It looks to be a regular thing, like Jumpin' Jack's beach and Thursday nights at the drive-in.

Naomi sets her cup down and begins pushing her way into the mix, pulling me along behind her. I quickly chug the rest of my beer and stall us for a second as I find a place to set the empty cup down.

In the center of it all, we dance. The girl's got rhythm, and I'm easily caught up in Nash's mix. When the crush of bodies becomes too much, and I find it hard to breathe, I leave, maneuvering myself back outside. I didn't tell Naomi I was going. I couldn't. A panic crept up on me and I had to get out. As soon as the fresh breeze hits my face, I take in a heap of air and lean against the house for support. Well, that was a first. I've never been claustrophobic before.

People are dancing out here as well. I continue to lean against the house, but notice a group of guys descending on me like wolves. I straighten up immediately and look for somewhere else to go, but they're on me in a heartbeat. Chaz is at the back of the pack, which has me curious.

"There you are," the leader says to me. "I've been looking for you all night."

I bark out a laugh. "Does that line usually work?"

He leans a hand against the house next to my head. "Always."

My stomach twists into a knot. He can't do anything with all these people around, but there's a disturbing darkness about him and it's invading my space. "Not interested."

I move to the left, but his other hand shoots up and lands next to my head, blocking me in. "Come on, gorgeous, don't be like that. Me and my friends are visiting for the weekend. Hang with us."

I pretend to give the idea some deep thought. "Yeah, no." I know I shouldn't provoke him, but his attitude is pissing me off.

"Zeke, stop." Chaz is suddenly next to him, pulling on his arm. "Leave her alone."

"Hey, guys." Colten pushes his way through the group, calmly nudging guys out of the way as he goes. "How's it going?"

"It's going just fine." Zeke runs the back of a finger down my cheek. I cringe and give him a shove, but he doesn't budge. "Just talking to this beautiful girl here."

"She is beautiful, isn't she? Do you mind?" Colten moves one of Zeke's hands off the wall and slides up next to me, putting an arm around my shoulders. "You ready to go, babe?"

The guy takes a step back. "This your girl?"

"She is."

"She didn't say nothin'. Maybe she's done with you." He moves in, standing nose to nose with Colten.

"Oh my god! Get over yourself." Taking Colten's hand, I shove my way through the group, pulling him along with me.

"Does your girl always lead you by the balls?" the guy hollers after us.

"Happy girl, happy world," Colten shoots back, undisturbed by the taunt.

I look back just as Zeke looks at his friends like, *What the hell?*

"What an idiot." Colten's laughing now.

"Wasn't that funny? The guy wanted to fight you."

"He could have tried."

"There were four of them," I retort.

He motions across the patio. At least six guys have their eyes on us. "They would have had their hands full instantly."

"Bullshit ego," I grumble to myself.

He stops me. "We've been havin' these summer parties for a long time, Tess. Those kinds of guys are always showing up actin' like jackasses. It doesn't always turn into an issue, but sometimes it does. And we're always ready."

Dawson walks up with Sri. "Everything all right, hoss?"

"So far. We'll see."

I lean in to Sri and quietly ask how it's going.

"Good." She blushes.

I give her an easy nod, not wanting to embarrass her further. "Nash is good," I say to her, changing the subject. "Does he ever deejay outside of town?"

"No. But he's got a big following on TikTok and Discord—Instagram, too."

I watch as Dawson focuses on something or someone over our heads. I turn to look, but can't see anything to be concerned about. He does have the advantage of height, though.

"Want to go in and dance?" Sri asks me.

"I was, but there were too many people." And after Zeke and his friends, I feel sort of—I don't know—off.

"Yeah, it can get crazy when Nash gets going."

"Hey!" some girl shouts.

I look over to see the same group of guys harassing another girl.

"Ready to take out that trash?" Dawson asks Colten.

"Right behind ya," he returns, his expression still easygoing.

As they move forward, so do five other guys. They surround the problem, and then it's all a blur. Some guy takes a swing at Colten, which he easily dodges. Dawson, towering above everyone else, takes a couple of hits in the gut, but then it's suddenly contained and the four idiots are being hauled around the side of the house. All except Chaz, who's following behind with his head hanging low. He seems too young to be out with those losers. Maybe one of them is an older brother.

Not long after, Colten, Dawson, and their friends return, laughing and shoving each other. The people at the party barely react to the melee, like it's all part of the show.

"Problem solved," Colten says, stopping in front of me with Dawson by his side.

"I see that." I laugh. "You're all very, uh, efficient."

"It's how it's always been handled," Dawson says. "Passed down from one townie to another."

"Well, that was fun," Sri jokes, and looks up at Dawson. Their height difference is almost comical. "You okay? I saw you take some hits."

He drapes an arm over her shoulder. "Don't you worry none. I'm just fine." A blush creeps across her cheeks when he grins down at her.

"What are you all planning for an encore?" I joke.

"We could roll out the Slip 'N Slide," Dawson says.

I stare at him. "You can't be serious." *That's like for little kids, isn't it?*

"Serious as a hellcat," he returns. "Come on, Colten. Let's set it up."

CHAPTER 22

A TEN-FOOT-WIDE PIECE of plastic is unrolled and staked to the lawn, with two tall sprinkler stations set up and angled at the plastic from the beginning to center and down to the end.

I stand corrected—there's an adult version.

As the water sprays, people come from all directions. Then it starts. One person at a time, some in pairs, they run and dive headfirst onto their stomachs and slide the length of the plastic. Everyone whoops and laughs, having the time of their lives. No one seems to care that they're getting drenched. I love it.

"Your turn," Colten says, shaking his wet hair all over me.

"I think I'll pass. It'll take more coordination than I am capable of." I can see myself attempting to land on my stomach and ending up on my face.

"Oh, come on," he says. "When will you get to do anything like this where *you* come from?"

Never.

"It's fun," Sri adds.

"I don't see you doing it," I say, laughing.

"We'll be right behind you." Her eyes are on Dawson as he walks our way, soaked.

"Let's go." Colten grabs my hand and pulls me to the end of the line behind Sri and Dawson.

I smile up at him. He doesn't let go of my hand as we wait our turn, which unfortunately doesn't look like it'll take long. Maybe he's keeping me from bolting at the last minute. I watch Dawson and Sri slide down the lengthy black line, tumble together, then jump up and run to the side.

Shit. It's our turn.

"This is crazy." I start to panic.

He looks down at me with a quick grin. "It's fun. You ready?"

"No! How do I do this?"

"Come on." He tugs my hand and we're running. He releases it right before we dive. I manage to get onto my stomach somehow and we're sliding and bumping into each other across the slippery stretch until we end up in a heap, with his heavy body landing on top of mine.

I stare up at him, grinning. "I like this part."

His eyes fix on mine for a split second before he jumps up and says, "Hurry," and pulls me along with him. The next couple nearly crashes into us as we step out of the way at the last minute.

"That was *so* fun," I laugh, and tug on his hand. "Let's go again."

He looks down at my wet clothes and groans. I follow his gaze and laugh. This tank is even more see-through than the one I had on at the beach party and I'm wearing the lacy bra again. I give a sultry smile like, *Are you sure you want to resist?*

He mumbles something I can't make out, but I think it involved a couple of swear words. I smile innocently up at him, enjoying his irritation. I shouldn't be the only one suffering from this attraction.

It was an unexpected, enjoyable evening from start to finish. Being that Colten was the designated driver, he gave me, Naomi, and Sri a ride back to my place in the truck's bed with Dawson riding shotgun. Another first for me. You can't get away riding in the open like this in the city.

"Thanks for dragging me out of the house," I say to Naomi while we wait for Sri and Dawson to say goodnight.

As I expected, the girls are staying over. It's as if we've been friends forever and this is the logical next step in the evening. How did I get so lucky?

"It was a fun night," Naomi says. "You didn't dance long."

"Too many people. I couldn't breathe."

"I heard you got hassled." She looks off into the dark, then back at me like she failed me somehow. "Sorry I wasn't there."

It's the second time I've experienced her protectiveness. Knowing someone has your back is a powerful feeling. "It's okay. Colten handled it. He was surprisingly calm, actually. It was impressive." I've misjudged her horribly. She's a truly unique person. There's no hidden agenda, jealousy, or any of the usual bullshit that comes with the other female friends I've had.

"He's good at that shit, a lot better than me." She cracks a smile.

Colten calls out my name, then waves me over. He's been waiting in the cab for Dawson.

I cross my arms on top of each other and lean onto his open window. "What's up?" My face is close to his. I almost pull back, but decide against it. I could so easily lean in further and . . . His eyes drop to my mouth, sending a shiver through me. I lick my lips in anticipation.

"I, um, wanted to tell you"—he turns his head, so he's looking out of the windshield—"my mother texted earlier and wants me to invite you over on Sunday. We're havin' a special dinner since Josie leaves this Thursday."

I stand up straight, my hands still resting on the open window, when his eyes find mine again. "Okay," I say. Disappointment rakes over me with painful reminders that this will never be.

"I'll pick you up around five?"

"Sounds good," I say absently, stepping away from the truck.

Why do I keep doing this to myself? I question on the way back to Naomi. He obviously doesn't want me the way I want him. I can't keep torturing myself.

"Oh," he calls out. "Mom also said to bring your laundry. She figured you'd be needing to do some."

"Okay. Thanks," I respond over my shoulder, not stopping.

"Dawson! Let's go," Colten snaps out.

"You ready?" I say to Naomi as I pass her.

"You okay?" She follows me up the steps.

"Yeah. I'm good." When I open the door to the apartment, I turn in time to see Dawson giving Sri a polite kiss on the cheek. I watch as she walks up the steps with a cheesy smile pasted across her face.

I'd like to have that smile.

"I'll sleep on the couch," Naomi says when we all walk through the door. "Sri can sleep with you. She's tiny, so it makes more sense."

"Works for me," I yawn. It's late, and the exhaustion is back. The little nap I took barely relieved the miles I put on my body today, not to mention the emotional drain. That was my fault, though.

But it's okay. I'm done. Colten is a fantastic person, and I'd rather be his friend than cause all this tension between us.

"So . . ." Naomi says, giving Sri a small shove. "You two finally connected?"

The goofy smile returns. "Yeah. We're going to hang out at the beach tomorrow. You two should come."

"You don't need us there interferin'. You should be alone with the boy. I have to work anyhow."

"I don't know what I'm going to do tomorrow. I hate days off," I say. All that downtime is difficult when my mind wants to drift to things I can't have.

"Come with us," Sri's sweet little voice pleads.

She's nervous, but she's also being nice. "No. Naomi's right. You need time alone with Dawson." I wink at her, causing her cheeks to pinken. It's nice to meet someone who blushes over a boy as much as I do. *Did*, I remind myself.

"You could come keep me company at Bell's," Naomi offers.

"I could do that."

But then what?

I could do a little shopping, I guess. Buy some decent underwear, for starters.

"Maybe you could help me come up with next week's flavor combination."

"That sounds like fun." I wonder how many forms of chocolate I could mix together and have it still considered ice cream?

I dig through the box with the extra linens, then make up the bed for Naomi on the couch. When I walk into the bedroom after brushing my teeth, Sri is already asleep.

My life has changed drastically since being abandoned here. Colten and his family are a gift. Sri is the sweetest human being on the planet and Naomi may be rough around the edges, but underneath, she's kind and a fiercely loyal friend. I'm so lucky to have these people in my life. My heart is so full after being empty for so long.

I've never known this feeling—contentment. That's the word I would use to describe it. Even not having Colten the way I want him, I still feel at peace, because he's still part of my life. Now, instead of waking up every morning and going through the motions, I look forward to what will happen next. And just when I think there is no way it could get any better, something new and spectacular happens.

CHAPTER 23

THE SUN always seems exceptionally bright when I'm not ready to wake up. But my bladder is screaming, so I don't have a choice. I look over to see Sri asleep on her stomach at the edge of the bed, her head facing the wall, with an arm disappearing over the side of the mattress. Careful not to wake her, I slide out of bed, then tiptoe to the bathroom. There's snoring coming from the living room. I peek down the hall and laugh silently at Naomi on her back, mouth open, her body splayed on the floor with one leg still draped on the couch. Hard to say from her position if she fell off or purposely moved to the hard surface for more room.

With my face clean, my teeth brushed, and my hair pulled back into a knot, I open the bathroom door, letting out a small shriek at the sight of Sri standing there rubbing her eyes. "Holy crap," I whisper, not wanting to wake Naomi. "You scared me."

"I'm awake," she hollers from the front room. "Coffee, I need coffee."

"Be out in a minute." Sri pushes past me, her body nudging me out of the way so she can shut the door. "Gotta pee, *bad.*"

Naomi's back on the couch when I walk into the living room. "How was the floor?" I tease.

"I'm used to it. I'm a restless sleeper."

I open the fridge and stare at the emptiness. "We'll have to go down to the Earl's for breakfast. I don't have much for food here."

"I could go for some waffles." She smiles dreamily.

"Waffles?" Sri enters the room. "You're making waffles?"

"No," I say. "We're heading down for breakfast. Is that okay? All I have are snacks."

Her face lights up. "Earl's cooking? Hell yeah!"

"Hey, do either of you have an extra hair tie so I can put this mess up?" Naomi asks. Last night's ringlets have turned into an explosion of frizz.

Humidity, Slip 'N Slide, and a restless night's sleep will do it. Mine wasn't much better. "I do. I got a new pack of them. They're under the sink. Help yourself."

"Thanks." She shuffles off.

"How'd you sleep?" I ask Sri, sliding my feet into my flip-flops.

"Surprisingly good."

"When I woke up, you were mashed against the wall. I hope I wasn't crowding you."

"Not that I know of. I'm a sound sleeper."

"I wasn't till I came here. It could be all the silence." *Or the overall peace this place affords me.*

"Ready." Naomi comes out with her hair in two giant knots

at the base of her head. "Sri. We'll have to leave right after we eat. I need to be at work by ten."

"No problem."

"Your hair is cute that way," I say.

She combines a grumbled thank you with the word "caffeine" as she slides her shoes on and pushes through us to get to the door.

"Not a morning person?" I ask. She turns and flips me off.

I *so* love her.

"Hey, girls." Twyla looks surprised to see us entering the diner together. "You're all up early for a Saturday."

"Morning, Miss Twyla," my friends say, one after the other.

Should I be addressing her that way?

"Morning, Miss Twyla." I try out the words. They sound odd coming out of my mouth.

"'Twyla' is fine," she tells me. "I've tried to get these two" —she jerks her head toward my friends—"to drop the 'Miss', but down here, it would be impolite."

"It's habit," Sri says. "We've been calling you that since we could talk."

Twyla touches her arm. "I know, baby. You girls have always had such good manners. So what brings you all out near the crack of dawn?"

"We were at a party last night," I say. "They spent the night and we woke up ridiculously early for some reason." I'm not hungover. I only had two beers, but I'm wiped all the same. "Anyway, Naomi was *whining* for coffee." I wink at her. "And then the idea of waffles got thrown in."

"You'll have to sit at the counter," Twyla says.

"No problem," I say, looking at how busy the diner is. "Do you need help?"

"No, no. I got it. Breakfast is simple, but if you could take care of your friends, that would be great."

"Sure thing," I say, already heading for coffee.

"I wasn't whining," Naomi says, eyebrows bunching as I set the mugs on the counter in front of her and Sri. They took the last two remaining stools. "I seem to recall someone else needing her caffeine fix last night when we came to take your sorry ass out."

"What can I say? Coffee is my silent best friend." I laugh and turn to the expo window. "Morning, Earl."

He glances over his shoulder while manning the grill. "You're up early today."

"We had a late night and we're craving your amazing cooking." I nod my head toward my friends.

He comes to the expo window and salutes with his spatula. "Well, hello there, young ladies. Do y'all know what you want?"

"Waffles!" we call out in unison.

"Bacon or sausage, or both?" Earl asks.

"I'm good with both," Naomi says.

Sri and I each add a "Me too."

"Coming right up," he says.

We all doctor our coffee with intense motivation, then sip slowly in silent bliss. I take care of the other people at the counter while I wait for our food.

"*Hey, Tess*," a voice booms. I look up to see Jeb holding up his coffee mug. "How about a refill?" I give him a raised eyebrow with a hand-on-the-hip glare.

"Please," he says, looking sheepish.

"Did I just hear that right, Jeb?" Twyla jokes as she passes him. "You said 'please'?"

"Ah, now, I ain't that bad." He stares into his cup.

"Well, we can up our manners no matter how old we are. I like it, Jeb, keep it up." She pats him on the shoulder.

"Yes, ma'am."

I take the coffeepot over and fill his cup. "I'm off duty, you know. Helping until our food is ready."

"I know. Just wanted to say hi and saw you with the coffee." His face cracks into a hint of a smile. "Killin' two birds with one stone," he chuckles. "I ain't never seen you this early."

"I can say the same thing." Jeb rarely comes around until eleven.

"It's too crowded here on Saturdays. I try to come before the tourists crowd up the place. You and your friends could sit here, if you want. Keep an ol' man company. I got this whole booth."

I look over to see Sri and Naomi, turned in their stools, watching our interaction. Naomi's scowling. This is her second encounter with Jeb. "Okay, but you be nice," I warn.

"Yes, ma'am."

"Come on," I say, walking over to my friends. "We're sitting with Jeb." Then I whisper, "He's okay, just really lonely and could use the company."

Neither one complains as they pick up their mugs and follow me back to the table. I sit next to Jeb. As I make the introductions, Sri and Naomi slide in across from us.

He dips his head in acknowledgement. "Nice to make your acquaintance." His kindness sounds rusty and awkward.

"It's nice to meet you too," Sri says, her smile bright.

Naomi grunts a hello. Those two are more similar than, I'm sure, either would care to admit.

"Order up!" Earl yells.

"Hey, did you eat yet?" I ask Jeb.

"All taken care of," he says. "I was just on my last cup of coffee."

"Okay. Be right back." I climb out of the booth and head to where the food sits under the warmer. "That was fast. Thanks, Earl."

"Family and friends get priority," he says with a friendly wink. "Hey. That's real nice of you girls, sittin' with ol' Jeb."

"He's grown on me." I smile as I stack two plates on one arm and grip the other in my hand. "This looks amazing, Earl." He's added sides of blueberries, fresh-cut strawberries, and whipped cream to our plates.

"Enjoy."

"We *will*," I say.

The conversation is light while we eat. Jeb is a perfect gentleman. And even though he doesn't say much, I can tell he's enjoying the company.

Twyla comes by with the coffeepot. "You all good? Need anything? More coffee?"

"I've had my fill, thanks," Jeb says to Twyla, who awards his polite reply with a big smile just for him.

"I'll take half a cup," Naomi says, "then I have to get ready for work." She turns to me. "Can I use your shower real quick?"

"How about I fill you a cup to go?" Twyla offers.

"Thank you. That'd be great."

"Cream and sugar?"

"Yes, ma'am."

"I'll take the bill for everyone," Jeb says.

I almost bust out laughing at Twyla's shocked face. "All this politeness!" she says, recovering. "You'll do no such thing. It's on the house."

Everyone objects, but she beams us all with a smile and walks off.

"Well, I best be off," Jeb says. I scoot out of the booth so he can be on his way. "Thanks for the company. I'll see you Monday," he says to me.

I smile up at him. "You bet."

"You come by Bell's sometime," Naomi tells him. "Try some of my homemade ice cream, ya hear?"

"I might just do that. Well, it was nice meetin' you both," he says, then ambles his way over to the door.

"That was nice of you, inviting him to have ice cream," I tell Naomi. I don't like that he's alone. It'd be nice if he could make friends with her before I go. Bell's would be another place for him to visit, hang out.

"No worries. I'm always looking for new customers. Can I have the key to the apartment?" she asks me.

"I didn't lock it."

Sri fishes her car keys out of her purse and hands them to Naomi. She must have brought clothes to change into.

"Y'all hanging here until I get back?" Naomi asks.

"Yep," Sri replies, lifting her mug. "Still some left."

"When are you and Dawson going to the lake?" I ask when Naomi's gone.

"Not until one. Why?"

"I need to go into town to grab a few things. Do you want to come?"

"Sure. I haven't been to any of the shops since I've been back. Have you gone to Bonnie Bee Goods yet?" I shake my head no and her eyes light up. "You'll love it. *So* many cute things."

"Clothes or knick-knacky kind of stuff?"

"A little bit of everything, why?"

I look over my shoulder to make sure no one is looking, lift my shirt up a little, and pull up a swatch of light-blue cotton with a wide, white band.

"Okaaay?" she drawls out, her eyebrows raised like, *Why the hell are you flashing me your underwear?*

"My stuff left with my car, and all I could find at the general store were these lovely briefs. That was a little over a week ago. I haven't been back in town."

"Oh. I'll take you to a place that should have what you need. Things have turned out okay for you here."

I smile. "Better than okay."

"And this guy you were with . . ."

"Dax?"

"Was he . . . abusive?" she asks tentatively.

"No. Just a dick and the biggest mistake of my life so far."

"I'm sure everyone has one of those, eventually. Mine was Justin, a second-year premed student—sickeningly handsome and arrogant as hell. Felt I should worship the ground he walked on, but servitude is not my thing."

I laugh. "Good for you."

"So, you like Colten?"

"We're just friends."

"That's not what I asked."

I blow out a breath. I make sure Twyla isn't within hearing distance. "It's complicated."

"Isn't it always? I don't want to see him get hurt either, but if you really like him, don't wait to tell him. I wasted a long time not telling Dawson how I felt."

"Oh, he knows, but he's made it clear he doesn't want to get involved."

"I'm surprised. The way he is with you, I thought . . . well." She looks down into her coffee cup.

"I'll only be staying here until the end of summer, and I don't think he's interested in a long-distance relationship."

"I'm sure Delilah coming back didn't help." She gives me a sympathetic smile. "I'm sorry."

"Me too. But it's okay. I shouldn't be jumping into another relationship, anyway."

On our way to the next shop, we hear, "Hello, ladies." Chaz pushes his way between us and throws an arm over each of our shoulders. "It's nice seeing you again."

We both shrug him off, then I round on him. "Listen, kid, I'm sure you're real sweet and all, but we're really not interested." I know I sound harsh, but he doesn't get it.

His face drops. "Sorry. I know. I just wanted to say hi."

"Then just say hi," I snap.

"Are you here for the summer?" Sri asks in her usual sweet tone.

I give her a look like, *What the hell are you doin'?*

He frowns at me, but brightens when he turns to Sri. "We just moved here."

Crap, this kid doesn't know anyone. "Maybe don't try so hard," I say, feeling bad for him, but *sheesh*. "And maybe introduce yourself to girls your own age—politely, with respect. Not this macho bullshit."

Sri hooks her arm through his and walks. "What she means is, relax and be yourself. Don't try so hard. Do that, and I'm sure you'll make friends just fine. Where did you move from?"

He's a couple inches taller than Sri and looks down at her like he's hit the jackpot. "Dallas."

He still doesn't get it. "How old are you?" I ask.

"Fourteen."

Tough age. Those raging hormones aren't helping. "I'm new here too. Just here for the summer. I work at a diner outside town called Earl's."

"I've seen it, but I haven't been."

"Best food in town," I say.

"Yeah?"

"Come on in sometime. I'll buy you a burger."

He winks at me. "Now you're talking."

I roll my eyes. "Chaz?"

"Yeah?"

"Knock it off."

"Oh, right. Sorry."

"We were just heading over to Bell's for some ice cream," Sri says. "Do you want to come?"

"Really?" He looks between us, radiating a look of pure joy.

Crap. I know that expression—one deprived kid to another. "Sure. Why not?" Maybe Sri can introduce him around.

.   .   .

"Seriously?" Naomi barks out as soon as she spies the kid as we walk in.

"Naomi, this is Chaz," Sri says.

"I know who the little runt is."

Chaz's expression . . . it breaks my heart. "It's okay," I tell him. "I've been told her bark is worse than her bite."

Sri walks behind the counter and grabs Naomi by the arm. "Can I talk to you for a minute? In private."

"The ice cream is made right here." I redirect his attention by pointing to the chalkboard sign of flavors. "Naomi concocts a lot of the flavor combinations herself. Go ahead. Pick one. My treat." I can hear their muffled argument in the back over the music that's turned down low. "You can't go wrong," I continue. "They're all amazing, even vanilla." I laugh to myself. "Personally, I go for anything chocolate. Hey. Was that your brother who was being a jerk at the party last night?"

His face turns bright red. "I'm sorry he was like that to you. I tried to get him to back off," he says, his expression earnest. "He's okay . . . sometimes. When he doesn't drink."

So that's his role model?

I hope the guys pummeled some sense into the jerk.

"We'll help you out." Naomi returned from the back with Sri behind her. "*But . . .*" She points a finger at him. "You can't be all weird and comin' onto every female with a heartbeat. Got it?"

Chaz stands up straighter. "Y-yes, ma'am."

"Well, all right." The corner of her mouth twitches up. "You decide on a flavor?"

"Well, I was thinking, uh, can I have a scoop of 'Everything but the Kitchen Sink,' please?"

"Make that two," I say.

"Three." Sri holds up a hand.

Naomi said I could help her create a new flavor today. Maybe she'll let me and Chaz create our own version of Death By Chocolate. It was nice of her to invite me to hang out. Should be interesting. Hanging with Naomi usually is.

CHAPTER 24

COLTEN PICKS me up for Josie's special Sunday dinner in a beautifully refurbished Porsche convertible.

"Where have you been hiding *this* beauty?" I thought he was being sarcastic when he picked me up for the BBQ and said he left the Porsche at home.

"Found it at an auction. It was a graduation gift to myself. Someone had started the process, but only completed the interior. I took care of all the nuts and bolts and then took it to Charlotte to get painted. There's a body shop there that specializes in vintage cars. Just got it back a couple of weeks ago."

I hold up my bag of laundry. "Where should I put this?"

"Behind the back seat works. I'd make sure the bag is closed tight. You don't want your stuff blown from here to my house."

I do as he says, open the door, then slide onto the leather seat. "*Wooo.* Hot!" I prop myself up—the bare parts of my legs burning.

"Sorry about that. I shoulda put a towel down before I left— wasn't thinkin'."

"It's okay. Just give me a second." I slowly ease myself down and buckle up. "I'm good now."

He leans against his door, looking at me. "I don't think I've seen you with your hair down. It's pretty."

I smile at the compliment, but don't let myself get worked up over it. I'm done with all that. "Thank you."

"This car would have been great for the movie," I say as we drive through town.

"I'm so used to needing the truck for work, I didn't even think of it. I'll be sure to bring it next time."

When we turn onto the lake road, I drop my head back on the headrest to take in the sun as it flickers through the tops of the trees. I breathe in deep the smell of earth and green. The ride has been silent, but I don't mind. Sometimes, the quiet speaks louder than words. Right now, it tells me we're comfortable being in each other's presence. I like that, the natural rhythm of us. Thinking about it, I realize the only time it's not there is when I'm forcing us to be more than we are. I'm glad I let my hopes of us go. I'll still have to fight the attraction, but I won't be questioning his every move, hoping, or wishing it means something.

He turns onto a dirt road that leads us to a large house with a picturesque backdrop of the lake. The layout and style blend well with the natural surroundings—single level, natural wood siding, dark green shutters, stunning gables, large windows.

"Come on." He shuts off the ignition and climbs out of the car without opening the door—not an easy task with such a long body.

I open my door and he's there with a hand out to me, laughing. When he pulls me up, I ask, "What's so funny?"

"Your hair, uh . . . The convertible, it . . ." He reaches out and smooths the side of my head from top to bottom, making my breath catch in my throat. "It's kind of everywhere."

"Oh." I let out a small, uneasy laugh. Keeping my mind in the friend zone is going to be harder than I thought. "This is why I don't like leaving it down."

He reaches behind the seat for my dirty laundry, while I attempt to comb my fingers through my wind-tangled hair. Giving up, I pull a hair band off my wrist and pull it into a messy bun.

"I can carry that," I say, following him across the driveway.

He slings the bag over his shoulder. "I've got it."

The double front doors are hand-carved trees over frosted glass. The workmanship is exquisite. As soon as we enter the house, Josie's there, grabbing my hand and pulling me along with her. "Come see my room."

I stumble behind her, trying to keep up. "Hold up, kid," I say, laughing at her exuberance. She takes me down a hall that parallels the main room. My eyes dart around, taking in neutral, light walls, natural wood trim, and all the light. We've passed a couple of bedrooms and a bathroom. One must be Colten's, because neither room is big enough to be the master. Maybe he'll show me later. I hope so. A bedroom says a lot about a person—neat or messy, sentimental, a place to escape or just lay your head down. Does he have pictures of friends, girlfriends, dirty magazines under his bed?

"What do you think?" She steps into her room with arms out wide.

I expected pink walls plastered with posters of adorable baby animals and a bed full of stuffed animals. Instead, I'm awed by the two floor-to-ceiling bookcases flanking large patio doors. The view of the lake is stunning, and so is the impressive telescope tilted toward the sky and the deck it sits on. The colors in the room are soft, earthy tones, not girly at all. "Did you decorate or your mother?"

"Mom. Decorating isn't really my thing."

"And the books . . ."

"All mine."

I look through the selection. She likes to keep what she reads. There are beginning- level chapter books all the way to Chesler, Fitzgerald, Nietzsche, Hemingway, the entire *Harry Potter* series as well as the *Twilight* and *Hunger Games* series— an eclectic mix.

"You have a wide range here."

"True. There's no particular genre I subscribe to."

"You sound like an old woman. Speak preteen."

She laughs. "*Fine.* I enjoy all books. Come on." She takes my hand and tugs me out of her room. "I'll give you a tour of the rest of the house." I follow her, continuing down the hallway.

"This is Mom's studio." She walks into a large open space with a vaulted ceiling and a wall of windows. So far, every room seems to have a view of the lake. The lighting is outstanding.

"Do you think she would mind me looking around? I'd love to see her work."

"You go right ahead," Twyla says, springing up behind us.

"Oh, hey." I startle, feeling a little embarrassed about wanting to snoop.

"Colten said Josie nabbed you at the door. I thought I would come save you if need be."

"*Mom*," Josie huffs.

Twyla gives her an affectionate pat on the cheek. "I'm just teasing, baby."

I notice several canvases stacked against the wall. "Do you mind?" I point, itching to have a look.

"Not at all."

She uses lots of bright, chunky colors to mimic real life, similar to the pieces in the diner and gift shop. "You're a fan of impressionism."

"Always have been. I like reality, but it's even better stylized with bold strokes and color."

"They're impressive. Are they displayed in any galleries?"

"No. I don't have time to peddle my work in big cities."

"It's a shame. You have genuine talent and could do well."

She smiles. "That's quite a compliment coming from a fellow enthusiast."

I shrug a shoulder, moving to her worktable. "You make jewelry as well." I touch a delicate pair of silver earrings woven into a loose ball with small, round, blue stones at the center. "Where do you find the time?"

"I've never needed a lot of sleep." She takes a dangly orb and begins inserting it through the hole in my earlobe. "When the house is at rest, that's when I get my best work done." I touch the earrings as she steps back to inspect. "Perfect. They're yours."

"Oh, no. I couldn't." I begin to remove them.

"You absolutely can. Those little ears of yours have been bare since you got here. The holes might close up." She taps my nose gently. "You know . . ." She takes a step back. "At first I wasn't sure about having you with us, but now I can't imagine it any other way."

There's a slight jab at the first part of the comment—the second has me floating on air. "I wish I didn't have to leave at the end of the summer." I can't remember ever being this happy.

"You have a goal, as you should. It's important to keep it no matter what." She stares at me pointedly like, *Right?*

She must think that Colten and I are a thing. We're not, but why would she be against it? She made a similar choice.

"Colten told me how you left California to be with Earl." She seems to be content in her choice.

"Yes, but I *completed* my degree. You've barely started on your journey."

"But my journey led me here." I know this is crazy talk. She's right. I have plans. And why am I arguing? It's a non-issue.

Maybe because if it were, and Colten and I were together, I would want her to be on my side.

"Am I missin' somethin'?" Josie looks back and forth between us.

"Not at all," her mother says, turning her to the door. "Come on. I'm sure your dad has dinner ready."

"Great. I'm starvin'," Josie says. "I can't wait to see the dessert he made for me. He's been keepin' it a secret." She runs off.

The thought of staying here past the summer started when Colten said "this place couldn't hold me, that it would never be enough." I'm not generally a stubborn person, and I don't need to prove him wrong, but when a person has been starved and suddenly finds themselves fulfilled, it's hard to think about going back to depravity.

"I know I'm not your mother . . ." Twyla starts.

"Thankfully no," I say on a laugh. "She's horrid."

She chuckles softly and places an arm around my waist. She squeezes me to her side as she leads us out of the room. ". . . But I think it's important to tell you . . . giving up on your dreams before seeing them through, just because you found something you maybe didn't have before, would be a mistake."

"If you're thinking this is about Colten, it's not." I think it's important to clarify. "We're friends getting to know each other. When I said I wish I could have stayed, it was because I've found something I've never had before—a family, real friends, community, a place I feel I belong." Understanding crosses her features. "I've never been around a family like yours. Love and kindness are given so freely, so easily. It's hard not to want what you have." I smile tentatively. "And I hope Colten and Josie know how lucky they are."

"Oh, my sweet girl." She briefly cups the side of my face. "I think they do, but if not, they'll realize it one day."

"Now that I know how it can be, I'll never settle for less in my life."

She waves a hand in front of her face. "That's the sweetest thing anyone's ever said to me. Come on. Let's go eat before you make me cry."

. . .

I lean back against my chair, rubbing my stuffed belly. "That was *sooo* good." Earl made the best ribs and best sides I've ever had.

His smile stretches from ear to ear. "Glad you liked it."

"Can we have dessert now?" Josie asks, barely containing her excitement. "I've been patient all day. I haven't peeked once. *I swear.*"

"Good girl." Earl gets up. "I'll go get it. Anyone want coffee?"

"I'll have a small cup if you're making some," I say.

"I think I'll have some too," Twyla says, getting up. "Colten? What about you?"

"No, I'm good." He taps my earring. "Did Mom give you these?"

"She did." I smile, proud to own something that Twyla made.

"They're pretty." He brushes a loose strand of hair off my face and behind my ear. I freeze at the touch, not sure how to react. He seems to realize the intimacy of his actions and drops his hand.

"Only a couple days left," I say on a deep inhale as I turn to Josie. "I'm excited for you."

Her face lights up. "This camp is amazing. It's a powerful think tank and I get to be a part of it."

"I was thinking more of campfires, canoeing, and arts and crafts."

"*Pfft.* No way. That's baby stuff."

"Hardly. I loved Camp Timberlake. I went there every summer until I was twelve. That's where I learned to swim, build a campfire. Kissed my first boy—" I wink at Josie.

"There will be no boy kissing," Earl declares, carrying a chocolate cake that puts all other cakes to shame. It's huge, covered in a light whipped chocolate frosting, and decorated with fresh strawberries and chocolate shavings.

Josie claps her hands and squeals, "I get to cut it!"

"Absolutely." When he places it in front of her, it sits higher than her head. She stands and Earl hands her a giant knife. "Be careful."

She glares at him like, *Seriously?* "I've been helpin' in the kitchen for how long?"

He kisses the top of her head. "I know, my sweet."

Twyla sets a fragrant, steaming mug of coffee in front of me. "Thank you," I say.

"You bet."

"I want to propose a toast." Earl moves to his seat and picks up his mug. "To my not so baby girl"—he gives Josie a warm smile—"who's growin' up so fast it's hard to keep track. We'll all miss you. And to Tess . . . her abandonment has been our gain. Welcome to the family."

The unadulterated acceptance has me biting my lip to stop the tears pricking at the backs of my eyes. Earl clinks cups with Josie, then me, then the process continues until we're all included.

"I want a huge-ass piece," Colten says as soon as Josie picks up the knife.

"Don't you always," Josie retorts.

He places his giant hand on top of her head and gives it a wobble, then with both hands, messes up her hair.

"Hey. Just for that—" She cuts the tiniest piece possible and hands it to him.

"There's always seconds," he says, accepting it gracefully.

"Not if we eat it all first."

She cuts a quarter of the cake in one slice and passes it in my direction. I bark out a laugh. "No way! I can't eat all that. Give it to your dad."

She hands it to Earl, who passes it to Colten.

"Hey!" Josie gives an indignant pout.

"Sorry, kiddo. I don't need to add another ten pounds to this belly." He rubs the tiny mound.

"Your belly is perfect." Twyla kisses his cheek.

In turn, he nuzzles her nose with his. "You're being kind."

Colten quickly takes a bite of the enormous slice, declaring ownership. "Oh, man, that's good."

I get the next slice, which is still too big, but reasonable.

The cake is six layers of alternating chocolate, vanilla, and strawberry, with fillings to match each layer. The first bite is beyond heaven, and not another word is spoken until we've finished. A culinary work of art like this deserves our full attention. Of course, Colten finishes before I'm a quarter of the way through mine. Josie's not far behind. I would have thought something as good as this would have slowed their speed-eating. Apparently not.

"Did you even taste it?" I ask Colten.

"Every bite."

"Oh really? All three?" I joke. "Those were the biggest bites I've ever seen."

"As opposed to your mouse-size nibbles?" He cuts off a tiny corner of my cake, giving me a pitiful expression as he takes the tiniest of bites, mocking me.

"I'm savoring it." I give him a shove, then motion to his parents' plates, which are as full as mine.

"Don't waste your breath," Earl says. "I've been on them since the beginning."

Colten ignores him, takes a massive chunk off my cake, and shoves it in his mouth.

"Hey!" I smack my fork against his with each word of "Don't. Touch. My. Cake," then tap it against his nose, smearing it with frosting.

His eyebrows shoot up. "This is a side of you I've never seen before." He chuckles while wiping off his nose.

"You threatened my dessert," I say, laughing. "No one touches my food but me."

"Territorial of food. Got it." He drags a finger through my frosting, then puts it in his mouth, sucking off the chocolate. "*Mmmm*. Delicious," he taunts.

"I will be respectful to your family and not start a food fight, but be warned, I'll get you back." I grin at him mischievously.

One side of his mouth lifts in a slow, wicked smile like, *Bring it on.*

CHAPTER 25

COLTEN OFFERS to take me down to the dock after we finish, an invitation I happily accept after Twyla and Earl won't let me help clean the dishes. I need to move before I go into a food coma.

The house has a wraparound porch set on a section of land that bows out into the water, allowing numerous rooms to have a killer view. That's why every room seems to have a view. The master must be on the other side of the house. It would have a killer view as well.

There isn't a beach, just green grass leading to large boulders edging the water, and a dock with two boats tied to it —a small motorboat on the one side and a speedboat on the other.

The sun has set, but the sky is just getting interesting. I stop when I reach the end of the dock, wrap my arms around my full belly and breathe deep.

"Nice, huh?" Colten says from behind me.

"Amazing," I say briefly over my shoulder, taking it all in.

"Do you want to go for a boat ride?"

"I'd love to, but it's getting dark."

"Just a short one."

"Okay." I can't remember the last time I was on a boat. We've never had one, but the families I grew up around, during our summers in the Hamptons, did.

He unties the larger boat and jumps in, holding a hand out to me. When we're settled in the bucket seats, he takes a set of keys from his pocket and starts up the engine. Giving me a quick smile, he pulls away from the dock.

We move slowly at first, until we're a good distance from the shoreline, and then he punches the throttle and sends us flying over calm waters that mirror the sky in shades of blue, pink, and orange.

Stunning.

The air is warm and fresh and I feel like throwing my arms up, squealing in delight. With no expectations, disappointments, or loneliness, I feel nothing but absolute peace—freedom. I realize that the sensation is foreign to me.

As we round a corner, the lake expands and stretches far into the distance.

"Can you waterski?" Colten asks, breaking the silence.

"Yes. Wakeboard as well, but it's been a long time, and I was never very good."

"If you want, we could go sometime when we're both off work."

Another fun time to look forward to. I'm sure our friends will come with us. "I'd love to."

I wonder why he hasn't suggested it before, then I remember I haven't been here that long. So much has happened —all good things for once. I smile into the wind. I know reality will find me eventually, but for now, I can't imagine life getting any better.

The thought of all this ending has me studying Colten's profile, committing every curve and angle to memory. He must see me watching him, because he glances over. His expression is hard to read as his eyes hold mine a moment before he turns his focus back to where he's going.

After meeting Colten, I realize that Dax and the others I've dated were there to fill a void—a need for affection, a few kind words, the chance to connect. I was terribly unaware that there could be so much more.

"Are you ready to go back?"

No. But I say, "Whenever you are."

"It's gettin' dark and you're shivering."

I hadn't noticed the ball I've rolled myself into. "You're right," I say, my teeth chattering now. It's cooler on the water.

"Here," he says, slowing the boat to a crawl and motioning me over. "Want to drive? You can sit in front of me. My body heat will keep you warm on the way back."

Seriously? Being that close to him could kill me. I can't believe he suggested it. He must not have thought this through.

I should probably tell him no thanks, but my body is already climbing over as he adjusts the seat back.

I park myself between his straddled thighs, rest my back against his chest, and grab the wheel. Heat radiates from his body, but the warmth is nothing compared to the inferno raging inside me. As I contemplate how my body tucks perfectly against his, I realize he hasn't moved. Is he even breathing?

Serves him right for offering up this position.

I turn my head to look over my shoulder, but he's so close I can't see his face.

He clears his throat. "Um, ever drive a boat before?"

"No, but I imagine it's similar to driving a car."

"It's easier." He clears his throat again. "There aren't as many obstacles, especially at this time of day." He pushes up on the throttle a little, his arm brushing mine. "All right, can you feel the tension?"

Ah, hell yeah! But I don't think he means from our bodies molded together.

I'm aware of my legs bouncing and make myself stop. *Frick.* What do I do with all this adrenaline? I'm buzzing with it. I continue the boat on a straight path, trying not to fidget. Colten reaches for his phone from a narrow ledge below the wheel. As he leans forward, his body drapes around mine, and I hold back a groan. I've never felt this kind of sensual torture before. When he rights himself, he's holding the phone up above us, telling me to smile.

"I'm not one for this kind of stuff," he says, "but I'd like something to remember you by." He takes the shot and sets his phone back.

"You make it sound as though I'm leaving tomorrow."

"You never know."

"I'm staying the summer." *I hope.* When he doesn't answer I ask, "Can we go faster?" This back-and-forth between his words and his actions is giving me whiplash. Maybe speed will help clear my brain of wanting him to feed my need for release.

"You're in control."

No. Not even close.

I push up on the throttle a little at a time until we're flying once again. It's not sex with Colten, but it takes a distant third or fourth place.

I wish I didn't have to leave at the end of the summer. If I stayed, Colten might allow this relationship to follow its natural course.

Maybe I could blow off school for a year and stay here and work. Lots of people take time off before starting college. A gap year, I think it's called. It's not like I'm giving up on my goal, just deferring it.

"We're getting close," he says, reaching around me to ease down on the throttle and then grips the wheel—his hands next to mine. I relax my grip, lean my head back on his shoulder, and look at the stars beginning to dot the sky.

"Almost there. Can you get ready to jump out? I'll pass you the rope. I'm sure the queen of Camp Timberlake will know how to tie up a boat." His deep chuckle vibrates through my body.

"Sure." I crawl over into my seat, chilling instantly. "I remember a *few* knots."

He pulls up alongside the dock. When I climb out, he hands me the rope, and I tie the knot as best as I can remember.

Colten steps out of the boat and stands next to me, inspecting my work. "Perfect." He faces me. "You're still cold."

I know. I'm shivering again.

He rubs his hands up and down my arms for warmth. "We better get you inside."

His touch has me searching his eyes, hoping the simple

gesture has greater meaning, even though I've told myself not to look for it anymore. He's about to move away.

"Wait, Colten. I—"

Before logic gets in the way, I stretch up on my tiptoes and press my lips to his. I know it's an insane move, but I couldn't stand the need any longer. His lips are soft as I thought they'd be, and oh so warm. The word *selfish* pops into my head. Several pounding heartbeats later, I realize he hasn't moved and isn't kissing me back. The fire in my body that sent me on this deluded path is doused instantly, then smothered completely when he grasps my arms and sets me away from him.

He looks a little stunned. *Angry* might be a better description.

"I'm sorry," I say, regret washing over me in uncomfortable waves. I've never been so humiliated. It's all my fault, though. I shouldn't have done it.

He doesn't say anything, only breathes deep and runs a hand through his hair.

Why isn't he saying anything?

His silent glare has me continuing to kick myself. *Please, just say something.* My throat knots up at the implications of what I have done. "I—I—"

He steps into me, grips the back of my hair, and crushes his lips to mine. The brief pain mixes with pleasure as my heart pummels against my ribs. Blood is rushing to my head, making my legs weak. I reach up and wrap my arms around his neck for support. The moment I do, he pulls me in tighter against his body, the intensity of his need happily matching my own. My hands slide under his shirt, sliding across tense muscles that quiver under my touch. His reaction excites me, empowers me. I've never felt so high. I need more, I need—

He's pulling away, breaking the kiss. He grips my hands and tugs them from around his neck.

"I didn't want this," he says, breathing heavily as I stand lifeless, my heart ripped out of my chest by his words. He kisses my forehead like it's some sort of consolation prize, then takes a step back.

I stare at his hands, clenching and unclenching. The torment in his expression as he looks out onto the lake speaks to my own. "I mean, I did. It's just . . ." His eyes meet mine. "We can't."

"Don't do this," I beg, finally finding my voice. I can't take it anymore. "We can figure—"

"No." He cuts me off and clasps his hands on top of his head, turning to face away. "We have to leave it at this."

"But . . ." I hurt in ways that are more painful than all the years my mother tormented me combined. "Can't we talk about it?" I can barely get the words out. We just have to work it through.

"Tess, please. Let it go, okay?" The defensive walls are back up. "If this goes where I think it could go . . . The pain of losing you . . ."

I reach forward and take his hand in both of mine, needing him to feel me. "It's already going to be painful, and me leaving for school doesn't have to be the end," I plead for his understanding.

"It's *four years*," he says. "And I have a life here, a business to run. I don't want a long-distance relationship."

"Why?" Tears of hopeless frustration prick at my eyes. "It

doesn't make sense. I could spend my holidays and summers here. There's FaceTime, phone calls, texts."

He shakes his head no.

"Why are you being so stubborn?" I holler, feeling like I'm going to explode from needs that will never be met. "I'm not Delilah! We can *do* this."

He stares down at me—his expression raw. "Maybe you can, but I can't." He turns and walks toward the house.

I gasp at the finality. Turning his back on me feels like a death blow. How can he do this? Just walk away so easily? My body slumps, wanting to drop to the ground and curl in on itself. I'm no stranger to rejection, but this is next level.

"Okay," I say to his back. "I'm sorry for pushing you into something you didn't want." Either that or I'm not worth fighting for.

He stops and turns. "It's not that I didn't want it, Tess. Fuck," he growls, anger radiating off him. "I want it more than my next breath. Can't you see that?" I open my mouth to speak, but he holds up a hand, stopping the words I was about to say. "I just can't. This is done. Over, okay?"

I nod in defeat. "Okay." There's nothing I can say or do to convince him. I have to accept his choice—really accept it this time.

From an overwhelming high to a deep, deep low—up and down on that tortured emotional rollercoaster. I follow him back into the house, stepping off the ride for good, because the alternative hurts too damn much.

Josie is still in the dining room. "How was it?" she asks us.

"I'll be right back," I tell him. "I need a moment."

I walk to the bathroom next to Josie's room as quick as my

legs will carry me. There's probably a half-bath closer, but I don't want to ask him where it is. I might break down in front of him if I do.

After locking the door, I stare at my reflection, trying to piece my mind back together. I choke on a sob and the tears break free.

What the hell do I do now?

And how can he just push this all away so easily? I'm dying inside.

He won't even talk about it.

"Pull yourself together," I tell the dejected image staring back at me. I don't want his family to think something is up between us. I grab a wad of toilet paper and wipe my eyes and blow my nose.

My hair is half out of its bun. Partly from being windblown, but more likely from our intense kiss. I fix it as best I can, then stare at my reflection. "We're just friends." I attempt a smile, then shake my head. "Yeah. That'll convince them," I say sarcastically.

I take a couple of deep breaths and shut off the light. On my way back to the celebration, I pass Josie's darkened room, then stop. I turn around, backtrack until I stand in the entrance of Colten's bedroom. The hallway is mostly dark, with only a small amount of light filtering in from the main room. I can't make out much more than the outlines of Colten's king-sized bed and a desk next to large patio doors similar to Josie's room.

I stare into the darkness a moment longer with arms wrapped tightly around my middle. I should get back. With a heavy sigh, I turn and head back to the dining room.

"Ready for Monopoly?" Josie asks. Everyone has reassembled at the table.

I plaster on a smile and hope it's better than the one I attempted in the bathroom. "Sure. Which game piece do I get?"

The monopoly tycoon, Josie, kicks all our butts. I try my best to let what happened with Colten go. It's Josie's night, and I want her to enjoy it. So instead, I focus on their incredible family dynamic. I revel in Twyla and Earl's easy love for one another, and tell myself to be grateful for what I have instead of being miserable that I can't get what I want. A fear creeps in, suddenly uneasy that I lost more than what I want. What if I lost his friendship as well?

The drive home is silent. I stare out the side window at the dark blur of trees, then up at the sky. No stars tonight. Maybe a storm is coming. The town lights eventually come into view and I watch as the storefront windows whiz past. Regardless of my earlier self-talk about being grateful for what I have, I feel empty—the thrill of being here gone.

When we reach the base of my steps, I'm out of the car with a mumbled *see ya*, not wanting to make things any more awkward than they already are.

As always, Colten waits until I unlock my apartment door before driving away. My mouth is dry and my chest aches as I mourn for something I'll never have. I pull a glass from the cupboard and fill it with juice from the refrigerator. It helps the dry throat but does nothing for the ache.

How could I have been so stupid?

I've wrecked everything.

Part of me knows Colten is right, that a long-distance relationship might not work. The other part thinks he's being weak. What's four years when we have something this amazing, something this intense? I mean, this isn't an everyday connection—even with my limited experience, I know that. I'm ready to fight for it, to do whatever it takes, and he's giving up before we even get started?

Frick, this sucks!

Why did I have to kiss him?

I walk to my bedroom with the plan of getting ready for bed, but I'm restless. I turn around and come to stand in the living room, not sure of what to do with myself. I refill my glass and stare out the kitchen window into nothingness.

There is a knock at the door. I whip my head around, my heart racing with adrenaline at the sudden noise. I rush to the window overlooking the stairs. Colten's truck is parked below. I whip the door open, ecstatic that he came back, only to fall flat when I see the agony in his eyes.

"What are you doing here?" I ask carefully.

He doesn't answer, just stares at me with that heartbreaking expression.

"Colten?"

He reaches me in two giant steps, wraps his body around mine, and squeezes tight, burying his face in my neck. "The further away I got, the more agonizing the pain—my chest, it hurt." He lifts his head and rests his cheek against the top of my head. He holds me tighter, making it hard to breathe. "I tried to stop myself from walking up those steps, but I couldn't. I need you, Tess, and I can't fight myself anymore."

He grips my head between both hands, then lowers his

mouth to mine as if his life depends solely on our connection. My hands slide under the back of his shirt, feeling his skin for the second time today. The sensation curls in and around my body, leaving me wanting more.

He kicks the door closed and reaches over his head for his shirt, breaking this kiss only long enough to pull it off. He reaches for mine next. Before I know it, we're skin to skin with lips, hands, tongues, and teeth, fighting for purchase as he walks me backward down the hall.

When we reach my bedroom, he scoops me into his arms. I bury my head in his neck and inhale the scent of him while kissing along his jaw and neck. Colten moans in pleasure as he lays me on the bed and settles his upper body above mine. He props his head in his hand as his eyes roam the length of my body. "Beautiful," he says as his fingers deliver velvety touches down my cheek and breast.

Don't slow down now! I feel like I'm going to internally combust. I grip the back of his head, bringing his lips hungrily against mine. My hands reach around his back, flattening and flexing on the surface as his upper body slides over mine restlessly. He's holding back.

When he breaks the kiss and sinks his head into the crook of my neck, breathing hard, I wonder if he will pull away from me again. I might tie him to the bed if he does. I'm that turned on.

He lifts his head, his eyes finding mine, warm and searching. "How can I be falling so hard?" My heart trips, then soars. "I tried to stay away, but after you kissed me tonight, all the reasons we shouldn't be together faded into nothing."

I cup his cheek in my hand. "The reasons don't matter anymore."

He presses a sideways kiss into the palm. "No. Not anymore." Then dips his head, pressing soft lips against mine.

How will I ever get enough?

His body slides over mine with a kiss that starts slow and languid, but quickly ignites until were nothing but a tangle of limbs twisted in the sheets, fighting a desperate battle for connection. In this moment, there is no past, no future, only an ecstasy I never thought possible.

CHAPTER 26

COLTEN LEFT SOMETIME in the early morning. I didn't hear him go. It was the sense of loss that woke me. I stretch out, smiling to myself as the early morning sun filters through the window. I never got around to closing the curtains.

Colten gave me more last night than I thought humanly possible. The connection was undeniable and the intimacy more than I ever expected. But I wish I had seen him before he left, so I would know if he had regrets or not. Last night, we didn't talk about where we would go from here. *We didn't talk about much of anything,* I laugh to myself.

I guess I'll let him take the lead. As long as he doesn't pretend it never happened, because that would tear me to shreds.

I drift off a little more until my alarm goes off. Colten must have set it, thankfully. I shower and get ready for work quickly, as I'm in desperate need of coffee.

"Morning, sunshine," Earl calls from the expo window when I finally make it into the diner.

The endearment never ceases to mush me. "Morning, Earl."

"What'll ya have?"

"I think I'll just do toast and coffee."

"That's not enough to hold you. How about some bacon and fresh fruit to go with it?"

"Perfect." Who am I to argue with such obvious wisdom?

I move behind the counter to pour a cup of coffee. Twyla comes up and hip checks me. I look over at her cheesy grin.

"What?" I say, afraid she knows what Colten and I did.

She shrugs a shoulder with an all-knowing smile and moves past me to get a bottle of ketchup, then leaves without saying a word.

Damn. I take a sip from my cup, watching her.

No way Colten would say anything. Mother's intuition? Or maybe she caught him coming in at the crack of dawn. She told me she doesn't sleep much.

So embarrassing.

Well, at least she's happy about it. Earl seems oblivious, unless he's just good at hiding his thoughts.

Please don't let him know.

I'm leaning against the counter, waiting for my food, when Josie comes up to the register. "Last night was fun," she says. "I'm glad you came over."

"Me too." *The afterparty was even better.* My cheeks heat at the thought. *How crude.* I didn't mean to think it. The words just popped into my head. The night was . . . Wow! I don't think either of us slept much.

"What's wrong with you?" Josie asks, punching numbers into the register. The drawer opens, she makes change for a customer's bills, then pushes it closed and leans against it.

"Nothing." I try to stifle the cheesy smile I know I'm wearing. "Are you stuck here today?"

"Yeah. But I don't mind, especially since I'm leaving soon." She grips the money in her hand. "Were you homesick when you went away to camp?"

"Heck no. My parents aren't like yours, though." I lean in. "Not as nice."

"Oh." She looks at me with a curious expression.

"Yeah. Unfortunately, we can't choose our parents. Don't you worry, though. You're going to have a blast. You'll be too busy to miss anyone, and before you know it, it'll be time to come home."

"I hope so."

Earl sets my food in the window and Josie leaves to deliver the change. He's made a happy face with two thick slices of orange for eyes with kiwi slices and a blueberry for pupils, a triad of banana slices for the nose, two strips of bacon for the smile, a slew of honeydew wedges for hair, and fanned strawberries for ears.

"Aw," I gush. "Thanks, Earl. That's so cute."

"Josie loves that." He shrugs a shoulder. "Thought you might as well."

"If I could reach you through this window, I would give you a big fat kiss. Thank you."

His grin reminds me of Colten's. "I'll take a raincheck, and you're welcome."

I sit at the counter with my plate and a steaming hot mug of deliciousness. "What do they have you doing today?" I ask when Josie comes back around.

"The usual—prep, bus tables, run the register for the gas station, man the gift shop."

"It'll be a super easy Monday with you here."

"Same goes to you. Havin' you around has really helped Mom a lot. I wonder if she'll hire someone after you leave, now that she's had time to see what it's like to have regular help. My bet is she will."

I hope not. I want to work here whenever school's out.

Leaning back on my stool, I try catching a glimpse of Colten in the garage, but I don't see him. My anxiousness builds as I eat, wondering if he changed his mind about us last night. Time has a way of making people see things differently.

I take a last sip of coffee and gather my dishes. The sooner I clean up, the sooner I can see how things are between us.

Ugh! I ate too fast.

"Can you take the counter?" Twyla asks when I come out from the back. "A large group just showed up."

"Yeah. Sure." Unbelievable. A gang of bikers filled every seat in the time it took me to clean my stuff and run a load through the dishwasher. Unfortunately, seeing Colten will have to wait.

We've been running for a solid hour and my head is dizzy, trying to remember what everyone wants and needs, when there's a loud crash. I look over and see Josie lying on her back with broken plates and food all around her. My first thought is that she slipped and I run her way, but Twyla pushes past me.

"Call nine-one-one!" she screams. "Earl!"

"Did she hit her head?" I ask.

"Call nine-one-one!" she yells at me with terror in her eyes. Earl runs from the back and is at Josie's side. He's checking her vitals as I rush to grab the portable phone by the register and frantically dial the numbers. There are only three, but my hands are shaking so hard it's difficult. I watch, waiting the long seconds it takes for someone to answer.

Josie is lying on the floor, her skin white. Earl is delivering chest compression while Twyla gives her mouth-to-mouth.

"Nine-one-one, what's your emergency?"

"A little girl passed out. They're giving her CPR. I'm at Earl's Diner in Jasper Creek."

"Are you in danger?"

"No. But you need to come now."

"What is your name?"

"It doesn't matter!" I scream, terrified. "Just *send* someone."

"Help is on the way. Please don't hang up. Can you give me your name?"

"It's Tess," I heave out, now that I know help is coming. "My name is Tess. The little girl that passed out . . . her name is Josie. She's eleven, almost twelve, but has a history of heart problems."

"Someone get Colten!" Earl yells.

"I'll be right back." I drop the phone, push through the people who have gathered, and run to the garage.

"Colten!" I yell, bursting through the door. There's a compressor going. I scream his name again. He looks up and smiles, then sees the horror on my face.

He rushes to shut off the pump. "What's the matter? What happened?"

"Come quick. It's Josie."

He pushes past me. I follow in his wake and see his parents are still working on her.

"Dad!" Colten hollers.

"Get the AED," Earl yells.

He does as he's told and comes back with a small box. Colten takes out scissors and cuts Josie's shirt up the middle and places pads on her chest as Twyla and Earl continue to work on her. The machine prompts everyone to move clear. Her little body convulses after the shock, and Earl continues to pump her chest while Twyla injects the lifesaving air into her lungs.

Colten takes Josie's hand in his, telling her she has to wake up. He says he'll let her win at chess. She can have the biggest piece of chocolate cake ever. He'll clean her room forever. On and on he pleads, offering up everything he can think of, if she'll just wake up.

A hand lands on my shoulder. I turn to see Jeb's concerned eyes. I didn't know he was here.

"They're doing everything they can," he says. I turn into him, burying my face in his bony chest. I hear a gasp from behind me.

"I've got a pulse," Earl calls out.

"Josie," Twyla cries.

I straighten up in time to see the relief on their faces. Earl pulls Josie against his chest. She gasps, her face contorted with pain as she grabs her side.

"Oh honey, your ribs. I'm so sorry." There are tears running down his cheeks as he gently lays her back on the floor. She attempts to reach up and touch him, but she's too weak. Twyla drops her face in her hands and sobs, her body shaking. Colten leans back on his heels, looking broken, and his tear-filled eyes find mine. I want to go to him, to all of them, but it's best to stay out of the way.

One of the bikers hands Earl a handful of clean towels. "For her head."

"Thank you," he says and gently lifts her head and slides them underneath.

I can hear a siren in the distance.

"Thank god," I hear Twyla say, and I know the feeling. I've never been happier to hear that sound in my life.

Earl kisses Josie's forehead. "Help's almost here, honey."

I look outside and see a few of the bikers near the street waving at the ambulance. When it pulls up in front, a lady in full leathers holds the door open. The rest stay where they are, averting their gaze to give the family privacy.

The EMTs hustle in and start assessing Josie instantly. Twyla is crying against Earl's chest. Colten has both his arms wrapped around his parents; his cheeks smeared with grease from hands buried in a car only moments ago. Their relief of Josie's consciousness is short-lived, replaced by the fear of not knowing if she will continue to survive.

The paramedics determine that she's stable, but her heart rate is weak and erratic. They need to get her to the hospital immediately for further tests.

The scene is horrifying, even blurred through a wall of tears. Jeb still has me around the shoulders, lending support as they prepare her for transport, then lift her on a gurney. She's so small.

"I'm okay," I hear Josie's faint voice say to her family as they wheel her out of the restaurant.

My knees buckle in relief at the tiny voice. I'm grateful Jeb still has hold of me.

Twyla catches my eye. "Earl and I are going with the ambulance. You and Colten stay and close the diner."

"The hell with that!" Colten rages. "I'm goin' with you."

"There isn't enough room," his father says. "But I understand your need to stay close to her. Just, I don't know, figure it out and come as soon as you can. We have to go." He's already moving out the door as he hollers back over his shoulder, "Drive safe, son."

Colten nods and looks down, broken. I rush over to him, throwing my arms around him and burying my face in his chest. He holds me so tight I can barely breathe—both of our bodies shaking.

Josie, little Josie. This can't be happening. My emotions cut loose with the dread of what may come, then realize my tears are probably making things harder on Colten. "I'm sorry." I pull away, wiping my eyes. "I can take care of things here. Just go."

He kisses the top of my head and breathes in a deep, shuddering breath. "Thank you. Are you sure?" He releases me. "I can't believe this is happening."

I hear someone clear their throat. I look over to see Jeb shifting from one foot to the other. "Son, you go on now and be with your family. I can help Tess here with whatever needs doin'. Don't you worry 'bout a thing."

"Thank you," he says, his expression beyond grateful. "I have to get my keys." He runs to the garage, shoving through the door, and then he's back in a flash, having shed his coveralls. He kisses the side of my head. "Okay. So—"

"Don't worry about anything here," I cut him off. "Jeb and I will shut down the diner, but keep the gas station open until its usual closing time."

"Okay." He briefly grips my hand before rushing away.

"Call me here when you get some news," I call out to him.

He runs back to me and kisses me on the lips. "Thanks again." Then he looks at Jeb. "To you both."

"You're not gonna kiss me too, are ya?" Jeb says, probably his attempt at lightening the situation.

"Hell no." Colten snorts, moving toward the door. "I'll call you when I can," he says to me, then he's gone, heading for his truck.

CHAPTER 27

"WELL, I guess it's you and me," I say to Jeb, wiping under my eyes.

"Listen up here, folks," he announces, surprising me. "Finish up your meals and Tess will take care of your bills. For obvious reasons, we'll be closin' down."

"Thanks," I tell him. "I'm not sure if my words would have come out as clear as yours."

"Don't you worry none. I'll start cleanin' this mess on the floor and then clear the tables. When you're done with all them customers, you can meet me in the back. I'll be washin' dishes."

"We have a machine for that."

"Well, they ain't gettin' in there all by themselves, are they?"

I kiss his cheek. "You're exceptional, you know that?"

He grunts as he works his way down to his hands and knees, the pain of the action evident on his face. "Leave it," I say. "I can do it."

"Go on about your business," he growls. "I'm already down here."

I grab a tray and set it by his side, then move to the register as customers line up. A giant of a man in a black leather vest, displaying tattoo sleeves on his bare arms, gets down on one knee to help Jeb, who growls at him like he did to me.

Stupid pride.

As I take care of customer bills, I notice another man, with severe scars on his face and down his arms, walk his dishes to the counter and set them down. The rest of the gang that isn't in line follow his lead. The thoughtful actions breathe new life into my battered heart. Twyla said this group comes through once a year. They must make a special stop for Earl's cooking. I'm grateful for the respect they've shown through this tragedy.

Motorcycles roar to life as the bikers prepare to leave. I thanked them all on their way out and briefly watch as they pull away one at a time, filing into a long line as they head out of town.

Jeb's taken care of the floor, so I take him to the back and show him how to run the dishwasher. I carry all the dishes and stack them next to him. While he deals with that, I shut everything off in the kitchen, then wipe down all the surfaces with disinfectant. Random customers come through the door needing to pay for gas, but it's easily manageable.

The phone rings.

"Earl's," I answer quickly.

"Tess, it's me."

My heart races at the sound of Colten's voice. "Is she going to be okay?"

"They had to rush her into surgery. It's gonna be a couple of hours yet before we know anything."

"Shit. Are you okay?"

"Not really, but what can I do?"

"You're there for your parents. I'm sure they're grateful."

"Yeah. I just feel so helpless."

"I know. I wish I could be there."

"Me too. Mom wanted me to say thanks. It gives them peace of mind knowin' you're takin' care of things. One less thing to worry about, ya know?"

"Yeah. No worries. And Jeb's been amazing."

"Tell him thanks as well."

"I'll do that. Call me when you know something, okay?"

"I will. Tess?"

"Yeah?" I hold my breath, scared that he'll say something that could destroy me.

"I—I'm so glad you're in my life."

I exhale, my chest swells with something deeper than I've ever known. "Me too."

We say our goodbyes and hang up. I pick up my rag and move behind the counter to finish up.

"So, you and the boy, huh?"

I pause before answering, images of last night race through my mind. "Yeah," I say. I ache, needing to be there for him, to hold him.

"That was quick."

I furrow my brow at him.

"I didn't mean it like that," he responds quickly. "I knew the moment I saw my Rosie that she was the one for me." His expression is sincere. "There's never been another."

"I'm sorry she's gone."

"No need to be. I just know how it can be to love someone that quick in every way possible."

"Oh, I don't—"

"You love that boy. I see it on your face every time you two are together. I may be old, but I'm not blind."

I laugh. "I'm not sure what love is." Even Maria was just there for the job. She cared deeply, but love? I might have loved her, now that I think about it, but then she was all I had.

"It takes many forms. There ain't no real way to define it, by my way of thinkin'. It's not there, then it is. And then it can be gone just as easily." I think of Josie, then of Jeb's wife and son. "You hang on to what you found, ya hear me? It don't come to us too often."

I walk over to him and kiss his cheek. "Well, you old softie."

"Ah, knock it off," he growls with a hint of a smile. "What else we gotta do?"

Sometime around six, I make us some sandwiches. I told Jeb he didn't need to hang out, but he refused to leave. Said he "wasn't leavin' me alone with no drawer full of money with all the crazies out there in the world." In truth, I appreciate the company. The wait is killing me.

Why hasn't Colten called?

"No news is usually good news," Jeb says, reading my mind.

I nod my head, hoping he's right.

I find a deck of cards in a desk drawer. He tries to teach me some new games, but I have a hard time concentrating. Finally, around eight, Naomi bursts through the door.

"Is she okay? I got here as soon as I could." She squeezes me in a powerful hug.

I fill her in and then she's on her phone with Sri, telling her to get her butt over here with a brief explanation.

Then she does the most amazing thing. She goes over to Jeb and pulls him in, shocking him with the same fierce hug she gave me—his expression is hilarious. "Thank you for being here. Y'know, steppin' up and all," she tells him.

"Well, I—" His face is bright red.

The phone rings and I run to pick it up. "Colten?"

"She's gonna be okay, better than new, actually." Jeb and Naomi come to stand beside me. "They found another hole in her heart. The surgeon missed it during her last surgery. They said it can happen when a heart is so small. But they've got it all now. They said she's going to be fine and shouldn't have any more problems."

I pull in a shaky breath. "Oh, Colten. I'm so relieved."

"What's he saying?" Naomi tugs on my arm. "She gonna be okay?"

I nod.

"Naomi's there?"

"Yeah. Jeb's still here too, and Sri's on her way."

"I'm gonna stay and help take care of my parents. They won't be leaving any time soon. I'm not sure when they'll open the diner again. But I'll be back sometime tomorrow afternoon. Can you man the gas station until I get there?"

"Absolutely." I want to do whatever I can to help.

"There's an extra set of keys on the bulletin board in the

office for the front door. Can you make sure I locked the door in the garage?"

"Definitely. I'll double check all the doors before I leave tonight."

As we say our goodbyes and hang up, Sri rushes through the door. "I got here as soon as I could." She wraps me in a hug. "How are you doing?" She steps back, looking me over. "Are you okay?"

"Great now. Colten just called."

There is a collective sense of relief as I tell everyone the news. It's been a rough day and I'm grateful to have my friends here—Jeb included, who has become an important part of my inner circle.

Everyone insisted on staying until closing. The cards were brought out once more and a simple game of rummy was played with the conversations centering around Josie. Apparently, she's always been a precocious child, her brilliance shining through as soon as she could talk. The more I heard, the closer I felt to the family that's so quickly become my own—a surrogate for the one I never had.

Naomi offered to stay the night, but I told her I was fine. I was ready to be alone and in desperate need of sleep. I checked all the doors and now stand at the base of my stairs, feeling the weight of the climb before I've taken my first step. The fatigue is overwhelming and I wish Colten was here to find me once again and carry me up.

The images of Josie on the floor and everything that happened flash through my mind. Life can be ripped from us at any moment. I'm thankful today wasn't the day.

I let myself into the apartment, chuck the keys onto the

kitchen table and make my way to the bedroom. Almost twenty-four hours ago, Colten and I were making love and life couldn't have been easier. Now I barely remember to set my alarm before passing out face down on the bed.

CHAPTER 28

WHEN I ENTERED the diner at seven the next morning, the images and actions of the previous day played out in my mind once again—Josie's small, unconscious body, the CPR, and the shock delivered by the life-saving machine that restarted her heart. It was a lot to take in so early in the morning.

Now I sit here, two cups of coffee later, still barely able to keep my eyes open, and take in the emptiness of the space. Without all the hustle and bustle, without the family—*my family*—it's nothing more than a business. It could be a trendy diner anywhere in the world. And it doesn't matter that it hasn't even been two weeks. They've pulled me in and made me feel like one of their own. I'm glad I can be here to help. I'd do anything for them.

It isn't long before people arrive, wondering why the Earl's is closed. Around eight, I break down and start serving coffee to go. I hadn't realized how many people come by for their morning cup. I guess since Earl roasts his own beans, it's well-known that we have the best coffee in town.

Throughout the morning, I'm touched by all the concern and thoughtful wishes. I'm glad the family isn't here to relive what happened with every visit. I tell them all that I'll let the family know they stopped by, hopefully saving Twyla and Earl the stress later on.

When the door opens for like the thousandth time, I'm startled, then happily overwhelmed when I see Colten's ragged face. "You're here!" I run over and jump into his arms. He crushes me in a hug before setting me down and planting his lips hungrily on mine. We're just about to rip each other's clothes off when we hear a vehicle pull up to the pump.

A slow, wicked grin curls his lips as they leave mine. "Let's lock the door. Free gas for everyone."

I wiggle my eyebrows. "Works for me."

"If only," he sighs, letting his arms drop from around my body.

I make a pouty face, which prompts him to give me one more toe-curling kiss before saying, "I'm gonna fix a sandwich. You want one?"

"Food? How can you think of food after *that*?" The only thing *my* insides need is more Colten.

"Couldn't you hear my stomach growling? I've barely eaten since yesterday. The food at the hospital was barely edible."

A somber reminder of our reality. "I'm so glad she's going to be okay."

He runs his hands through his messy hair. "Me too."

"What time is it, anyway? I'm kind of hungry too."

He pulls out his phone. "Close to one."

"A sandwich sounds great. I'll have whatever you're having." Then we can snack on each other in-between customers for the rest of the day. "If you want, you can take a shower upstairs when you're done eating. I would imagine it would feel good after your long night."

He pecks my cheek. "Great idea." Then disappears into the diner. I'm smiling to myself as I walk toward the window and look out.

That's weird. A limousine? Here?

Maybe some rich person got lost. As I watch, the door to the vehicle opens, pricking my interest even more. I see the dark hair first, then the eyes, and my heart sinks.

No, I scream in my head.

My entire being feels sucked dry of everything good as the man looks around, visibly irritated. I look over my shoulder to see Colten in the kitchen, then open the door to step outside. Maybe I can talk my father into leaving before Colten sees him. I don't want him to be part of the drama that's about to unfold.

"Oh, Tess. Thank god." He droops momentarily before righting himself again. "Do you *know* how many small-town gas stations I've been to?"

What is he talking about? And why is he here? He shouldn't be back from Europe yet.

Heavy legs guide me toward a man who could wreck my life as easily as his next breath. My father is an imposing man, tall with dark hair, who is used to dominating in the workforce.

"Why did I have to hear of your disappearance from the police?" he says angrily. "Why didn't you call me?"

"The police?" I choke out, my throat suddenly dry.

"Yes, your lovely friend Dax was pulled over for speeding in Florida, and when the police determined the car wasn't his, they took him into custody. Do you know that useless little shit blackmailed me with your whereabouts in exchange for a lawyer because he didn't want his parents finding out?" He shakes his head in frustration. "And *then* he didn't even know *which* town he left you in, only an approximate location. When it was determined his knowledge was useless, I told him he could forget the lawyer and that he's lucky I don't press charges. No one blackmails me and . . ." His words trail off as he studies me. "Tess, are you okay? You're white as a sheet."

I'm terrified. *Don't make me leave.* How do I explain? I need him to understand. "Yeah. I'm fine. I'm—"

"Get your stuff and let's go." He makes an impatient gesture. "I've wasted enough of my time. I need to get back to the office."

Of all the instances where I need him to listen . . . "Sorry you had to *waste* so much *time* looking for me." Anger rips through me so fast he steps back, eyeing me with sheer confusion. I'm not the passive daughter he's used to. "But I'm not going anywhere with you. I have a job and an apartment here." *And people—people who are more important to me than you will ever be.*

He looks at the structure dubiously. "Tess, I don't have time for this nonsense. Say your goodbyes—or whatever you have to do—and let's go." He makes a move to climb back into the limo.

"No." I'm not letting him take this away from me. "You've never cared about me or what I'm doing," I say with hands fisted at my side, "so stop acting like you do. I'm not going anywhere."

The bitter words stop him in his tracks. His face looks stricken when he turns. "Why would you say such a thing?

When I got the call from the police . . . Well, it scared the hell out of me. Who knows what that boy could have done to you? I flew back immediately and went to a lot of trouble and expense to find you. *Which,* I might add, could have been avoided if you would have just called me when that idiot took your car. It would have saved you from . . ." He flutters a hand toward the building. "This."

"Stop acting like you care, and this . . ." I mimic his actions. "Is the best thing that's ever happened to me. I'm not leaving."

"The hell you're not!" His face flares in an indignant rage— that someone had the gall to oppose him.

"Do you have my stuff?" I ask. At this point I couldn't care less about school, money, anything other than getting him the hell away from here. I'll take a year off and work, get financial aid, *anything* to be free of him and my mother.

"Yes. In the trunk," he says, flustered. "What does that have to do with anything?"

I walk past my father to the other side of the car and tap on the driver's window to get his attention. I move away as he opens the door and steps out. "Yes, ma'am."

"Could you please open the trunk?" I ask, then walk toward the back of the behemoth vehicle. I never realized how obnoxious these cars are. They should be used for weddings, graduations, and funerals, and nothing else.

"Stay where you are." My father barks the order at the driver.

"Look," I say to my father. "Just let me get my stuff and I'll come back in time for school. I can't handle going back to that hellhole you call a home and frankly, you can't make me."

"What's wrong with the penthouse?" he sputters. "Have you

lost your mind? *No.* You will come with me now! Your mother—"

"My mother what?" I challenge, continuing to seethe with anger. "She doesn't give a shit about me. She's nothing more than a sad excuse for a human being and far from *anything* resembling a mother."

"What are you talking about? That's just nonsense," he sputters.

I need this to end. Now's not the time to hash things out with him, and I know acting this way isn't helping my cause, but I sure as hell won't settle anymore. I just won't. I need to get my stuff and make him understand that I'm fine where I am.

I inhale deeply and exhale slowly, attempting to calm myself. He needs to see me rational, not enraged, if he's going to take me seriously.

"Sorry. I shouldn't have gotten so angry, but I'm happy here. I have friends. Please, just let me stay until school starts. I have a job and an apartment." I throw out with an optimistic smile, "Aren't you impressed?"

"Look, young lady. It's hotter than hell out here, and I've run out of patience. If you want your education paid for, you will come with me *now*."

And there it is. The ultimatum I've been dreading.

It doesn't matter. I've made my decision to stay. My parents are not healthy to be around, and I don't want or need them in my life anymore. I'm eighteen and free to make my own choices. School will just have to wait a little longer.

"Tess?" Colten says my name.

I hadn't heard him come outside. How much has he heard? "I need a minute," I tell my father.

"Do what you need to do, but I want to be back on the road in fifteen minutes." He turns away, dismissing us both, and climbs into the back of the black beast.

"So. That's your dad?" Colten nods toward the limo slowly pulling away. I assume to park off to the side.

As soon as it's gone, I rush forward and wrap my arms around his waist, burying my face in his chest. My stomach is in knots. I need his calming energy to help me through this. "Yeah. Nice, huh?"

"You need to go with him."

I rear back, staring up at him, confused. "What? No, I just need to make him see. If he can't, then it's fine. I'll figure it out without him."

"Tess, come on. You're not thinkin' straight. You can't give up on school just for me. It's ludicrous."

"No, it's not." Why is he saying this? "And I'm not giving it up. I'll defer for a year. I'll get a student loan and work for a year. I don't need him."

He stares down at me. "Come on, Tess. You're eighteen and angry that your dad is trying to tell you what to do. You should have called him. He has a right to be pissed."

My eyebrows shoot up in surprise. "What? Why would you say that? He has no right! I'm not leaving."

He rubs the back of his neck, clearly frustrated, which makes no sense. The answer is simple. Why is he acting like this?

"He has every right. He's your father, and he cares about you. If he didn't, he wouldn't be here." He takes my hands in his. "You don't want to cause all these problems for yourself. You've set a path for yourself. Who knows what will happen if you defy your father by staying? And if you don't see this through, you would regret it, and so would I."

"I just told you, I'm not giving this up." I hold one of his hands against my face. *Feel me.* "It'll be fine. One year won't change anything." I wrap my arms around his waist with his hands still grasping mine and smile up at him.

He removes our joined hands from behind his back and steps away from me. "Tess, I was serious when I said I don't want a long-distance relationship."

I stare at him, confused. "Yeah, but that was before we were, you know . . . together." I attempt a smile. He can't be serious.

"Nothing's changed." His face continues to be void of expression as he looks down at me.

"What are you talking about? Everything's changed. I don't understand. Then why did you . . . ? Why did we . . . ?"

"It was a mistake. I shouldn'a come up to your place the other night. I wasn't thinking straight."

My hand flies to my mouth as I choke on a sob. "No! You feel the same way about me as I feel about you."

"That's not the point!" He clasps his hands on top of his head as pain breaks out on his face. "I'm not explaining this right." He drops his hands. "We just met. It's not right for me to keep you here."

"You're not keeping me here. It's my choice to stay. And if this is some noble sacrifice, *stop.*"

"It's not just that. You need to see this dream of yours through—see where it takes you without me gettin' in the way. Ya know, influencing your decisions and all? You need to experience all that college life has to offer. And do it without lookin' back."

"You're exhausted. This thing with Josie . . . You're not thinking straight," I plead. He can't push me away. I need him.

"Tess! I don't want to live in fear of losing you, okay? That's why I was holding back all this time. But you got under my skin the way no one ever has. I tried to resist my feelings for you"—he reaches for me, but stops himself, looking devastated —"but I wasn't strong enough. Don't you see? That's why I can't do this. *Four years* I'll be wondering if or when you'll drift away, if you're only keeping up the relationship because you don't want to hurt me."

My hand grips my shirt over my heart. This can't be happening. I can't breathe.

"Manhattan is a world away from a life here, and over time, these two worlds will seem even further apart," he says, pleading for me to understand. "I don't want to experience that slow, agonizing separation."

"I'm not Delilah," I yell at him, somehow finding air, then turn away to look out onto the road.

"I know you're not." He grips my arm, turning me back. When I won't look at him, he lifts my chin until I do. "But the situation remains the same, and I don't want to deal with the potential fallout. I can't."

I grip my stomach. "So because of one young, clueless girl, you're going to throw what we have away? This is ridiculous! You can't paint me or anyone else with the same brush. Every situation is different. Why can't you see that?" I throw my hands in the air in frustration. "This doesn't make any sense." I *need* him, his family. They've made me feel whole. I'll be miserable without them in my life. "You can't just walk away from this." My eyes are welling with tears. I'm amazed I've held them back this long.

"It's the right thing for both of us. I know what I want and where I want to be. You're just startin' to figure that out. I'm not goin' anywhere. If your path brings you back to me, then it will be without regrets from either of us."

"How could I regret being with the person I love most in this world?"

"Look. Your dad is waiting." His expression has turned hard. "You need to go." He turns abruptly and starts walking back to the building.

Tears of frustration are falling heavily now. "Don't walk away from me." *Please don't abandon me the way everyone else has.* "I've decided!" He stops and faces me. "I'm not leaving you, and—and your parents, and Josie," I choke out. "After everything that's happened, Twyla needs me here," I say in a desperate plea.

"Please stop crying. You're killing me." He takes a step toward me and stops. "I'm tryin' to do the right thing here."

"The right thing? Shouldn't this choice be half mine? What you're doing is trying to control my future, just like my father."

"I'm nothin' like that man over there." He points at the limo. "Think about Paris, London—all the galleries. You can't have that life by staying here and waitressing."

"I'll find a way to have both."

"Not here, you won't! You just don't get it, do you? Come on, Tess. You just graduated high school. You can't pass over your future and live the rest of your life in some tiny town after knowin' a guy for two weeks. We hooked up once. Maybe you just got caught up in the moment. You know?"

My head jerks back like he slapped me. *"Excuse me?* You think I don't know my own fucking mind? How dare you!"

"What I *think* is that you're too young to make such an enormous decision after knowing me for such a short time. *Hell,* I barely know you either." He runs a hand through his hair, looking disgusted with himself. "What was I thinking? And you'll be bored with this place after another couple of months anyhow."

"Enough with the condescending bullshit!" I yell at him, then shake my head, trying to clear it of the lies he's hurling at me. They don't make sense with what I experienced two nights ago. "You're having second thoughts about me?"

"You'll thank me later," he says dryly.

"Really. And you know this, how?" I'm so angry right now, I could explode.

"Did you ever think that maybe you need love and affection so bad that you'll settle for anything you can get and that's why you end up with pieces of shit like Dax? How do I know I'm not just another body to fill the void?"

That one hit hard.

Bullseye.

A direct hit.

"You asshole! How dare you? If you think these things about me, why did you bother?"

"You were throwing yourself at me." He smirks. "It was damn hard to say no."

No more. I'm done being used and abused. I hurl myself forward, shoving him, then shove him again, harder. His massive body barely moving.

"Fuck you!" I scream in his face, then storm into the

building for the key to my apartment. Maybe he's right, and he's just another piece of shit on the list. Maybe he just hides it better than most.

He comes through the door just as I am about to leave. I shove past him, neither of us saying a word. How could I have been so stupid?

I let myself into the apartment and lean against the closed door. I can barely see through the tears streaming down my face. Naomi and Sri, Twyla, Earl, Josie, Colten—Jeb. The thought of leaving them all behind feels like the weight of an elephant sitting on my chest. I slide down my back to the floor and sob into my hands. I try to make sense of my conversation with Colten. Conversation, my ass. It was a fight. He was awful, and it makes me sick that he sees me as some desperate skank needing a love fix—a poor rich girl that never got love from her parents. "Fuck you!" I scream.

He doesn't know shit!

I've never been that person, have I?

Oh, shit. What if I have?

But it was different with him.

Gross! Was it pity sex? He knew how much I wanted him.

I need to get out of here. Wiping my eyes clear, I heave myself off the floor. There isn't much in the apartment that's mine. I throw my ugly underwear in the garbage, along with everything in the fridge, and tie off the bag. Then I grab a leftover plastic shopping bag, throw in my Mason jar full of money, along with all the other things I've acquired since I've been here, and set it by the front door. I change into the clothes I arrived in, strip the sheets off the bed, and leave them in a pile on the mattress. Since all the clothes that were given to me are freshly washed, I place them back in the bag and set them next to the sheets.

I take one last look around before stepping outside and locking the door behind me. After tossing the garbage in the dumpster, I set out to find Colten. I don't want to, but I need to explain about the apartment.

I find him in his garage, staring at the hoisted car. "I emptied out the fridge and stripped the bed. Please tell your mom that I left the clothes that were donated to me up in the bedroom."

"Okay."

When he doesn't say anything else, I huff out a breath, push the door open, then turn. "Tell your parents thank you. And give Josie a hug for me. Naomi and Sri . . . tell them what happened with my father coming and whatever else you want to say about me. I don't care. And Jeb. Please look out for him. He's just lonely."

"Tess . . ."

"Promise me!" I shout at him. Whatever else he has to say, he had his chance. I don't want to hear it.

He nods his head that he understands, and I'm out the door, stomping my way across the parking lot. I've been a fool. If he cared about me the way I thought he did, he would have fought for me—done anything he could to make this work. Instead, he ripped what we had apart with his vile accusations.

"Finally," my father says when I climb in.

I shut the door and stare out the window as the building disappears. That's when the pain becomes more than I can bear.

CHAPTER 29

Four Years Later

I BOLT UPRIGHT, awakened suddenly with my heart pounding and an aching sense of loss.

Colten.

The dream was so vivid. It's like it all happened yesterday, and the distance of four years never existed. We were walking in the cornfield across the street from the diner, holding hands. He stopped us, and looking deep into my eyes, leaned forward and kissed me. I could feel the softness of his lips and the intensity of who we were as the kiss fired up every nerve in my body.

Why? I flop back on my pillow.

I thought I was past this.

I pull myself out of bed and shuffle to the kitchen for something to drink.

For weeks after I left Jasper Creek, all I could think about was jumping in my car and driving back. I wanted Colten to tell me that he didn't mean the things he said, that we could make it work. People say stupid things in stressful situations. He'd been through a lot with Josie, then my father showed up unexpectedly.

I wanted to know the truth. But every time I had my car keys in hand, staring at the front door, I'd freeze. After my father showed up and brought me back home, I barely left my bed for weeks. I was already broken. I didn't want him to shatter me completely if his answers weren't what I needed to hear. So I stayed put. School started and eventually I lost my sadness in a world I loved—art. And when school got busy, I thought of him less and less, until I hardly thought of him at all.

I lean against the kitchen counter and chug a tall glass of orange juice. If I'd had more time with Colten that summer, would he have reacted the same way when it came time for me to leave?

I need coffee. I busy myself by preparing the fancy coffee machine with beans, then water, and flip it on. It grinds, then starts the drip process. I wonder what Colten's doing right now.

I picture him under a hoisted car in his sexy coveralls, his hands working expertly, able to fix anything. Those greasy coveralls were only hot because I knew what they were hiding underneath.

I can't go there. I should take a shower—a cold one. Maybe I can freeze him out of my mind. But after that . . . then what? With no plans for the day, keeping my mind occupied won't be easy. I adjust the water. Step one in operation Forget Colten All Over Again.

Ugh.

Damn dream!

Graduation was a week ago, and I've been decompressing ever since. My father was there, proud as could be. My mother, of course, was not in attendance. I haven't talked to her since my father divorced her.

I graduated with a double major as planned. My father's changed a lot since the day he found me. On the way to the airport, I unleashed hell on him. He listened to me rage for an hour about my mother, Maria, him. He never got angry or contradicted me. When I was empty, he held me and apologized for being oblivious. He said he felt horrible for making me leave Jasper Creek at such a crucial time for the family who took me in. I couldn't believe this was the man I thought I knew.

As I dry off, I mentally list all my favorite artists, their works, style and composition, most notable pieces—anything to drown out the thoughts of him. That was one of my tricks after coming home, especially at night when I would close my eyes and see him there.

I never reached out to Twyla—I could have called to see how Josie was—or my friends. I kept finding excuses not to. At first it would have hurt too much, then I was avoiding the awkwardness of too much time passing, then guilt set in. It was wrong not to contact them. I should have been stronger. It wasn't all about me.

I go for a long run, pushing myself to the brink of exhaustion. It doesn't matter what I do. The dream stays with me.

Our time together was short, but the impact it had on me was extensive. He became my first love, trusting him with all I am, then he rips my heart out in less than two weeks.

Damn. I can't get the dream, the image of him, out of my

head. I can see him so clearly, feel his touch. Every detail of my time with him called to the forefront of my mind. The ache of missing him is so strong—none of it diminished, neither is the crippling memory of the pain he caused.

By the time I get back to the apartment, shower again, run a few errands, I've decided.

"What do you mean, you're leaving?" Levvy asks in a panic. "You start your job at Sotheby's in less than a week. You can't leave now." She's obsessively organized. She'd need a week to make decisions about an event as simple as a road trip, and then a month to plan it. Levvy was my dormmate when I started at NYU. After our freshman year, we found a place together off campus.

"I know it sounds crazy. I've done what I set out to do, but now I need closure—I need to know."

"Know what?" She stares at me as though I have an extra appendage growing out of my head. "And who is this guy again? I've never heard you mention him before."

"I couldn't." *It would have destroyed all the barriers I had carefully built for myself.* "It had to be forgotten."

"You're insane." She plops down on my bed. "Okay, spill. I need to know everything if you think I'm going to let my best friend just walk out that door to who-knows-where."

I laugh because she honestly thinks she could stop me. She's like that—powerfully vocal, with the confidence to rule the world—but she's also compassionate and caring and would want me to do whatever would make me happy. She's like Sri and Naomi rolled into one. That's probably why I love her the way I do.

"I met him the summer after high school graduation, and in the short time we were together, he became everything to me."

I give her every detail. When I'm done, I'm even more resolved about my decision. "I'm going." I stand up abruptly. Moving to my closet, I pull out my suitcase and plunk it on the bed next to Levvy. I'm in a frenzy now. I have to see him and resolve this. If the dreams are back, there's a reason, and if I don't do this now, it could haunt me for the rest of my life.

"You mean *now*, now?" Her voice is almost a screech.

"Yes. If I leave immediately, I can get several hours in before I need to quit. I should be able to be there late tomorrow evening."

"Why don't you leave in the morning? Think about it a little more. Give yourself a chance to think this through—calm down a little. You said so yourself, things weren't left, uh, that great."

"I'm totally calm. You're the one who's panicking." It'll be hot there. I need summer things. Sundresses, definitely. "I have to do this. I've already waited four years too long."

"Listen to yourself. Tess! He dumped you, cruelly, I'd like to add. Come on. This is crazy."

I rush to the bathroom and grab the necessities, jamming them into my overnight case. "I'm not a hundred percent sure he *was* being cruel." I return to the bedroom, then turn on my heels when I remember I forgot my hairdryer. "He sent me away, basically called me fickle, playing off our night together as a fling, but it wasn't. There's no way. I think there was more to that day, and I want to know what it is."

I poke my head out of the bathroom and point my hairdryer at her. "It was so easy for me to believe the hurtful things he said because, at the time, cold hostility and rejection were emotions I was familiar with. The idea of someone caring enough to look out for my best interests by letting me go was not." I duck back in the bathroom to grab my makeup brushes. "I don't know what really happened—what the real answers are —but I owe it to myself to find out, because if I don't, it will haunt me for the rest of my life."

"You've come to this change of heart all because of a dream?"

I come back to my room and throw my hairdryer in my suitcase. "It's just, when he started digging into my open wounds, my insecurities." The negative memories batter against the positive ones from the dream. "I don't know what went wrong." Maybe this *isn't* such a good idea. *No.* I shake my head at myself. "I talked myself out of what I thought I felt that summer, that it was nothing more than a crush, a strong physical attraction. But it was more. The dream reminded me of that, but until I talk to him, I won't really know his side of it."

I dig around in the bottom of my closet for sandals and flip-flops. That's when I see the bag. The one I took when I left Jasper Creek. I didn't pay attention when I was packing up my room at the penthouse. Dad sold it and bought a smaller place after the divorce. When Levvy and I found this apartment, I moved all my stuff here and never unpacked everything. Most of it's stored in the back of my walk-in closet. Now that school's over, I wonder what the plan is. Levvy and I haven't talked about it.

More memories come rushing back when I look inside the bag.

The Mason jar still filled with all the money I made at Earl's Diner. The key to the apartment. In my haste, I forgot to return it. I turn the key chain over to read the inscribed words. *Wherever you go . . . come back to me.* I remember the first time I read it. I thought it was beautiful, but didn't give it another thought. Now it means everything. Sri's running shoes. I hope she wasn't pissed I took off with them. I was angry and didn't pay attention to what I was shoving into the bag.

"You'll lose your job." Levvy's still trying to get me to stay.

"No, I won't." I open my drawer and gather up underwear—nice underwear with matching bras. No granny panties. "I'll be back in time to start. It'll be fine. I'm just killing time right now, anyway."

She takes my arm. "What if you don't come back?" Her panic is amusing.

I stop what I'm doing and stare at her. "I've worked too hard to get where I am. It's not an option. Besides, they actively recruited me. If I'm as important to them as they make it seem, then being a day or two late won't change anything." Levvy opens her mouth to protest. "But I won't be," I assure her.

"What if you're wrong about all this?" She waves a hand, indicating my suitcase. "What if he found someone else?"

The thought never crossed my mind. "Then I'll know where we stand, hopefully have a nice conversation, and I'll turn around and come home. At least I'll get to see my friends, if they're still there, and things will get settled with Colten once and for all." I want to add "without regrets" but I can't. I have so many.

"What's this guy look like?"

I laugh. "I don't have a photo. My phone disappeared with my car, remember? But he's, well . . . his eyes, that mouth—"

"He's probably got a massive potbelly and losing his hair. You said he was a mechanic? He's probably toothless as well."

I turn from my closet and make a face. "*Ew.* I hope not. And that is so incorrectly stereotypical."

"He could be married. With kids!" she shouts at me as I run back into the bathroom for my forgotten razor.

"Like I said . . ." I zip the razor into a safe compartment in my overnight bag. "I'll see my friends, then come right back home. And if nothing else, it will be a nice long drive to contemplate my life and put the past where it belongs." I move to stare in my closet.

"Tess. This isn't you."

"You mean this isn't *you.*"

"You're methodical."

"Me? In some things, maybe. You're the one whose life has to be systematically organized."

"Whatever." She waves me off. "This is craziness."

"I don't know. Maybe it is, but I've been so focused on the endgame . . . now I'm realizing part of my life feels missing, unresolved. I thought this was where I would discover myself. Now I realize I already had—that summer. I need answers, or at the very least, closure." *I need him the way it used to be.*

But Levvy is right. That may not be an option. I need to prepare myself for that.

I pull out shorts and some of my favorite summer tops from the dresser. "I miss who I was and what we had. I know it might be too late, but I need to know one way or the other. If I don't do this, it will eat at me, and I won't be able to move on. You would go, wouldn't you? Come on. Tell me the truth. If you were me?"

She lets out a resolved sigh. "I'm an English lit major, a hopeless romantic by default. Of course I'd go . . . eventually. *After*—"

"I know. After careful consideration and planning."

"Yes, true, but I don't have a career plan. I'll probably keep going to school until I'm a professor. I mean, what the hell else can you do with a degree in English?"

"Go into marketing, work for a publishing company, write and publish that book you're always working on and trying to hide from me."

Her eyes grow huge. "You know about that?"

"We've been roommates for how long? How could I not know?" I close the lid to my suitcase, throwing my body across it so I can zip it closed. I might have over-packed.

"Why don't you call first? It's a long trip, Tess. Just call."

"No. I need to be there, to see his face and everyone else I left behind. I made friends that summer—really good ones. I never got to say goodbye." Hefting my bag, I set it on the floor. "If I call, then I may not go. This is too important."

"Okay," she relents. "I get it. Just be careful."

"I didn't just get my license, *Mom*." She twists her face and sticks her tongue out at me. "I'm twenty-two. I can take care of myself."

"I know."

"I'll be fine. Stop worrying." I gather up the rest of my things. "Come on. Walk me to the door."

CHAPTER 30

THE TRIP SEEMS to take forever. The anticipation is frazzling my nerves and making the drive seem so slow.

Maybe I *should* have called first, instead of just showing up and being like, *Surprise! I haven't talked to you in forever. So why was it you broke my heart again?*

This was a stupid idea. I could turn around, I guess. But what would that accomplish?

Nothing.

I need to know, right? Get answers, see my friends, apologize for bailing. Well, I didn't really bail. The circumstances were out of my control. And how could I have stayed connected with Naomi and Sri and not Colten? Just hearing his name would have killed me. Not reaching out was self-preservation. And selfish. It's going to be hard to face them. I hope they're not too mad at me.

The drive has allowed for too much time to think. A multitude of scenarios have played out in my mind—an equal number of good and bad.

I called my father on the way out of town to let him know I was going to visit Colten and his family. He was worried, since he was a part of the emotional fallout when I left. But I'm a different person now, and I'm trying not to have any expectations other than closure. I should be able to get that one way or another.

This is healthy.

It's the right choice.

I groan out loud. My mind is foggy. I'm tired and cranky from the shitty sleep I had last night, and I need more caffeine and probably some food. The hotel was fine. I stopped around one in the morning, but was too wound up and nervous to sleep. Finally, around four, I got out of bed, found an open restaurant, and had breakfast and loads of coffee before hitting the road. But that was nine hours ago.

When the exit comes into view, my nerves go from prickly to a full-on sweaty panic.

Jasper Creek

Population 6,150

I take deep breaths, attempting to calm my racing heart.

This is the right thing to do.

I need to see how this story will play out in real time.

It's going to be fine.

I can handle this.

The positive affirmations continue until the town is in front of me.

Wait. That's not right.

Where is the gas station, the diner? I couldn't have driven past it.

I pull into the side of the road. Looking over my shoulder, I don't see anything. No way I'd miss it.

Do I have the right town?

Of course I do! I wouldn't forget the name. I turn around and head back. That's when I see the large cement slab.

What the . . .

I pull into the empty parking lot, put the car in park, and jump out. This can't be right—but as I step up to where the gas pumps used to be, I'm slammed with the realization. It's all gone. I drop into a squatted position, feeling light-headed as the life drains out of me.

"No," I sob, terrified at what might have happened.

I need to find Naomi. Jumping up, I rush to the car. My destination, Bell's. I desperately hope that she's still there. It's the only place I can think of to go. If she's not there, I can try one of the other shops. Someone in this town will tell me what happened.

I'm relieved to see the sign. Bell's is still there. Anything could have happened to it in the time I was gone. I rush in, but don't see anyone. "Naomi?" I call out.

I see the mop of orange curls first. "Tess?" She's wiping her hands on a towel. "Are you okay?" She walks toward me, registering my frantic state. "What happened?" Her expression hardens. "What are you doing here?"

I grip her arm. "What happened to the station, to Earl's?"

The pain on her face has me fearing the worst. "It burnt down."

I feel like the earth just fell out from beneath my feet. Everything is spinning. "I think I'm going to be sick."

She wraps an arm around my waist, leading me to a chair.

"It's okay. No one got hurt. Riley!" she calls out. "Bring me a clean, wet rag. You better sit down, Tess. Your face is as pale as a white man's butt."

A stunning woman with mahogany skin and amber eyes, wearing a concerned expression, hands Naomi a cloth. "Thanks, babe," Naomi says and places the cloth on the back of my neck. "There you go, now. Breathe."

I try to catch a full breath, but it's caught somewhere deep. "What happened?" I force out, swiping at the tears rolling down my face.

"About two years ago, there was an electrical fire. The place was incredibly old. It's been in their family for generations."

"I know, but—oh my god. All Twyla's artwork. Colten's beautiful garage." I gasp for air after each statement. I'm hyperventilating. "Earl's Diner. The gas station. That place was their life."

"Tess! You need to breathe. You're scarin' the hell out of me." She pushes my head down between my knees. "Just shut up and breathe."

"Naomi," Riley admonishes. "Go easy. She's had a fright. I'm going to get her some water."

I do what Naomi says, not that she's given me a choice. I can't believe this is happening.

"That's it," she says. "Try breathing in for a count of three, then out for three. Good, that's better." Having my head down helps. The knot in my chest loosens. "Now in for four, out for four."

Riley sets a glass on the table. "How's she doing?"

"Better."

I push up against her hand. "Can I get up now?" She

continues to hold me down with considerable force. "I think I'm okay," I say, and push up against her hand again. "You can let me up now."

"Oh. Sorry."

I take a drink of water and smile up at Riley. "Thank you."

"You bet."

"Why didn't they rebuild?" I ask, calmer now.

"Well, after Josie—"

"She died!" I jump up.

"Damn it, Tess!" Naomi's out of her chair, pushing me back into mine. "*No.* Calm the fuck down." Riley places a hand on Naomi's shoulder with an expression that she should calm down herself. "Sorry," she says, looking down at me. "Josie's fine. But after the surgery, Colten told me his parents struggled with the regret of not spending enough quality time with their kids. Which is bullshit. He has the best parents of anyone I know. Anyway, that's why they decided not to rebuild, *and* Colten wanted to travel—" She pulls a couple of napkins from the dispenser on the table and shoves them into my hand.

"So where are they all now?" I blow my nose and wipe my eyes.

"They're all still at the lake."

I reach out and grip her hand. "And you're sure Josie's okay?"

"Yes! Josie's fine. Brilliant as ever." She yanks her hand free from my grasp and plants it on her hip, her eyes narrowing. "Why are you here? I've missed you and all, but you left and no one's heard a word since."

"I'm sorry. Colten, he—"

"Was an idiot," she snaps. "I know."

"Maybe you should have a seat," Riley says to Naomi. "Do you want some water as well?"

"No. I'm fine." Naomi sits across from me again and Riley moves behind the counter. "He filled me in on the basics after you left, but you could have called."

"I know. I'm sorry." I stare at the wad of napkins in my hand before looking back at her. "It all seems stupid now. Colten and I fought that last day. He said some mean shit. It messed me up. I didn't think I could stay connected with anyone involved. I'm sorry. I know it was a chickenshit way to react. That's one reason I came back. I wanted to make things right."

"I won't argue with the chickenshit part, but I get it."

"Thanks. I need to see Colten. Can we talk later?" I ask, standing.

"Sure thing, but, uh, he's not here."

My heart plummets. "What? Why?"

"He's still traveling, been gone close to what . . ." She addresses Riley while standing up from her chair. "Close to a year this time?"

"Sounds about right," she responds, walking back over to us.

"Oh." This is not the way this was all supposed to go.

"You go on to the house, anyway. They'd love to see you. It's okay. We can talk later. Oh, and, hey." She holds a hand out to the person next to her. "This is my partner, Riley."

"It's nice to meet you," I say, smiling at her, then Naomi. It's fantastic that she's found someone.

"You as well," Riley says.

"Wipe that stupid smile off your face," Naomi scolds me.

"Why? She's stunning." I look at Riley. "You're stunning,

by the way." Then, back to Naomi. "I'm just glad you're happy." I edge toward the door, eager to be on my way. "We'll catch up soon, okay? I'm so glad you were here."

"I bought the place."

"Really?" I beam. "That's huge. Congratulations."

"Thanks. The owner decided to sell." She puts her arm around Riley's waist. "We bought it together."

"That's fantastic." I move toward the door again and stop. "How is Sri?"

"Finished school and opened a pharmacy here in town. Her and Dawson got married a year ago."

"Oh, wow! No way. Okay. I'll track her down too. And Jeb? Is he . . . okay?" The sudden fear that he may have passed away has my stomach roiling. "Have you seen him?"

"That ol' coot?" She snorts. "He's been here hasslin' me almost every mornin' since the restaurant burned down. He took it hard when you left. That's what Twyla told me."

"If I don't see him, will you . . . tell him I'm sorry?"

"You come on by here tomorrow and tell him yourself. He knows as much as I do, but I'm sure it would mean a lot to him if you told him hi. He's not doin' so hot—aged quite a bit since you left."

"Okay. Tell him I'll be in to see him. Does he still come around eleven?"

"Yeah. About that time."

"Okay. See you soon."

"You better," she demands.

CHAPTER 31

IT TOOK me a while to find my car after leaving Bell's. I was in such a panic I forgot where I parked it. The drive was as picturesque as I remember. I should have asked Naomi for an address because I couldn't find the house at first. I'd only been there once, and it was a long time ago. Several wrong driveways later, I came upon a mailbox with colorfully painted flowers that sparked the familiar.

I park in front of the triple-car garage and climb the steps to the stunning front door of carved wood over glass that I remember so well. Images of the night I came for dinner roar through my head. So do the nightmarish events of the day I left. Time has faded the memories to where I'm not sure I recognize them clearly. But that's why I'm here. I need the truth.

I knock on the door and feel relief all the way to my toes when the doorknob turns. I'd be wrecked if no one answered.

"Tess!" Shock registers on Twyla's face before deep concern. "Oh, honey." She steps out of the house and pulls me into a crushing hug. "What's wrong?"

"It's gone," I sob into her shoulder. The realization hits me all over again. "The diner, everything. It's all gone." The best part of my life was set ablaze and there's nothing left but a cement slab to show for it.

"No one got hurt." She leans back. "That's all that matters. Come inside." She takes my hand and shuts the door behind us.

Leading me to the kitchen with a comforting arm around my waist, she deposits me at a stool in front of a granite countertop serving as the island. The familiarity helps ease the tension a bit. "Here, let me get you something cold to drink."

"I stopped at Bell's. Naomi told me what happened."

Twyla hands me a box of tissues and moves toward the refrigerator. "It happened late at night. There was nothing worth saving after the tanks blew—rocked the whole town. We had to demolish what was left. It took weeks to round up all the debris that was blown everywhere."

"That's hard to imagine." She hands me a cold glass of lemonade. I set it on the counter, then get up to throw away the wet, snotty tissues before settling back on the stool. "It's the only gas station in the town. What are people doing?"

"Didn't you see the shiny new Shell gas station?"

"No." I take a sip and lick the tartness from my lips. "After coming across that blank slab of concrete, everything else was a blur."

"They moved into town about a year after you left. All the locals continued to get gas at our place." A warm smile plays across her lips. "And of course, for the diner."

"*And* you served the best coffee in town."

She sits on the stool next to me. "That too."

"Naomi said you chose not to rebuild."

"That's true. After it all burned down, and we had some time to think, we realized how much work it had been, and what it took from us. It wasn't worth it." She takes a sip from her own glass. "This is such a wonderful surprise, but why are you here? Why now?" Twyla's no-nonsense attitude.

"I had to see him."

She nods in understanding. "We never understood why you two didn't keep in touch. Colten wouldn't give us any details. He just said that your father came to get you. We knew you had a deep affection for each other, anybody could see it, but then you were gone."

"That was Colten's choice." The resentment in my voice has me cringing a little. Her loyalty will always be with her son, and I don't want to piss her off. "Sorry. He, well . . . That's why I need to talk to him. We didn't leave each other on the best of terms. He wanted me to finish school. I wanted to stay and figure things out. He didn't want a long-distance relationship. I wanted it all. Now that I've got my degree—well, I just . . . I need to know."

"Honey, I completely understand. Like father, like son. I'm almost sure that's the same argument I got from Earl when he left to come back and help his dad run the station. I wanted to leave with him, but he wouldn't hear of it. He insisted I finish my degree and felt we needed some time apart to see things clearly—we were pretty hot for each other." She giggles. "The moment he left, I knew I would come here after graduation. I didn't tell *him* that. Men can be stubborn when they get an idea stuck in their head."

I chuckle, able to relate. "I'm sorry about leaving abruptly. But with Colten being . . . and my father demanding I go home .

. . I didn't feel I had much choice. I should have called you and Earl to say goodbye and get an update on Josie, but I was upset and angry, then afraid of digging it all up again once I'd finally buried it."

"I admit, I was hurt. But I knew there had to be a good reason. You're not a callous person. I just wish Colten would have told me the long version instead of the clipped one, void of the important details. I certainly felt the loss with you gone."

"Weren't you able to hire someone?"

She gives my hand a squeeze. "Oh, honey. That's not the loss I was talking about."

Wham! Right in the feels. "I missed you so much." The tears are coming again. When I lost Colten, I lost his family as well, making it harder to heal. It feels good to know Twyla felt the same way.

She leans over and hugs me. "I missed you too. I did try to find a suitable replacement, but just like before you came, it never seemed to work out. And then the place blew up. It was devastating at first, but now we don't miss it one bit. Sometimes things happen for a reason, I guess."

I grab another tissue and wipe my eyes. "Like my ex-boyfriend taking the exit and stopping at your place, all because my bladder was going to break?"

"Even that. Honey, you were such a breath of fresh air. You woke us up and made us realize we were stagnant—eat, sleep, work, repeat. That was our life." She tucks her hair that hangs shoulder length behind her ears. "There are a lot of beginnings in life—change sees to that. You were starting on one of yours. It made us want to have one of our own without even realizing it. The fire cemented it for us."

It's hard to imagine me impacting anyone. It was the other way around. "I'm glad everything turned out okay." I wipe the condensation on the side of my glass with the tips of my fingers. "So, Colten is traveling?"

"Yes. He's been gone for close to a year." Her eyes turn sad. "Before that, about six months. He always wanted to see the world. It's just not the same seeing it in pictures, and with the business gone, he took the opportunity. The timing was right, you know?" She picks at something on her jeans. "After you left . . . well, he changed. And when the place burned down, I think he started questioning what he really wanted out of life. With nothing holding him here, the possibilities were piling up inside him, until one day, he was heading overseas."

I wonder if one of those possibilities was coming to find me?

Man, losing his garage must have been hard on him. It was everything he was. A vision of the fire plays out in my mind—destructive, violent, devastating. "The fire. All those memories . . . gone. I can't believe it."

"It was hard to grasp at first, but what we came to realize is that your memories are here." She taps the side of her head. "And in here." She places a hand over her heart. "Nothing, not even the forces of nature, can take that away."

"I know you're right. It's just a lot to take in." I take another sip of my drink. "With the diner gone, what have you been doing with all your free time?"

"Art mostly. It's nice to create without feeling like I should do something more important. My paintings are being showcased in several galleries, mostly in the coastal resort towns."

"That's great to hear. Your work is captivating. The way it draws you into the moment. I'm sure people are buying it up."

She smiles, looking pleased. "I'm doing well."

"Have you ever thought of opening a gallery here?"

"Only as a fleeting idea. It's not something I would want to take on at this stage in my life."

"That's fair. How's Josie? Is she around?"

"No. She's a camp counselor at that brain camp she was supposed to go to before—before her surgery." The painful memory shows on her face. "Are you hungry?" She stands up. "You must be starving."

"No. I'm okay. But thank you." I should be hungry. I haven't eaten anything since breakfast, which was at a ridiculous hour. "What about Earl? What's he up to? I can't see him puttering around the house."

She laughs, sitting back down. "No. That wouldn't do. There's a fine-dining restaurant that opened in town. He went to work there as the head chef. He's loving the creativity of his work without having the responsibility of owning it. At least for now. That could change. We have the insurance money if he wants to start his own place. As I said, Earl and I don't really want to be tied to a business anymore, so I highly doubt it."

"Do you know where Colten is?"

"Last text we got, he said he was somewhere in Southeast Asia."

"He told me he wanted to go to Australia."

"He was there for several months when he left the first time, then decided he wanted to travel to Europe and Asia and away he went."

"Did he say when he'd be home?"

"No. He'll be sorry he missed you." *Will he?* "I can give you all his contact information."

"Yes. Please. And yours as well. I want to stay in touch this time." Disappointment grips me hard. Colten was supposed to be here. I stand up. My legs are stiff from the long drive. "After that, I should get going."

She grabs her phone off the counter and hands it to me. "Put your information into my contacts, and I'll text you with Colten's details."

I do as she says and hand her phone back. It doesn't feel right reaching out to Colten this way. "If I don't get in touch with him, could you let him know I was here?"

"Honey, I really think you should kick up that courage of yours or you'll regret it." She eyes me knowingly. "You came all this way to find him. You can't give up now."

I made the initial effort. He can reach out if he wants to take the next step. "If it was meant to be, wouldn't he still be here?"

"Honey, I can't answer. As much as I believe in that stuff, there are always exceptions. You can't use it as a beacon to guide you, only to shed light."

"I suppose." I'm too disappointed to think about reaching out to him.

"Have you booked a place to stay for the night?" She takes my empty glass and sets it in the sink.

"No. I think I'll get back on the road, drive until it gets dark, and then stop for the night." Crap. That won't work. I'm supposed to see Naomi tomorrow, and Jeb.

"Now that's just silly. You just got here. Have dinner with us and stay the night. Earl would be so upset if he missed you. He went over to Raleigh to hit up the farmer's market and will be back soon." She touches my arm, looking hopeful. "What do you think? Spend the night? You could stay longer if you like. The lake is beautiful this time of year—well, you remember."

I glance at the wall of windows that showcase a breathtaking view. I smile. "Yeah, I remember." She's right, staying until tomorrow makes more sense. And I don't want to miss Earl or let Naomi and Jeb down, plus I still need to see Sri. "Okay. I'll stay the night if you don't mind."

"*Pshhh!*" She waves off my thanks. "I'm just so happy you're here. Why don't you lie down for a bit? You look like you're about to keel over."

"Maybe just a quick nap. I didn't get any sleep last night."

"You can stay in the guest room, and I'll wake you up when dinner is close to being ready." Twyla places a hand on my lower back, guiding me. "We'll have a nice visit, and you can tell us all about school."

The last thing I remember is walking into the bedroom and taking my shoes off by the bed.

CHAPTER 32

I WAS in a deep sleep when Twyla tried to wake me. She said it was like trying to wake the dead. With next to no sleep the night before, it wasn't a surprise.

The sun has set; the sky leaning closer to a deep, smoky blue. Before leaving my room, I texted Levvy to tell her I had made it and let her know Colten wasn't here. I added a sad face emoji and told her I would stay the night and head home tomorrow.

After washing my face, I turn the corner into the main room and the aroma hits me. Oh, man, that smells good!

Earl is bustling around the kitchen with soft jazz playing in the background. He cuts up something green and throws it into a frying pan, giving it a well-rehearsed flip, adds a pinch of this and a shake of that, another flip, and then sees me. "Tess!" He turns the heat down on the stove and with two giant steps, I'm enveloped in strong arms. The greeting feels like I've come home. He sets me away from him, looking me over. "You look great, Tess."

"Thanks. You haven't changed at all."

He winks at Twyla. "You're being kind."

"What can I do to help?" I ask.

"How about you and Twyla open a bottle of wine, or would you prefer a beer?" He moves back toward the stove.

"Wine sounds great."

"So, fill us in," he says, returning to his creation.

"Wait. Let me get the wine first." Twyla rushes out.

"Are you happy?" Earl asks.

"Mostly." My response surprises me. "Happy enough." That doesn't sound much better. I thought I *was* happy until that dream, and coming back here has reminded me of everything I left behind.

Twyla is back and reaching into the cupboard for wine glasses.

"I missed you guys," I say.

With a bottle in one hand and three glasses in the other, Twyla gives me a side-armed hug and kisses the top of my head. "We missed you, too."

"So, you finished school?" Earl chops, whisks, flips.

"I did." I take a sip from the glass Twyla hands me—fruity, but not too sweet. "Thank you. This is good. I got a full-time position at Sotheby's."

"Good for you. Is that what you want?" Twyla asks, looking a little surprised. She knows I wanted to work at a gallery.

"Not exactly. But it will look good on a resume. And I interned there for three summers, so it was a natural progression. I enjoy the hustle and bustle, the prestige. Besides, I'm too young to manage a gallery. No one would take me seriously."

"You could work at one, work your way up," Twyla suggests.

I shrug. "This was an excellent offer." I can afford to live independently of my father. Our relationship is great, but it's still something I need.

"What will you be doing?"

I take another sip of wine. "It's mostly administrative work, organizing meetings, stuff like that. I'll be the assistant to the directors of acquisitions. I'll learn a lot about the purchasing process."

Twyla clinks her glass to mine. "Congratulations."

"Thank you." I smile, but suddenly feel lacking.

It was the right choice, right?

Seemed like it at the time.

Now, after hearing myself recite my job description, I'm not sure.

Thoughts for later. Right now, I'm just so excited to be here. "So, what's for dinner? It smells amazing."

"Sautéed mushrooms with white corn polenta and horseradish over roasted pork tenderloin and a couple of other goodies I'm throwing together."

"Yum. You didn't have to go through all this trouble."

Earl winks. "But I get to show off for you. It's a new creation. I'm trying it out to see if I want to add it to the menu at Bernard's."

"You're enjoying working there?"

"With full creative license, I'm in heaven. I create a new menu every week. How's New York?"

"Busy, crowded, *loud*. Same as always. You two should come up sometime."

"Neither of us are into crowds," he says, "though Twyla would love the art museums and galleries."

"Speaking of art." I point my glass at Twyla. "I'd love to see what you're working on."

"Go show her your new studio," Earl says over his shoulder.

"New studio?" I pump my eyebrows excitedly.

"We built a she-shed since you left," Earl explains.

"A what?"

Twyla sets her wineglass down. "Come on. I'll show you."

Out the back door, I follow her to the left and see a log-cabin-like shed with a front porch bracketed with thick log railings. There's a wonderful smell of evening green—heat mixed with a touch of dew. It's so quiet. I come from the noisy and entered the serene. You can hear yourself breathe.

She flips a light switch on the wall when we enter. The first thing I notice is the bright white vaulted interior with large skylights, then the sliding glass door that leads to another porch overlooking the lake. She has a potter's wheel, an easel set up with a painting she's working on—something scenic—a desk, a daybed, several shelves with her supplies, and empty and painted canvases in layers leaning up against one wall. It looks a lot bigger in here than it does from the outside.

"I'm speechless, and a little jealous. I would have loved this as a kid growing up."

"It'd be an expensive playhouse. But thanks. I love it too."

"Hell. I would have lived in it. Anything to get away from that mausoleum my parents called a home."

She touches my hand. "How are things with your parents?"

"My dad and I are great. That summer and how it played out cemented our relationship. My mother doesn't want anything to do with me. After I clued him in on all her crap, my father filed for divorce."

"As he should. She sounded dreadful."

"Still is." I lean closer to the painting. "This is impressive."

"Aw." She grins big. "Aren't you sweet."

"I'm excited to hear that you took the initiative to get your work into the galleries."

"Me too. It's fun *and* lucrative." She picks up a sketchbook from her desk. "Can I show you something?"

"Absolutely."

She flips a couple of pages past the beginning and hands it to me. It's a picture of me, sitting at the counter in the diner, talking to Josie.

My heart flips with joy, then sinks a little, wishing I could go back to that time. I look so happy. "Are there more?"

"Yes. Go ahead."

I sit down on the bed with the pad in my lap and turn the pages, taking it in one page at a time. There is another sketch of me sitting at the counter with Colten, laughing, probably at something he said. There are some of Earl behind the expo window, and some of Colten in his garage under a car in deep concentration. Seeing him drawn just as I remember gives me a stab in the heart.

"This is all from memory?"

"No. They're from photos I took with my phone."

"I never noticed you taking pictures."

"I'm sneaky that way," she laughs.

There's one of me standing next to Jeb, full attitude, giving him hell. The stunned expression on his face is priceless. I know she didn't have a camera when this happened, so some are from memory.

"Naomi said Jeb switched his late morning coffee to Bell's."

She laughs. "That's because I kicked him out of my house."

"What?" I laugh in surprise.

"Yep. I was worried about him. I hadn't seen him after the fire, then the old coot showed up at my house about a month later, expecting breakfast."

"Seriously?"

"Crazy old man. I fixed it for him, gave him a coffee, then told him if he ever came to my house again, I would have him arrested for harassment. He thought that was hilarious. Honestly, I think it was his way of checking on us."

"Did he ever come back?"

"No. When Bell's started serving breakfast and lunch, he became Naomi's problem."

"She's the perfect person to handle him," I say. "I bet Jeb loves sparring with her."

"Yeah, she has a tough streak, like you do. Hers might be a little bolder, but you, without a doubt, can hold your own."

"I didn't know I had it in me until I met Jeb." He was my tipping point, an introduction to the new me. I found my voice that summer, and I've used it well ever since.

Dinner was outstanding. It was great to catch up—to hear about Josie. Twyla showed me pictures. She's grown up and so beautiful. It's not surprising given the family's genetics. "She looks tall."

"Five nine," her dad says, gathering plates off the table. "Had a growth spurt at fourteen."

I start to get up. "I can help."

"No. Sit and relax. I got this," Earl says.

"Do you want to see some pictures Colten sent us?" Twyla asks.

Nervous flutters whirl in my gut. Do I?

What if he's changed beyond recognition? It hasn't been *that* long. I slap on a smile and hand the phone back to her. "I'd love to."

I watch as she scrolls through photos. What if he's fat . . . or bald like Levvy said?

Would it matter?

I don't know.

A chaotic mix of joy and anxious nerves has me shifting in my seat uncomfortably. We were together for such a short time. I want to remember him the way he was . . . or maybe not. A slap of reality might do me a world of good.

"Start from here." She hands the phone across the table to me. "These are the most recent, from Vietnam."

The photo is scenic. I've never been to that part of the world. It's beautiful. *Swipe.* The beaches are stunning. *Swipe.* And the mountain roads are so narrow. *Swipe.* My heart slams against my ribs at an image of Colten looking over his shoulder as he sits on a rock with a stunning mountain range behind him.

Did a girlfriend take this photo?

I hope not. The familiar ache of loss is edging back. I want to ask, but it feels wrong. As I continue staring at the photo, Twyla leans forward to see which one has caught my eye, so I angle the phone toward her.

"That's one of my favorites," she says. "Colten met a group of friends at a hostel and traveled with them for a couple of days."

I pinch my fingers on the screen and spread them wide to zoom in on his face. Everything about him is the same—that grin that always sets my nerves humming, the bluey-green eyes. His hair is a little longer, wavier, and touches the back of his neck. He's got lots of facial scruff. I zoom back out again. He's thicker, less boyish, more manly, and still in great shape. I scroll through more photos—leaning on a motorcycle with another breathtaking view behind him, playing soccer with a group of locals at the ocean. "He looks happy."

"He is. I'm so glad he did this," Twyla says.

I continue to scroll as Earl clears the table. "And Colten hasn't said when he'll be back or what his plans are?"

"No. We actually haven't heard from him in a couple of weeks, but that's not unusual."

I hand her back the phone. "Dinner was amazing, Earl. Thanks again."

"I'm glad you liked it. I will be adding it to next week's menu, for sure."

"It'll be a hit."

I look at the other empty chairs. It feels weird being here without them—Colten and Josie. The pictures made me feel raw. Seeing him . . . I didn't know how I would react, but the sense of loss feels like a punch in the gut. If he was here, there would have been some resolution to our past, but now I'm an open wound again.

This sucks.

"Sweetie, are you okay?" Twyla asks, looking concerned. "Your cheeks are a little flushed."

"I'm okay, just hot I think. Probably the wine."

"Why don't you go on down to the dock and get some fresh air? Earl and I will finish cleaning up."

"No. I'm fine. Let me help."

"Not today, my girl," Earl says. "You look worn out. You go on. It's a beautiful night."

"Okay." I get up from my chair and head to the back door.

"There are some jackets in the mudroom," Twyla says. "It still gets cool by the water at night."

I remember. "Thanks."

I grab a well-worn, blue jean jacket off the hook and slide my arms in. Immediately, I'm flooded by the scent of Colten. I look down and recognize it as the same one he lent me when we went stargazing. I pull it tightly around my body and breathe in deep, taking the assault on my senses as a painful but welcomed gift.

No moon tonight as I step outside, and with minimal light coming from the house, the stars are breathtaking. You just don't see this in the city.

I sit cross-legged on the end of the dock and lean back on my hands for an easier view. As I gaze up at the sky, I look for star clusters I'm familiar with, then the few Colten taught me. I remember desperately wanting to kiss him that night. When it finally came, it was more than I ever expected, and when we made love, I never thought we would be separated again. And here we are four years later, thousands of miles apart, and complete strangers.

I lie on the dock for a better view of the sky. Looking back, thinking about the day I left so long ago, I can see where it might have gone wrong. I was racked with insecurity. Both of us were throwing up shields for protection, and neither of us handled the situation well.

So now what?

He didn't want me to reach out until I was done with school. Here I am and he's halfway around the world.

Well, when does life ever turn out the way we want?

Not very often, that's for *damn* sure. But once in a while, we get lucky. That veer off the road turned out to be an excellent detour, something truly spectacular. And even though my relationship with Colten was a mixed bag, I wouldn't have changed it for anything. The experience opened my eyes to possibilities I never knew existed.

Do I let go, or pursue him further?

I don't friggin' know, but *I am* getting cold. I heft myself up and walk my way up the dewy grass to the house.

Twyla smiles when she sees me. "Just in time for dessert."

"*Ugh.* I'm so full." I stretch back, circling a hand over my stomach. *It's an Earl dessert,* I remind myself. "But it'll be worth the hurt."

"Good girl. Do you want coffee?"

"No thanks. With the nap I took, I'd be up all night."

"I have herbal tea."

"I'm good, thank you, though."

"All right. Have a seat. Earl and I will be right back."

"You guys don't have to wait on me."

"I enjoy having someone to care for. Now sit," she orders, her nurturing smile spreading over me like a warm blanket.

"Yes, ma'am." I want to be like her when I grow up. I laugh to myself because *I am* grown up.

Minutes go by and Earl is setting an artful dessert in front of me. "It's too beautiful to eat," I say, laughing.

He chuckles. "I'm sure you'll find a way. And before you go on about all the trouble it took, you know how much I love to create. Thanks for giving me an added incentive." He kisses the top of my head, sending bubbles of happiness through my system.

He mushes me most of all. "Lucky me," I say.

"And me." Twyla enters, placing a mug of coffee next to her husband as he takes his first bite. "If Earl and I didn't work out every morning, we would be as round as we are tall."

Coffee or not, I can't sleep. After staring up at the ceiling for several hours, I get up and go into Colten's room next door. I've only ever been on the threshold, but it was dark, and I couldn't see much. I walk to the side of the bed and turn on the lamp. Natural wood, white walls—same as the rest of the house, except his room is accented in shades of blue. A computer screen sits on his desk with car-part catalogues spread haphazardly, just the way he left it.

Not being able to help touching his things, I organize the catalogues into a neat pile. I'm surprised Twyla could stand the mess. Maybe leaving it that way gave her the sense he'd be back at any moment. I mess them all up again.

There's a bulletin board over his desk with reminder notes, photos, concert tickets. I lean in, examining each photo up close. I recognize most of his friends, though they're all a lot younger, mostly goofy poses, then my breath catches. On the lower right corner is the selfie he took of us on his parents' boat. The night we made love. The beginning of everything I thought we could be and never were.

My hands are a little shaky when I unpin it. That night was everything to me. I lie on his bed and inspect the photo further, replaying every detail from the moment he picked me up for dinner to falling asleep in his arms.

I went on a few dates in college, even kissed them goodnight, but there was nothing there. No one has ever made me feel the way Colten did.

The thought of never experiencing it again makes me sad.

When my eyes finally feel heavy, I turn onto my side. I set the photo on the night table, scrunch Colten's pillow up under my head, and wrap myself up in his blanket. Like his jacket, his scent is still there—pine, fresh air, and something uniquely Colten.

CHAPTER 33

MY CAR IS PACKED. It's late morning. I woke up in Colten's bed when the sun blasted my eyelids. Realizing where I was, and not wanting Earl or Twyla to see me there, I tiptoed back to my room. I knew I should get my stuff together and get going, but I flopped down on my stomach, feeling awful from the crappy sleep, and was out again before I knew it.

Twyla and Earl talked me into staying for breakfast, which extended the visit. I didn't mind. I love being spoiled. It's a rarity for me.

Feeling jittery from all the coffee, I tell them I want to take one last look at the lake before I go. I need to get to Bell's. Jeb is probably waiting for me.

When I walk out onto the dock, the sun is scorching hot. I better not stay out too long. The boat Colten took us out on is tethered and bobbing in the water. The sight of it has a bigger impact in the bright light of day.

What if I never see him again?

The decisions we made all those summers ago have been

haunting me since the dream. I wanted to resolve this so I could move on, and now I'm stuck. Even an email would only be a start, and it would be impersonal. FaceTime would be best—terrifying, but it makes the most sense. But it's just not good enough. I need to see him, talk to him face to face—feel him.

I roll my shoulders—they're knotted up with tension—then rock my neck from side to side, attempting to ease the stiffness.

"Tess?"

The sound of his voice has me whipping around, not believing my ears. He's standing at the entrance of the dock, his hands in the front pockets of his jeans, waiting while my heart trips over itself.

He looks the same but different—different even from the pictures Twyla showed me. His hair is even longer, and he has a full beard. I struggle to accept what I'm seeing. It's like I've conjured him out of thin air.

He opens his arms to me. "You came back."

Without a second thought, I run and jump, throwing myself into his arms. He catches me easily, his grip firm as I wrap my legs around his waist. I'm holding on like my life depends on it. Even feeling our bodies mashed together, I have a hard time believing he's real.

He's here.

Realizing the boldness of my actions, I release my legs and let my body slide down the length of him. "Sorry. I've—"

He grips my face and crushes his lips on mine, cutting me off.

"I—I've wondered," he says between kisses. "I never thought I would see you again. I'm so sorry that I screwed everything up."

I hear words coming out of his mouth, "never," "sorry," but nothing is really registering other than the sparks igniting throughout my entire body. I grip the back of his hair, needing something to ground me, but it doesn't help. His hands slide under my shirt and over my back, his lips brushing over my jaw, then down my neck. The dream that brought me here has become a reality.

My chest is tight. I can barely breathe. I need him over me, in me, under me.

"Tess," he says in a drawn-out whisper before finding my lips again.

The sound of my name brings me back. This is not a dream, not the past, this is reality, and suddenly I feel lost and incredibly overwhelmed.

I don't want to stop, but there are questions that need to be asked, things that need to be said. I put my hands on his chest to separate us and take a step back for added distance. "Please. I need a minute."

He nods. We stare at each other, breathing hard while we search each other's features, neither of us able to believe the other is here.

"Wow," he says.

"Yeah." I exhale my first full breath after seeing him.

He steps toward me and takes my hand. "I can't stand here and not touch you."

"I know, and I want so much to let go of our last moment together, but I have so many questions. You really hurt me." I stare at his chest, afraid that if I look into his eyes, words that need to be said won't be. "I need to know why. Why did it end the way it did?"

He wipes his free hand down his face. "I've asked myself that so many times. My reasoning made sense in the moment, but none held an ounce of logic a few days after. For what it's worth, I'm sorry." He glances over my head at the water before his eyes settle back on mine. "With everything that happened with Josie, I never got to think past the night we made love, and then your dad was just—there. I felt like our futures were on the line and decisions needed to be made. What started as me being unselfish and lookin' out for your future quickly backfired when you kept fightin' me. Then all this shit started fillin' my head, all these doubts, fears, and insecurities. They were all firing at once, and I couldn't think straight. Words were spewing out of my mouth before I gave them much thought. And then I couldn't take them back when I saw the damage they caused. I didn't even mean what I was saying.

"After a week, I thought, well, at least you'll do what you set out to do, but I felt dead inside. You left with a piece of me that day. I know it sounds cliché, but you did." The back of his fingers skim along my jawline, sending an aching need through my body. "I thought about trackin' you down, then talked myself out of it—thinkin' there's no way you were gonna want to talk to me after how I behaved, and it seemed cruel after letting you go. My views on our relationship hadn't changed, so what would be the point?" His eyes roam the length of me, settling on my face once again. "*Damn*, it's good to see you."

My smile feels wobbly right along with the rest of me. His answer is everything I needed, but now what?

I didn't think this trip through. My insatiable drive to see him got me here, but I never considered what would happen if our connection was just as intense as when we met.

"Can I hold you again?" His crystalline blue eyes search mine, looking vulnerable.

How am I supposed to think logically with him looking at me that way? I step forward with my arms stretched out in front of me. We lock in an embrace with my ear resting over his heart. Its racing speed matches my own.

He squeezes tight and kisses the top of my head. "Did you finish school?"

"I did."

"Are you happy?" he asks.

There's that confusing question again. Being near him, his touch . . . I'm happy *now*. He leans away. I assume, to see why I'm not responding, as if my expression will tell him everything. But I keep my face hidden in his chest, not wanting him to read what I don't understand myself. "I'm about to start a full-time position at Sotheby's."

He rests his cheek on top of my head. "Then it was all worth it," he says, sounding firm in the idea that all the right choices were made. "How long can you stay?"

There's that splash of cold reality. I slide out of his embrace. My legs feel like cooked noodles. "I was on my way home . . . now, actually. The car is loaded. I start work on Monday."

"It's only Thursday. You can stay another day, right?" he asks, looking hopeful.

Can I?

I still have time. Not a lot, but some.

This could be bad. I didn't expect it to get so real this quick.

"Yeah. I can stay another day, but I will need to get on the road by tomorrow so I can have time to prepare for my first day of work."

"Perfect. I'll take it." He gives me a quick squeeze, smothering me against his chest before releasing me and taking a step toward the house. "I'm so glad you're here."

"Me too." I follow along next to him. I am so screwed. "Did your parents know you were coming home?" I can't imagine they would have kept that from me.

"No. I wanted to surprise them. I only saw them for a minute because I bolted out the back door as soon as they told me you were out here."

"Then it's good we're going in." He holds the door open for me. "I need to call Naomi, anyway. Jeb is waiting for me at Bell's, and I'm late. I hope he won't be too disappointed. What time do you think it is?"

He leans back and looks up at the sun. "I'd say around one."

"Do you want to come to Bell's with me or stay and visit with your parents?"

We step into the house. "With you, of course. I can see them any ol' time."

"Okay." I hug him again. I can't get enough. "I'll meet you in the kitchen when I'm done?"

"You bet." The smile he gives me has my heart thrashing around in my chest.

This trip could be the end of me.

Colten is sitting at the kitchen island talking to his mother while Earl whisks eggs. I take a moment to focus my breathing before I enter. Seeing him . . . it's all so overwhelming.

Catching sight of me, Colten tilts his head, looking intrigued by my thoughts. I give him a reassuring smile and continue my way into the kitchen and sit on the stool next to him.

"Tess," Twyla says from the open refrigerator door. "Can you believe it?"

"No," I laugh. "I'm still in shock."

She points the carton of juice at her son. "Why didn't you tell us you were coming home?"

"Where's the fun in that?" he laughs, then leans over to me and whispers, "You good?"

I nod my head as Twyla comes around the counter and fills his glass with orange juice. But really? I'm far from good. My head is a jumble of emotions.

How do I process this?

Where do all the pieces fit?

I know I should be happy that he's here. And I am. It's just . . . Holy crap! It's really him.

Four years and we're sitting here, together.

It's hard to grasp.

"I missed you so much." Twyla kisses the top of his head. "You've been gone forever."

"Great surprise, son." Earl pours batter into the waffle maker.

"Is your stuff by the front door?" Twyla puts the juice back. "I better get it in the wash. I'm sure it's ripe."

"You don't have to do that. I can get it later."

She grimaces. "No way! Who knows what bugs are crawling in there."

"There aren't any bugs." He looks mildly insulted. "It wasn't like I was livin' on the streets."

"Were you staying in hostels?" She rests a hand on her hip.

"Yes. Always."

She nods her head in confirmation. "There could be bugs. I'll be right back."

"What did Naomi say?" Colten asks.

"I told her we'd be there tomorrow at eleven. Jeb already left." I feel shitty about not showing up when I said I would. "I can leave right after."

"Okay." He pops a grape into his mouth with a big, cheesy grin. "Looks like I have you for another twenty-four hours."

"Yep." I give a small smile—my stomach suddenly feeling nervous. That's a lot of time to fall deeper than I already have.

"So where didja fly out of?" Earl sets an omelet and a large plate of waffles in front of Colten.

"Ho Chi Minh. You would love Vietnam, Dad. The people are so friendly. It's super cheap to live and the places you can visit from there are amazing."

"We really enjoyed the pictures you sent—all of them," Twyla says, coming through the kitchen with his backpack and disappearing again.

Earl leans against the counter. "You must be exhausted—jetlagged and all."

"I'm okay. I'm sure it will hit me later."

"How did you get home from the airport?" Earl gathers up the vegetables and returns them to the fridge. "We would have picked you up."

"Well, after I flew into Charlotte, I took a bus to Raleigh, then hitched the rest of the way. I wanted to surprise you," he says quickly at his dad's puckered brow. "And I got lucky. You're never gonna believe who picked me up, Tess. Remember that annoying little kid, Chaz?"

"Uh." I have to think back. *At the beach. His brother pestered me at the party.* "Oh, yeah. Seriously?"

"Crazy, huh? He's working construction over in Raleigh and was comin' home for the weekend. He got off a day early because they were waitin' for an inspector or something."

"Is he still the same?" It's hard to imagine him anything other than he was, a scrawny teenager with acne.

"Not at all. He's a good kid. Well, not a kid anymore." Colten shovels another bite of food into his mouth. "He asked about you—always does, every time I see him. Which isn't often, but I've seen him grow and change over the years."

"When was the last time you ate?" I ask.

His cheeks are full when he smiles at me, making him look like a chipmunk on his luckiest score ever. *So cute.*

"You were lucky." Earl scrubs the frying pan. "You could have been out there waitin' forever."

And I would have missed him.

I think back to the conversation Twyla and I had about those seemingly meant-to-be moments. They've happened at a few crucial times in my life, the one with Colten being the most relevant, but I don't believe in fate, that things are destined, pre-planned. So how does *that* work?

Colten swallows his bite and takes a sip of his juice. "Naw, barely waited at all. And with these charming good looks? *Pfff.*" He grips my stool, pulling it toward him. It makes the most horrible scraping sound against the tile. "Right?" he says, wrapping both arms around my body, trapping my arms and squeezing hard."

I look up at him. "Wow. You've become overly sure of yourself." My words come out distorted from the lack of air in my lungs. He laughs at the sound and loosens his grip as he kisses my cheek, then releases me completely to take another bite.

This all feels so normal and at the same time, not at all.

Earl smiles at the two of us. "I called the restaurant and told them I wasn't comin' in tonight."

"You didn't have to do that, Dad. We have lots of time."

"My son is home." He gives Colten a look that says no other words are needed. Family comes first.

"My god." Twyla comes back into the kitchen pinching her nose. "Have you *washed* your clothes since you left?"

"On occasion," he muffles through another mouthful.

"I was tempted to take it all out to the firepit and burn it."

"I told you I would do it."

She waves him off. "So, what did I miss?"

"Not much. Colten's been shoveling food into his mouth nonstop," I say, nudging him with my shoulder. "Where are you putting it all?" I lift his shirt, getting a brief peek at his tanned washboard abs before he smacks my hand away playfully.

"There ain't nothin' that beats Dad's cooking," he says like it's a given.

My eyebrows raise. *I can think of something.*

Don't even go there!

He gives me a steamy half-smile, which prompts me to take a sip of his juice as heat pulses through my system.

Damn, he read my mind.

"Tell us about some of your adventures," Earl says. "And how was the food? We never got many details. Our FaceTimes were always so short."

Colten wipes his mouth on a napkin. "Let's see . . . the last time I talked to you, I was still in Thailand."

"Yes. You were somewhere near Bangkok."

"Right. Food was amazing almost everywhere I went. I visited a lot of the coastal areas south of there, then decided to head to Vietnam. I flew into Hanoi, which is in North Vietnam, and bought a motorcycle for next to nothing. I met a guy from Germany at the hostel who did the same thing, and we ended up travelin' south together, ultimately ending up in Ho Chi Minh city. Had my life flash before my eyes a few times along the way."

"Don't tell me that!" Twyla glares at him.

"You asked about my adventures." He laughs. "Anyway, from there, my German friend and I flew to several islands nearby, then parted ways after we were slipped some drugs in a bar."

Twyla's hand flies to her chest. "Colten Morely Reed."

Morely? I laugh to myself.

"I'm not impressed." Earl's tone is hard. I've never seen him remotely angry before.

"I know, I know. The bartender must have slipped something into our drinks. That's the only time our bottles were out of sight. My friend was dragged out into the streets. While he was getting his ass kicked, a bunch of girls from the hostel recognized me stumblin' around out of my mind and took me back to recuperate. I was out for twenty-four hours.

"By the time I was right in the head, my friend was gone. That's when I decided I was ready to come home. I sold my bike for the same amount I paid for it and hopped on the next plane with a decent airfare. It took me close to three days to get here, but I made it." He throws up his hands in the air like, *Ta-da!*

Neither of his parents are smiling. "You were lucky, son," Earl says, his voice still strained.

He drops his eyes to his plate. "Yeah. I know."

My mind is racing through all the could-haves and it terrifies me. I guess this kind of thing could happen anywhere. Still . . .

"What about your German friend?" I ask, needing the rest of the story. "It seems odd he would leave without saying goodbye."

"He was scheduled to fly out the next day. We were celebrating when it happened. I texted him when I was finally conscious, but he'd already left. Apparently, he woke up in the hospital but was still able to make his flight."

"Well, I'm glad you're home. Safe." Twyla reaches across the counter and squeezes her son's hand.

Earl is back to cleaning, probably giving himself time to settle down. Colten is twenty-four. It's not as if he's an irresponsible teenager. I wonder if it's hard to accept your children growing up.

"So, Tess." Earl shifts his attention to me. "I'm glad to hear you're stayin' a little longer."

"You are?" Twyla beams. She had missed that part of the conversation. "That's fantastic."

I'm happy the mood has lightened. The tension felt out of place in this family—the situation with Josie excluded.

Colten rises and takes his plate to the sink. He rinses it and puts it in the dishwasher. "Is it okay if I take Tess out on the boat?" he asks his parents.

"You just got home," I say, not wanting to take him away from his family.

"I have them forever. I only have you till tomorrow."

I wonder how much despair the human heart can withstand? Leaving him again could break me for good this time.

"You go on ahead," Earl says. "The boat's runnin' a little rough. You might need to give it a tweak at some point."

"Sure. I'll give it a listen."

My head tilts. "A listen?"

"You can tell a lot about an engine by the sound," Colten says.

"*Ahh*, Master Reed is one with the force." I climb down from my stool.

"A *Star Wars* reference?" he says, surprised. "I think I'm in love."

CHAPTER 34

EARL AND TWYLA won't let us help clean up and shoo us out the back door. Colten takes my hand, linking his fingers through mine, as we walk toward the dock. I wish I could stop asking myself, where is this all going?

We settle into the boat—Colten behind the wheel, me in the seat next to him. He grabbed his favorite ball cap before we left the house. It looks even more ragged than when I saw it that summer so long ago. It must have made the travels with him. Colten turns the key, and the engine comes to life.

"It's idling rough. I'll have to pull off the cover and get in there."

Sounded fine to me. Those expert ears, I guess.

The boat moves slowly away from the dock. When we are clear, Colten pushes up on the throttle, sending us flying over the water.

Déjà vu. It's like we're starting over exactly where we left off four years ago. The night before it all went to shit.

It's a beautiful day. The sun is peeking in and out of large puffy clouds, which is a good thing because it's crazy hot. I wish I'd thought to put sunscreen on.

"I needed that," Colten says as he slows the boat to a crawl. "To let go, fly across the water, to have room. It's crowded, noisy, and polluted in Vietnam. Not in the rural areas, but in the cities where I spent most of my time." He closes his eyes and breathes in deep, looking blissful. "Listen to that silence."

"I know. I've missed this."

"Me too." He turns, locking eyes with mine, relaying something deeper.

I shift my eyes toward the shoreline. I don't know how to handle what's happening. Colten is not going to follow me to New York.

"So, are you home for good?" It's time to see where his head is at.

"I think I've gotten the travelin' out of my system for now. I'm ready to get back to work."

Damn. "Will you open another garage? I guess you'd have to unless you wanted to work for someone else."

"Probably." My heart sinks. "The land is still ours. I'm thinkin' maybe two bays this time. But no gas pumps. It's too disruptive, and I don't want to hire employees. Besides, we got the Shell gas station. Did Mom go on about it? She usually does."

"Not really, just that it was here." Now more than ever, I need to steel myself against the feelings that are still beating strong.

I can do it.

I have to.

"I couldn't believe it when I walked in the front door and

Mom told me you were here," he says. "When I told y'all I was ready to come home because of the drugging incident, that was only part of it." His eyes roam my face, taking in every detail before continuing. "I knew you were done with school, if you'd stayed on your original timeline, and I thought, well, in case you came back . . ." He shrugs a shoulder. "I never really expected you would, but I wanted to be here if you did."

I'm blown away by his admission.

He came back for me?

I want to crawl into his arms and submit to everything I still feel for him. But we're back at the beginning—our lives moving forward in two separate locations.

He takes my hand. I watch as his palm slides against mine, his fingers linking us in a solid bond. My eyes drift closed, wanting to absorb the sensation of his touch, but I can't have this, and it's a mistake to think that I can. I pull away, but he holds firm.

"Why did you come back?"

I can see the need for confirmation in his eyes. That I still feel the same way and we can finally be together. But who gives it all up, him or me? This isn't fair to either of us. "I had a dream. It was about us, and painfully vivid. Every feeling, every memory, hit me like a tidal wave. So I jumped into the car, needing to see you. There was no forethought. I just came, then Earl's was gone, and you—"

He pulls me over onto his lap, unleashing more feelings for me to fight. Damn him.

Is he purposely trying to make this more difficult?

I almost groan out loud when his fingers trail up and down

my forearm with feather-light pressure. He's going to suffer as much as I am when this goes to shit.

Why is he acting like we have all the time in the world?

I mean, he fought so hard to keep us apart four years ago. And now he . . . what, doesn't care about the backlash of separation?

I am *so* confused right now.

"When you left . . ." He pauses. "I had too much time to think. It wasn't good. Mom can tell you—maybe she already did. I was like a walking zombie for several months. There were days, in that first year, I wanted to jump in the car and hunt you down. I told you that already. Sorry if I'm repeating myself." His fingers move to the top of my thigh, drawing invisible designs, leaving raised bumps in their wake. "I kept running that last day over and over in my head, playin' out ways I could've handled it better."

I swallow hard against the sensations he's creating. *Focus!* He said he could have handled it better. "Yeah, me too."

But thinking back, I'm not sure what I would have done or said differently. He set the stage and didn't give me any leeway to change his mind.

"I looked for you on social media," he says, "but your last post was right before I met you. Part of me was happy you weren't keepin' up with your accounts. Seeing you movin' on would have killed me."

"I know what you mean. I looked for you as soon as I got my phone back." I reach up absentmindedly and twirl a lock of his hair around my finger. Stop it! I drop my hand. "I wanted to have a link if I needed it. But I couldn't find you."

"It's under *Coltenbefixinthings* on Instagram. Not an easy

account to find." I laugh at the name. "I know. It's stupid. I was thirteen when I made it and I haven't posted since high school." There's silence as we tug slowly along, following the shoreline. "Are you excited about your new job? I guess I kinda asked that already. Maybe I'm more jetlagged than I thought."

"It's fine, and yes, I am." I move back to my seat, needing the space. It's probably the thought of leaving Colten that's got me feeling down about the new position. "We should probably head back. I didn't put any sunscreen on and I can feel my skin frying. Besides, I feel guilty about taking you away from your parents."

"They're fine."

"I know, but still."

"Okay." His index finger reaches out and pushes lightly on my cheek to test the flush. "Yeah, you're getting burnt." He takes off his ball cap and sets it on my head. I remember the same thoughtful action at the Jasper Creek Fourth of July BBQ. I adjust the tightness and pull my ponytail through the back as he steers us toward home.

Colten had a short nap. He tried to get me to join him, but I opted out, saying I had some emails I needed to respond to. I didn't. I just couldn't handle being in such an intimate situation. Who knows where it would have led? And, well . . . I just couldn't.

Earl cooked up another killer meal. We talked and drank wine, drifting from one conversation to the next. After dessert, we FaceTimed Josie. She was excited to see her big brother home and shocked when I came into the frame. I got to tell her I was sorry for not saying goodbye. She gracefully waved it off and said she understood. She's so grown up—sixteen, driving and talking about quantum mechanics. I can't believe it. We promised to exchange contact information with her mother. Regardless of what happens with Colten, I'm not letting this amazing being become a memory again.

Where Josie has changed drastically, Colten is very much the same, with only subtle differences. The long hair, the beard, and he looks older—less boy, more man. But there's something else. Maybe it's all the traveling. When you spend your whole life in one place and then you're suddenly out in the world, it has an effect.

"Your mom and I are going to go to bed." Earl wraps an arm affectionately around Twyla's shoulders and kisses the top of her head.

It's getting late. I know *I'm* exhausted. Colten must be dead on his feet. I hate the thought of our night together ending. We only have tomorrow afternoon and that's it.

"Have a good sleep." Colten hugs them both. "Hey, just wondering . . ." he says to his dad. "Is my truck going to start?"

"It should," he answers. "I've been driving it off and on like you told me to."

"Thanks, love you."

"Love you too," they say.

His mom breaks free from Earl and gives her son another hug and kiss. "I missed you," she whispers.

"I missed you too." Colten pulls her in for another hard squeeze. "It's great to be back."

"Well?" Colten says to me after his parents walk to their bedroom. "What do you want to do now?"

"It's getting late. You should get some sleep."

"I had a nap." He brushes my cheek with his fingers. "I was thinking we could go for a drive and look at the stars."

I involuntarily lean into his touch, my eyes already drifting closed. When I realize what I'm doing, I straighten and take a small step back. "All right. Are you sure you're not too tired?"

He's wearing an expression of confusion, probably wondering why I pulled away. "No. I'm good. You?"

"I'm fine. I should grab a jacket, though." I turn away and walk to the back door, grabbing the one off its hook that I used last night. He looks at it as I push my arms through the sleeves. "Did you want to wear it? I can grab a different one."

"No. I don't need it." He nods his head at the jacket. "It looks good on you."

I smile and close the two sides of the front over each other and hug the material against my body. "It's comfortable." *And it's yours.*

It's a nice, warm night, but windy with the truck windows down. Colten reaches over and takes my hand in his. They're softer than I remember. The callouses have smoothed out, but the thrill traveling up my arm is the same.

Damn, damn, damn. I'm going to be fitting the broken pieces of my heart together when I leave tomorrow.

Not much I can do about it now. I'm too far gone.

It's not long before we turn off the lake road onto a bumpy one. As soon as he parks, I know where we are. He grabs the blankets from behind the back seat and runs to my side, but I'm already out of the truck.

"You ready for some stargazing?" he asks, holding out an arm to me.

"With you?" I smile big, linking my arm through his. "Always." The excitement of getting to spend time alone with him floods my mind with memories. Some feelings never change.

He drops the tailgate, chucks the blanket in, then jumps up, holding a hand out to me. I plant a foot on the edge and he hauls me up. We open the blankets, making a comfy space, then lie side by side. He clasps his hands over his chest. Mine stay at my sides as we look up at the stars in awe as a gentle breeze brushes my cheek.

The sky is clear, and without a moon, it's exceptionally dark. The crickets and frogs are in concert, playing a soothing melody that I could easily fall asleep to if I wasn't so wound up. It's been a roller-coaster of a day with my emotions running rampant, and my thoughts racing as they work to solve the puzzle of us.

"Do you remember the star clusters I taught you?" Colten's deep voice rumbles through the dark as he turns his head in my direction. A sensual chill courses through my body at a wisp of his breath that touches my cheek.

I tilt my head to the side, facing him, his brilliant eyes shining in muted grays in the dark. "I was out on the deck last night, searching." My eyes drift away to the sky, pointing out and naming the constellations I remember.

When he doesn't respond, I turn my head to see if he's fallen asleep. He hasn't. He's staring at me with an intensity of warmth and longing that steals my breath. When he reaches over and cradles my cheek and runs his thumb over my lower lip, I know that stargazing will be much later on the agenda. And as much as I want to resist, I know the pent-up need inside me won't let that happen, no matter what my better logic dictates.

As I lie naked on top of him, thanking the universe for his existence, I struggle with knowing this is the beginning of the end, then instantly berate myself. I'm an adult. I can be rational about this. It's important to take happiness as it comes, and we both needed this time together, regardless of the consequences. Closure can take on all kinds of forms.

I lift my head at his slow, steady breathing.

He's asleep. I chuckle to myself as I attempt to move to his side without waking him. He pulls me back.

"You fell asleep." I press my lips above his chest.

"Sorry. I've gotten good at sleeping in all kinds of positions."

I prop my head on my crossed hands and stare at him with raised eyebrows. "Really?" My mind conjures up images of women wrapped around Colten's beautifully sculpted body.

"That came out wrong. Don't look at me that way." He pinches my bare butt.

"*Ow.*" I giggle.

"I mean when traveling. I can sleep just about anywhere."

"Got it." I kiss the hollow at the base of his neck "Not me. I need all the comforts of home."

"Speaking of home. How are things there?"

"The condensed version is that Dad and I had a long talk and worked things out and he divorced my mother, who, in turn, doesn't talk to me anymore."

"Okay. Some good, some bad."

"No. All good." I swirl my fingertips over the wisps of hair that sit between nicely sculpted pecs. "Having her completely out of my life has been the best thing for me."

He sighs. "That feels so good." He takes my hand and kisses the tips of my fingers. "You better stop. I don't know if my body can go another round on this ribbed truck-bed."

"I could be on the bottom this time." I lean up and nip his bottom lip with my teeth.

He looks up at the sky and groans. "Let's go home. I want you in my bed."

I kind of like it out here—it feels a little daring out in the open—but he's already up and pulling his jeans on. I pause a moment to enjoy the view.

When he sees me, he grins with a chuckle deep in his throat. "Come on, Tess. Let's go home." He holds out a hand to me, pulling me up against him.

I take advantage of the nearness and kiss him until his hands are roaming my body and his chest is heaving. "Okay. We can go now," I say playfully.

He lifts me up. When my arms slide around his neck, he pulls my legs up so I'm straddling him. His jeans are still open.

Oh, lord. It's payback time.

Back at the house, we take our time. We talk, kiss, and explore each other's bodies as we fire up and cool down over and over. Four years is a lot to catch up on. I don't let myself think about the future, just enjoy the moment as if it could go on forever and nothing outside of us exists.

I tell him about Levvy, school, and more details about the

talk with my dad and how it all played out. He tells me how ridiculously happy Dawson and Sri are, and gives me the condensed details of their wedding. He explains how Naomi met Riley at a BBQ at Jumpin' Jacks beach and gives details about the fire and his version of how it rocked his family. I enjoy his colorful tales as he verbally maps out his journey abroad, starting with Australia, then Europe, followed by Asia, giving bits of details from each location.

"I probably don't really want an answer to this," he starts, "but I'm going to ask anyway." The tips of his fingers trail up and down my back. "Have you been with anyone since we were together?"

With my upper body settled between his legs, I touch my lips to his abs. "Not intimately. You?"

"No." He smiles, looking pleased, or maybe relieved. I can't tell for sure. "I went on a few dates on my travels, but they never amounted to anything."

"For a guy, isn't that a long time to, you know . . . go without?"

He lifts his head off the pillow to look down at me with pinched eyebrows. "That is so sexist," he says, laughing, then turns us both to lie on our sides. "And what about you? That's a long time to, you know . . . go without." He smirks. "And I don't do flings, remember?"

I smile sweetly at him. "I remember."

He brushes a fingertip over my lower lip. "Besides . . . they weren't you."

Love dances along the inner walls of my heart as his words validate all that we were. I touch my lips to his. "Thank you for that."

He tucks a loose strand of hair behind my ear. "I wasn't pumping your tires. No one has touched me the way you have."

How did we let this go?

"My feelings for you haven't changed," I say, the words coming out easily, with no fear, making me wonder why. "I may have shoved them down deep, but that was purely survival."

I'm hit with a parallel reminder of my childhood. I learned how to block the longing for love, but the rejection carved all kinds of invisible scars. When Colten rejected me, those scars should have embedded a little deeper than they did. Somehow, I must have known there was more to the story, and I was waiting for the moment to finish what we started—to live our lives together as we were meant to.

"I suppose our meeting was a gift as well as a curse. It seems like a lifetime ago and yet only yesterday." He rolls me onto my back, caresses my lips with his. "But you're here now, and I'm not letting you get away this time."

I want to ask what he means by his last statement, but his lips have my mind shifting to other pleasures, and then to nothing at all.

CHAPTER 35

I WAKE up with Colten's heavy limbs draped over me, his face nestled in the crook of my neck, his breath tickling me on every exhale.

Being with Colten is better than I remember, and that's saying a lot because I have fantastic memories. The connection felt deeper, more intense—tender one moment, rough and demanding the next.

I will miss this. All of it. I can't believe I'm leaving today. My heart already feels like it's breaking.

What was I thinking about last night—scars and my parents, something Colten said? I try to remember the exact thoughts I was having before he whisked my mind into sexual oblivion, but I can't. It felt important, though.

He stirs, then lifts his head, smiling at me. "I could get used to this."

Me too. That's the problem.

Is it time to talk about our situation?

Before I have time to get too deep into my thoughts, he rolls himself on top of me, pressing me into the mattress. There's a kiss on my lips, slow and lazy, which continues down my neck, between my breasts, and down to my stomach before he stops and looks up at me, eyebrows pumping. My worries are once again wiped away.

We shower together, exploring all the sensitive areas, reveling in one another's touch until the water runs cold and we're shivering and pruned. We dress and venture out in search of food. It's around ten and we're both starving.

"Morning," Twyla says, coming into the kitchen as Colten pulls eggs from the fridge. "I can make you breakfast." She slides into his arms for a hug, then comes over and squeezes me as well.

"That's okay, Mom. I can do it."

"I know you can do it, but I can do it better. Move over." She hip-checked him out of the way. "How does a veggie scramble sound to you two?"

"Great," we both say.

She opens the fridge and digs through a drawer, pulling out all kinds of veggies. "Colten, you're on toast duty."

"Yes, ma'am." He gives her the military salute, and she swats his butt playfully with the spatula she just pulled out of the drawer. "Where's Dad?"

"He went in early to get the prep work done for this evening's meal. He should be home in an hour or so." She dices and slices with an easy fluidity.

I realize I've never seen her cook before. I suppose you pick up a few things living with a chef.

"What are you two up to today?"

"Well. I need to pack and get over to Bell's as soon as we're done," I say. "Jeb is waiting and I should get on the road." I look at Colten, surprised he doesn't seem affected that I'm leaving. Maybe he's just resolved to how things are?

"Oh . . . Can't you stay another day?" Twyla begs.

"I'd love to, but I really should get back."

"I understand. Well, that's sweet of you to make Jeb a priority."

Guilt and a bit of sadness works its way past my overdosed sexual high. I should have been there yesterday. I feel like I let him down, again. "He was so kind that day that everything happened with Josie. I'm not sure if Colten told you, but he stayed and was an enormous help. He wouldn't leave my side." And then I just left without a word. *I suck.*

"I think Colten mentioned he was there, but at the time, I wasn't really listening. I wish I would have been kinder to him when he showed up at my house that first day, but he caught me by surprise. He became a better person for knowing you, Tess. You touched something in him. I'm sure he misses you."

"I miss him too—the grizzly old buzzard."

"Why don't you call over there and let them know we'll be there in thirty," Colten says.

"Here. You can use my phone," Twyla says, already dialing the number.

Breakfast was great. I've had omelets, but not a veggie scramble. It's just sauteed veggies and cheese in scrambled eggs. So much easier. I'll have to remember that. I cook, but I'm not great at it. Maria only taught me the basics and how to read a recipe. I wish I would have gotten around to asking Earl for some tips like I'd planned. We always think we have more time than we do.

I've packed up my car and left it behind as Colten drives us into town. We will say our goodbyes at the house when we're done visiting everyone.

We talk about all kinds of random things on the way—still having so much we need to catch up on—and before we know it, he's parking in front of Bell's. The time is going too fast.

"Well, look what the cat dragged in," Jeb says, turning on his stool when we walk through the door.

"Hey, Jeb." Seeing him fills me with a warmth set aside only for him. "Sorry I missed you yesterday."

"Eh." He waves me off. "You got a hug for this old man?"

"You bet." I rush to his side.

His frail arms wrap around me and squeeze me like a long-lost family member. "I missed you, kid."

My throat thickens and tears prick my nose and eyes. "I missed you, too." I pull away with a deep inhale, willing the thick emotions away, not wanting to create a scene that would most likely make Jeb uncomfortable.

His hair is thinner and completely white, the lines on his face etched deeper, his cheeks hollower, and the dark circles under his eyes make me wonder if he's taking care of himself.

He nods at Colten. "Welcome back."

Colten holds out his hand to him. "Jeb." They shake in greeting as Colten takes a stool and pulls me between his legs, linking his arms around my stomach.

Jeb cracks a smile. "So I see you two finally stopped dancin' around each other?"

I look over my shoulder and smile at Colten. He pinches my side playfully, causing me to flinch and let out a small yelp.

"My boy finally smartened up," Naomi says, adding her all-knowing grin.

"How's it going, Nomi?" Colten asks her.

"You know I hate when you call me that." She gives his shoulder a shove, which moves me to the side with him.

They haven't changed a bit.

"You back for good?" Jeb asks Colten.

"Yes, sir, I am. Came back yesterday. I almost missed Tess."

A bittersweet response. It would have almost been easier if I'd left earlier that morning and our paths never crossed —almost.

"Well, that was lucky." Naomi winks at me.

Colten kisses the top of my head. "It was."

Naomi plants her hands firmly on the counter in front of us. "Ice cream?"

"I don't know if I have any room." Even though my mouth is watering at the thought. "We just ate a massive breakfast."

"Hell, yeah!" Colten says.

"Your stomach is a bottomless pit," I laugh, leaning my head back to nuzzle my cheek next to his now-smooth face. He shaved his beard off this morning. He said it was getting hot and itchy.

"This is dessert. You're gonna say no to Naomi's ice cream?" he teases me.

"*Fine.* Just a small scoop." I concede to my desires for the second time today. My mind drifts to Colten's body melding with mine under the bedsheet. I clear my throat and sit up. "What's this week's creation?"

"Apple Crumble and Choc-o-riffic Zing."

"Ooh, two specials," I say. "I'll take the Choc-o-riffic, of course. What's the zing?"

"Coffee."

"Sweet! I can always justify the need for a little more of that."

"I remember." Naomi gives me a conspiratorial wink, then turns to Colten and her expression goes flat. "Vanilla?"

He laughs. "No. I think I'll try the Apple Crumble."

Naomi runs from behind the counter to the front door and sticks her head out, looking up at the sky.

"What're ya lookin' at?" Jeb hollers at her.

"Seeing if pigs are flyin'."

"Girl, you finally done lost yer mind," Jeb cackles, shaking his head.

"Ha, ha," Colten says as she walks back. "My tastes expanded on my travels." Her eyebrows shoot up at him from behind the counter.

"New tastes in food," he clarifies. I can visualize the eye roll he's giving her behind my back.

After digging and scooping in the barrels of ice cream in the display freezer, Naomi sets a massive single scoop in front of me, and a triple scoop in front of Colten. I immediately take a bite and sigh. Nothing beats her ice cream. Well, maybe some of Earl's desserts. And sex with Colten—nothing beats that.

Colten angles his body behind me so he can use both hands to get at his treat. I move to get up, but he grips the back of my shorts. "Stay," he says, to which I respond with a contented grin.

"Where's mine?" Jeb asks, looking cross.

"You didn't say you wanted any," Naomi barks at him.

"Aren't you supposed to ask?" he snaps back.

"Fine," Naomi huffs. "What do you want?"

"Vanilla."

She throws her hands in the air. "Why I even bother is beyond me."

"What the *hell's* wrong with vanilla?" he yells.

"Trust me," Colten says. "Don't ask."

"This is so good," I say to Naomi, attempting to divert us from where this conversation is heading. "I taste the chocolate and coffee, obviously." I narrow my eyes. "Peanut butter, banana, coconut and . . ."

"Pecans." She sets two scoops of vanilla in front of Jeb. "Want any nuts or hot fudge on that?" she asks him.

He waves his spoon at her. "Why would I want to go messin' up a good thing with all *that* crap?"

I laugh, then say, "You should taste some of the Apple Crumble. It's your two favorite desserts put together." He eyes me dubiously. "Just try a taste."

"Fine," he growls.

Naomi digs out a spoonful and hands it to him. He eyes it before taking a tentative bite. His bushy eyebrows lift in surprise, and he puts the rest of the spoon in his mouth.

"Can I have this instead?" He pushes his untouched bowl of vanilla toward her.

"Absolutely." She looks pleasantly surprised. "I'll do anything for a convert."

"You should sell this to the restaurants for their dessert menus," I tell her.

"She has." Riley comes from the back and wraps an arm

around Naomi's waist. "Hi, everyone. I was in the middle of making the egg salad for lunch tomorrow."

I look over at Jeb to see how he's handling this relationship. I could see him making a snide comment—he's rural and old school.

Well, maybe he did in the beginning and Naomi put him in his place, because he seems fine with it. I'm proud of him.

We have a nice visit. Colten and I do most of the storytelling, more Colten than me, since he's the one with the adventures to tell. It's wonderful being here again. The only thing that's missing is Sri.

"You said Sri opened a pharmacy in town?" I ask Naomi.

"Yeah. Across the street and to the right. Colten knows where it is."

"I'd like to stop there next if that's okay," I say over my shoulder to him.

He kisses my cheek. "I go where you go."

I wish.

"You two look good together," Naomi comments. "You stayin' this time?" she asks me.

"Uh . . . no." I frown. "I start my new job on Monday. I need to leave as soon we're done with our visit. And I say hi to Sri."

"*Huh,*" she returns with a head nod. What she's really saying is, *You're leaving again, breaking my friend's heart, and you suck.*

But last time it was all him, he did the heartbreaking. All I did was what he told me to do—leave. And he's a big boy. He can make his own decisions. He knows I need to leave.

And he still hasn't acknowledged it.

He hasn't even asked me to stay. Not that I would, but . . .

Maybe he thinks that since we slept together, I'll change my plans. I can't imagine he wants me to just drop it all now and come live here.

The thought is tempting. Which surprises me.

"You ready?" he says in my ear when my ice cream is all gone.

"I suppose I better get going." I stand up. "We're going to head over and see Sri," I tell Naomi.

"I should be gettin' on as well," Jeb says, the pain evident in his eyes as he struggles to get off his stool. I quickly take his arm, lending support. This time I don't care if he wants the help or not. "Will you be back this way again?"

"I don't know." The thought makes me ache all over. I'm afraid to look at Colten because I might fall apart. "Do you have a phone?" I ask Jeb. "We could stay in touch."

"I'd like that." He cracks a shy smile that almost does me in. I take a deep breath to hold back the tears.

Naomi finds us paper and pens and we exchange phone numbers, then we all pull out money for the ice cream. Jeb fights us and wins, even though Naomi insisted it was on the house. "A celebratory treat," she says.

We say our goodbyes, hugs are shared, and the tears well in my eyes no matter how hard I try to fight them off.

"That was hard," I say, following Colten after we part ways with Jeb outside.

He drapes an arm across my shoulders, pulling me against him. I loop my arm around his waist and lean into his side, wondering when we're going to talk about the inevitable.

I'm stalling. I wonder what his excuse is.

CHAPTER 36

WE HEAR a loud squeal as soon as we enter the drugstore, then see Sri running down an aisle toward us with her arms out. She squishes me in a hug before moving on to Colten.

"Naomi told me you were back," she says to me, "but I hadn't heard *you* were." She eyes Colten.

"Just yesterday."

Colten takes my hand in his, pulling it up and kissing my knuckles. She nods in satisfaction and says, "Dawson is going to be super excited you're home. We should have a BBQ at the beach. It's too late to organize it for tonight, but tomorrow or the next day works."

"Oh, I have to leave right away."

"What? *Nooo*," she drags the word out, disappointed. "You can't. You just got here. Why do you have to leave?"

"My job starts Monday."

"It's only Friday. Come on. Stay for one more day. We'll have the BBQ tonight."

If I leave early the following morning and drive late into the next night . . . but I'll be bagged the next day when I start work. *Screw it.* "I guess I can stay one more day."

"Are you sure?" Colten says. "Tess starts her new job at Sotheby's."

She hugs me. "Congratulations!"

"Yeah. It's a great opportunity." Once again, I'm not getting that same excited thrill I once did.

"Great. Okay." I can see the gears turning in her head. "Good thing about owning your own business, I can close a little early. I should be able to be there by six-thirty at the latest. Dawson can meet you all there earlier, since he's off work at five. I'll text Naomi."

"We'll bring the potato salad," Colten says. "I'll get the recipe from Dad. Tess and I can make it. Can you cook?" he asks me.

"When I have to. I mostly get takeout."

"Why don't you tell everyone to bring their own meat to grill and a side," Colten tells Sri. "We'll make it a potluck. That's the easiest."

I can see the relief wash over her. I don't blame her. It's a lot to put together on such short notice.

"Okay." A customer comes in. "I better get back to work. I'll see you all later tonight."

I give her another hug. "See you soon."

"It's so good to see you, Tess." She grips my hand, then releases it, leaving it to help the customer.

"You too," I say over my shoulder.

Colten places a hand on my lower back, guiding me in front of him. Another closure ticked off the list. I've spoken to everyone I left behind. It's been a busy couple of days.

He picks up my hand when we're outside. "Where to now?"

"Back to your house, I guess. Sounds like we have some potato salad to make."

My stomach is in knots. One more day will only add to the pain of leaving. I don't understand how Colten can be so calm about this. I'm doing my best to leave the pieces of us alone—not attempt to fit them together, because I know they don't fit. But my brain keeps changing the angles in hopes that somehow they will.

When we get home, he pulls me by the hand into his room and shuts the door. He's unbuttoning my shorts. "Uh . . . Shouldn't we start cooking?"

He pulls his shirt over his head. "Later."

My head is in the crook of Colten's shoulder, his arm draped around my waist, securing me to his side. A bed has never felt so good. "You've been quiet since we left town," he says, "except when you were screaming my name in delirious pleasure."

I smack his belly. "I was not. Your mother could have come home, I was purposely quiet." He responds with a chuckle. I look up at him. "Colten? What are we doing?"

"Having the best sex of our lives, I thought." His hand slides over my rear, giving it a soft caress. "And maybe some more gettin'-reacquainted time."

I pull a swatch of chest hair. "I mean after that."

"Ow! I know what you meant. Tess, there's never been anyone else. I let you go once, hoping you would find your way back to me when the time was right, and you did. Are you mine?"

"It's not that simple."

"Yes, it is. Are you mine?" he asks again.

"Always, but—"

"That's all I need."

"But I'm leaving tomorrow."

"So, I can't come with you?"

I sit up and stare at him in shock. "What?" The thought that he might follow me was fleeting and mostly a fantasy. "You would do that?"

"I can fix cars anywhere."

"But you said you were happy to be home, and that you wanted to build a new garage."

"You're my home now. As long as I'm with you, I've got everything I need."

"Why didn't you say this before?" I choke on the words. The emotions are getting the better of me.

"Before what? This all just happened. I needed to know what *you* wanted." He slides a hand up and down my arm. "Tess, I've waited four years hoping you would come back. You think now that you have, I'm going to let you go? I told you I wasn't. *Hey.* Why are you crying? I hope those are happy tears."

"Very happy. I'm also stunned, amazed, surprised, relieved, and a little scared. What about your family?"

"I'm a grown man. It's time for me to leave the nest. Why are you scared? Are you not sure about us?"

"No. I am. Maybe scared isn't the right word— overwhelmed? But in a good way," I quickly amend. "You're sure you're okay living in New York?"

"I can live anywhere as long as I'm with you. I love you, Tess."

I squeal and cover his face with kisses as tears stream down my face. "I love you too. So much."

He's mine, and he's coming with me. I've never been this happy.

"We can tell my parents tonight when my father gets home," he says, laughing under the barrage.

"But you just got back from traveling."

"I'll stay a week, ten days. That will give me time to visit everyone before I head your way. I'll need to buy a car. I don't want to take the Porsche, and I'm not sure I want to drive the beater that far."

"We won't need two cars in the city."

"Okay. I guess I can take the bus up. It's not like I have a lot of belongings."

"But it will take longer for you to get to me."

"True." He nibbles my earlobe. "I'll fly." Then flips me onto my back, covering me with his body, and sending me into a fit of higher-than-life giggles. His lips find mine, but they're only a starting point as he kisses a trail down to my belly button, then—

"Just so you know . . ." I interrupt the heat. "I have a roommate. Her name is Levvy." He lets out a moan and drops his head on my stomach. "*Oof.*"

"And we want to talk about this, why?"

"I can't help it. My mind is going a mile a minute." I push at his shoulders so I can sit up. "This is so exciting. We have lots of plans to make. We'll have to stay in the apartment with my roommate until she finds another place, or we do. I don't want to leave her with all that rent."

"Whatever you think is best." He gently lays me back.

"I can't believe you're coming with me."

"Uh-huh." He rolls me on top of him.

"We should—" My words are lost against his mouth.

We spend the afternoon in bed. It isn't all physical—we talk and make plans. I'm glad Twyla and Earl are out of the house. It would have been embarrassing otherwise. When we finally climb out of bed, we make our way to the kitchen to scrounge up something to eat. Colten is starving.

"You two have been keeping busy?" Twyla asks, entering the kitchen. I choke on my water as she sets grocery bags on the counter. "Are you okay?" She pats me on the back.

"Yeah. Just went down the wrong pipe." I notice Colten's lecherous grin, and I want to throw something at him. She's going to know. Probably already does. *Ugh.* I want to hide.

"We're gettin' together with friends at the beach for dinner tonight." Colten reaches into a bag and begins putting groceries away. "Gonna do a potluck thing. I want to make some of Dad's potato salad."

"Okay. Uh . . ." She looks through the refrigerator. "Yeah. We have all the ingredients. I can make it for you, if you like."

"No. That's okay. It'll be something fun for Tess and I to do together."

"You're staying another day?" Twyla clues in, looking thrilled.

"Yeah. Sri talked me into it." I sit on a stool with my drink. I'd help put things away, but I don't know where they go.

"I've decided to move to New York to be with Tess."

Twyla's hand stops midair, a box of pasta hovering near a cupboard shelf. "Uh." She sets the box on the counter and turns to us.

"I thought we were waiting until tonight and tell your parents together," I hiss. How could he throw it out randomly, blindsiding his mother that way? She's still staring at us.

"I'm too excited. I couldn't wait that long." He sits next to me and takes my hand in his.

Twyla clears her throat, getting our attention. "It's okay, Tess. He's never been one to hold on to big news." She leans her back against the counter and crosses her arms over her chest. "Is this another one of your big adventures?" She directs the question to Colten.

I slide off my stool. "I should leave you two to talk."

He clasps onto my wrist. "Stay."

I stay where I am, but wish I was anywhere else. This is personal, and she's not happy about the announcement.

"Colten, are you sure you're not changing one quest for another? You haven't settled since the fire. That newness can be addicting. Are you sure this isn't some sort of avoidance behavior? It was our home. We spent more time there as a family than we did here."

"The fire had an impact—a huge one. Everything I was disappeared with that building. When the initial trauma settled, I wasn't sure what my next step was. Traveling was an opportunity to see the world—stretch my legs, experience new things, and sort myself out. But deep under all that was Tess, and maybe the waiting was making me restless." He takes up my hand. "Now that she's here, I feel as though the final missing piece of my life has fallen into place. She has an amazing job in New York." He kisses my fingers. "She loves me as much as I love her. What else can I do but follow her?"

Tears well up in Twyla's eyes as she assesses Colten.

Crap, what have we done? The thought of hurting this amazing woman . . .

But what if she opposes this move?

What if he picks his family over me?

What if it's the other way around? They'll hate me. *Ohh.* This doesn't feel good. My nerves are making me feel sick.

"You're right." She walks over to us, smiling through her tears. I grip my stomach and breathe an enormous sigh of relief. "I'm happy for you both. All a parent wants is to see their children healthy and happy. I'm so thankful I have both." She sniffles as she hugs us one at a time. "Well, I'm going to go call your father. I can't keep this news a secret either."

I whack his chest with the back of my hand when she leaves. "You could have at least warned me."

"I'm sorry. It was a spur-of-the-moment decision."

"This should be a private conversation between you two."

"Why? It involved you."

I shake my head at his lack of finesse. "I know, but shouldn't you have talked to her on your own, in case she wanted to tell you that you were being an idiot and making the biggest mistake of your life?" Which she kind of did.

The side of his face scrunches like I'm a moron. "You know my mom. She has no problem speaking her mind."

"Okay. You're right about that."

He pulls me between his legs. "Do you forgive me?"

"This time." I nuzzle his nose. "Next time . . ." I let the words hang with a shrug of my shoulders.

He bumps my chin with the side of his knuckle. "You know I'm going to mess up, right—make mistakes?"

"We both will." I drape my arms over his shoulders, locking my fingers behind his neck. "I've heard the best part of fighting is the making up. So, I'm not worried."

"Me neither." He slides a hand into my hair. Taking hold of the back of my neck, he brings our lips to within an inch of each other. "You want to go practice makeup sex?"

I place a hand on his chest, grinning. "It's time to cook."

I call Levvy with the news. She's shocked, then excited. Leave it to the hopeless romantic to understand. I text her a picture of Colten I snapped randomly. She responds with *Oh my god, he's hot* and lots of derogatory emojis. She's fine leaving or finding another roommate. We decide to discuss it more when I get back.

I debate whether to call my dad, then decide to talk to him when I get home. If he's not in town, then I'll FaceTime him. I'm not sure if he'll take the news as easily as Colten's parents did. He was the one who had to deal with the fallout after Colten broke my heart. He may not be too receptive to him being in my life again.

Life is a crazy ride with all its ups and downs and twists and turns. I could never have predicted how things would turn out coming back to Jasper Creek. I came motivated by the past, without thinking through the consequences. It could have been a disaster of epic proportions, and it was heading that way until this afternoon. I guess sometimes you have to let go and allow the wheels to fall off, then pick up the pieces wherever they land. Mine didn't fall very far this time, thankfully, and I got everything I wanted in the process.

I know it won't always be that way, but I'm damn thankful for this one happy beginning.

CHAPTER 37

WE BOILED eggs and left them in the refrigerator to chill in a bowl of ice water since we're a little short on time. Colten peels potatoes while I cut them into bite-size pieces. While they boil, we talk more about the move.

When the potatoes are cooked, we drain them, add the pickle relish, chopped eggs, onions, celery, and dressing, then mix all the ingredients together before setting it in the refrigerator to cool for the two hours we have left before the BBQ.

Twyla comes into the kitchen as Colten hands me the last pot to dry. "I was thinking. We should go through your stuff that's been collecting since you were little. I think it's time to purge some of it. Especially since you're moving away."

"Now?" He leans against the counter.

"Not now, but before you go. I was out in the she-shed and started thinking about it. I'd like to do it before you go—doing it over FaceTime will be a pain."

"What kind of stuff?"

"Oh my god." Her face gets animated. "Hordes of toys, books, clothes."

"Clothes? Why would you keep my old clothes? It's not like they're going to fit."

"I don't know. It's mostly stuff from high school. I thought maybe you might change your mind."

"No. You can donate them. Donate everything. But you might want to save the T-shirts and cut them up for rags. You can use them in your studio."

"Are you sure? You don't want to even look at anything?" She looks so sad. I think the things she saved are more important than she's letting on.

There was *nothing* left of my childhood when the penthouse was being packed up for the move. Colten is being an insensitive idiot.

"Mom, if I haven't used any of that stuff in however many years, I doubt I'll have a use for them now."

"I guess you're right," she sighs, turning to busy herself.

He walks to her, wraps her in his arms, and kisses the top of her head. "I'm sorry. You are the best mother in the history of the world." He bumps her chin up so she'll look at him. "I can look at whatever you want me to look at, but the toys . . . maybe you should keep them for when the grandkids come over."

"Grandkids?" I choke mid swallow. "Aren't you getting a little ahead of yourself?"

"Maybe." He keeps an arm draped over his mother's shoulders and cocks a grin at me. "But I *do* want kids, don't you?"

"One step at a time, but yes, someday for sure." I shoot him a glare for putting me on the spot. Shouldn't this be a private conversation?

Twyla pats his arm, moves to get a glass from the cupboard, and fills it with water. "I'll look through everything and keep what makes sense. And don't worry about the other stuff, I'm just being overly sentimental. If there's anything I think you might want, I'll ask you."

"That works."

I'm only half listening to their conversation. I'm still hung up on the kids thing. Up until this moment, I've never thought about having children. With no romantic prospects and having just graduated from college, why would I?

Kids . . . with Colten?

He hasn't even mentioned marriage. Do I even believe in the ritual? It's not like you need to get married to have kids.

"I'll go through my room before I leave, though," I hear Colten say. "Get rid of stuff I don't need and pack up memorabilia I want to save."

"Oh, honey, you don't have to do that. I'm not kicking you out."

He laughs. "It's okay if you want to turn my room into an exercise space. Isn't that what parents usually do when their firstborn flies the coop?" Her eyes well with tears that quickly spill down her cheeks. "Mom. What's wrong?"

I snap to attention and watch as she waves him away and takes a drink of water.

"I was just kidding." He takes her hand and pulls her into a hug.

"I know," she says against his chest. "It's hard when your kids grow up."

"I have to use the bathroom." They need space. "And I want to change for the BBQ. I'll see you in a bit."

"We're not all grown up," I hear Colten joke on my way out of the kitchen. "Josie is still a teenage pain in the butt."

Twyla seems like the type who would leave her kids' rooms intact forever. If my parents would have stayed together, my mother would have gutted my bedroom the moment I left, and my mother didn't do memorabilia—she hated clutter.

I guess it doesn't matter now. We'll be making our own space and our own memories. I'm excited. I can't wait to show him New York. I hope he likes it there. I know he said that home is wherever I am, but he may hate it. *Crap.* I hope not.

Dawson is banging the final stake into the sand when we walk out onto Jumpin' Jack's Beach. The volleyball net looks ready to go. "Hey, man." He gives Colten a back-slapping man hug as soon as we reach him. "Welcome back."

"Yeah. Good to see you. You remember Tess?"

"Hell, yeah." He swoops me up and spins me around in a tight hug before setting me on wobbly legs. "How ya doin', beautiful?"

"Good." I giggle, loving the easygoing familiarity. "It's nice to see you." He's not as skinny as he once was. There is more muscle since the last time I saw him.

"Do you wanna pull that table over?" Colten asks and nods in the direction of the trees.

"Yeah, let's do it."

Colten sets down the cooler loaded with the potato salad, drinks, and hotdogs, then hands me the plastic bag filled with hotdog buns. I watch as they push and shove each other on the way up the beach.

I'm a little nervous about how everyone is going to take our news. Will they resent that I'm taking away one of their own, permanently? The guy has been deeply rooted to his friends since birth.

I set the buns on top of the cooler and spread out the blanket I brought from the truck. The heavy table is dragged over with taunts of strength and lack of manhood. Then they're off to Dawson's massive truck to get his cooler and propane grill. When we parked next to the monster, Colten said Dawson must have bought it when he was out of the country, because he hadn't seen it before. I laugh, picturing Sri trying to get in and out of it.

I get lost in the tiny waves that splash and roll lazily up the beach until a rush of noise hits me. I turn my gaze to see Colten and Dawson, each holding a handle, struggling to carry the largest cooler I've ever seen, followed by Naomi, Riley, and a guy I don't know who's carrying a smaller cooler.

"I brought the ice cream," Naomi says, and tells the new guy to set it under the edge of the picnic table.

"Nice. Isn't it going to melt?" I ask.

She opens the lid, then shuts it quickly as smoke billows out. "Dry ice."

"Good to see you again." Colten shakes the new guy's hand. He's of medium height, dark-brown hair, blue eyes, and jacked.

Naomi leans over to me. "You don't remember him, do you?"

"Should I?"

"That's Chaz."

My eyes bulge. "No friggin' way."

He comes over to us. "Hey, Tess. Good to see you."

I wrap my arms around his neck and give him a big hug. "Look at you all grown up—and good-looking." His cheeks are rosy red when I release him.

"Don't say that," Naomi scolds. "The boy already has a big head."

"I do not." He stares at his shoes a moment, clearly mortified. "How long ya stayin'?" he asks me.

I give his arm a squeeze with a *don't mind her* expression. "I have to leave tomorrow, early."

"Oh," he says, his disappointment clear. "I was hoping to introduce you to my girlfriend. She was going to come home with me this weekend, but she wasn't feelin' well."

"I'm sorry to hear that. I would have loved to have met her. I hear you're a carpenter?"

"Yeah. I, well, Naomi set me up with her older brother. I trained on the job as an apprentice. Been doin' it comin' on three years now and love it."

He can't be more than eighteen or nineteen. *How did he finish school?*

After Chaz has wandered off, Naomi pulls me aside. She tells me Chaz's brother was sent to jail for rape charges and his mother's drinking got out of control. Chaz didn't do so well after that. Naomi helped him get his GED and set him to work with her brother in Raleigh.

To think I disliked her at first. I'm so proud she's my friend.

"You took what I said about keeping an eye on him seriously," I say.

"I like him. He's a good kid. Just needed a little direction and a couple of kicks in the ass."

"Didn't he have a little sister?" I watch as the guys huddle around the grill.

"Yeah. She went to live with an aunt while her mother went into rehab. It wasn't easy on Lorelai—that's his sister—but she seems to be doing okay now that her mother is back and staying dry. They live outside of town. Chaz comes home most weekends to help any way he can. He's been a great influence on her."

"All thanks to you raising him right." I look at her, and then at Riley. "You think you'll have children someday?"

"I feel like I already do. Riley and I have been workin' on an outreach program over at the New Life church for lower income kids. We make sure they stay on the straight and narrow and not get lost in the system, ya know? Sri is involved too, giving them crazy science experiments, and tutoring when needed. Twyla does art projects with them. I was hoping Colten would set up a volleyball program now that he's home and maybe even teach the older kids basic auto mechanics."

"Oh, yeah . . . right." I stumble over my words.

She leans away, eyeing me. "He's going with you, isn't he?"

Shit. I can't lie to her. "Yeah. We were going to tell everyone later."

"Let's eat!" Dawson yells.

"Can you not say anything?" I grip her forearm, pleading. "I want to let Colten do it."

She doesn't look happy. "Yeah."

"I'm sorry," I say, feeling bad.

"For what?"

"Taking him away."

She dismisses my words with a flick of her wrist. "I'm used to Colten being gone. It's not that. I guess I was hopin' maybe you would settle here." I stare at her in awe. She ignores my expression, links an arm through Riley's, then mine, and says, "Let's go see if the food is almost done. I'm starvin'."

"Shouldn't we wait for Sri?" I ask, but she's already leading me toward the table of food.

"She'll be along shortly."

And there she is—a flash of yellow in my side vision.

"I made it," she calls out, waving, her little body glowing in a bright yellow sundress as she runs toward us with sandals in hand. "What did I miss?" Dawson is carrying a large plate of grilled meats. She kisses him when he lowers his cheek to her. "I'm starving. I hope you weren't waiting for me to eat."

"We didn't," Naomi says. "Everything just got cooked."

"Come here, baby," Dawson says, "I got a big one for ya." He pumps his eyebrows and holds up a thick hotdog packed in a bun.

She shakes her head and laughs. "You wish."

"*Oooh!*" Everyone sounds off at the insult.

Sri drops her head against his arm affectionately and takes the hotdog. "It's perfect. And thanks for knowing the way I like it." She looks up at him with a lecherous grin.

"Are we done with the innuendos?" Naomi complains. "Because y'all are making me sick."

Everyone laughs and begins eating as quips and good-natured jabs are thrown around. I'm going to miss this. I've never had a tribe—somewhere I belonged.

When the food is demolished, Colten unfolds himself from

the picnic table and stands up. "Okay, I've got an announcement."

Sri grips my hand almost painfully. "Is he proposing?" she whispers excitedly in my ear.

I laugh an exaggerated, "*No.*" Then think, *Frick, I hope not.*

"So all of you know the story of Tess, or the basics of it. She's come back to me and I want to tell you"—he looks around at everyone—"that I love her today as much as I did when she was abandoned on our doorstep all those years ago." He locks eyes with me.

Oh shit. He wouldn't.

He holds a hand out to me, helping me stand up next to him. "I've decided to move to New York to live with this amazing person." He kisses the side of my head. "And I hope y'all will be happy for us."

Cheers erupt all around, while I breathe a sigh of relief, happy that no one seems resentful, and that this wasn't a proposal—not that I'm opposed, necessarily. I just want to start with us living together.

What if he's a revolting slob, or has nasty habits that turn into deal-breakers?

I can't imagine that happening, but I need the time together to find out.

There's lots of hugging and back-slapping before Naomi yells, "Who wants ice cream?"

"Why did you look so scared?" Colten pulls me away from the group when everyone crowds around Naomi.

"I thought you were proposing."

"Would that have been so bad?"

"No, well, yeah, in a way. First things first, I want to make sure we're as compatible as we think we are."

"You take all the time you need, but I know what I want." He grips my chin and brushes his lips over mine.

"They say you don't really know a person until you live together."

"They say that, huh?" He slides his arms around me, pulling our bodies together. "And who are these brilliant philosophers?"

I crane my neck back and give him a sly smile. "People."

"*Ahhh*, people," he mocks, as if it all makes sense.

"Smart people," I amend.

"Fine, we'll listen to your *people*. But, Tess . . ."

I stare up into the stunning eyes that haunted my dream only days before. "Hmm?"

"You are it for me."

My heart swells to the point of exploding. "That's good, because I love you so much it hurts."

He pulls me tight against him.

"Hey, you two lovebirds coming or what?" Naomi bellows. "If not, I'm closing the lid up, so the ice cream doesn't melt."

As I sit back and watch the scene, I'm struck by the power of it all. The closeness and the trust. I want this in my life.

At least I know I will always be able to come back.

CHAPTER 38

"LET'S take the boat out and watch the sunrise." Colten sweeps the hair that's fallen onto my face behind my ear.

I'm lying on my stomach, snuggled against his side. I lift my head, open an eye, and peer up over his body. There is barely any light in the sky. I drop my head on the pillow, moaning. I've never been a morning person, but the thought of going with him is sort-of-maybe oddly tempting.

He nudges me as he stands up. "Come on sleepyhead, time's a-wastin'." I grumble, playing hard to get. He nudges me harder. "Let's go. It'll be worth it. I promise."

"Do I get coffee first?" I muffle into my pillow.

"Not if you want to see the sunrise." He pokes me in the ribs, making me flinch and squeal. "Coffee takes too long to brew."

I turn my head to a half-naked Colten. What a vision. "Okay, *fine*," I grouch, and barrel-roll myself off the bed to a standing position.

He smacks my bare butt playfully. I yelp, my eyes wide open now. "Get that cute little ass of yours movin'."

I tweak his nipple. "You wanna go?" Clenching my fists, I hop around like a delinquent, provoking a fight.

"No, but this is quite a sight," he says, referring to my nakedness. "Is your butt okay? I didn't mean to smack it that hard."

"Do you want to kiss it and make it better?" I say, wriggling my eyebrows at him.

"If I do, we'll never get out of here." He pecks me on the cheek. "You need to get on the road."

"Fine," I grumble teasingly.

"Race ya." He runs around the room, scooping up his clothes. I follow his lead, competing to see who can get their clothes on first. We end up pushing and shoving each other all the way to the back door. The next contest seems to be who can reach the doorknob first.

He wins and hands me a jacket with a smug look on his face.

"Yeah, yeah." I walk past him as he holds the door open for me.

We step out onto dew-covered grass. The air is already thick with humidity. I breathe deep, as I always do when I'm hit with the fragrant rush of green. I need to get my fill. It's a gift that I won't have in the city—*we* won't have in the city.

Colten unties the boat and helps me in. "I've got to fix this before I leave," he says when he starts the motor.

The water is as smooth as glass as we slowly pull away from the dock. The sky presents itself in muted shades of pinks, purples, oranges, and blues. There's no hurry as we take in the silence of the morning.

I watch as the colors in the sky become more vibrant and find myself mesmerized by how they blend and scatter in the reflection of our wake. If only I had the talent to capture it on canvas.

"So, two more days, and you start your new job." Other than the sound of the engine, Colten's question is the first thing to break the silence.

"Yeah, I guess," I say with a sigh.

"You guess?" He looks over at me, surprised.

"Well, I interned there for three summers, so it's familiar. I really want to manage a gallery, but I'm young. This is a good start and it'll look good on a resume." Almost the same words I said to Twyla. They sound rehearsed—not as truthful as they once did.

Is that really what I want to do for the next several years? Live in the city, fetch coffee, run errands, execute orders?

I've been on autopilot for so long, I don't know.

I look around me. I'm awake now and the view grips my emotions. This is what I want to see every morning when I wake up.

The sudden realization knocks the wind out of me.

"Tess? Are you okay?" He takes my hand and squeezes it. "All the color just drained from your face."

I take several deep breaths. "Holy fuck! I don't want to work at Sotheby's." My face suddenly burns red-hot and my tongue feels dry in my mouth. "I need water. Do we have any water?" I fan my face.

"I don't know." He stops the engine, moves to the back of

the boat, and fumbles with a seat cushion. "Maybe there's some in the cooler." He lifts the lid to a hidden space and pulls out a bottle and cracks the top before handing it to me. "I don't know how long these have been in here. Does water go bad?"

I don't care. I chug the contents. "What am I going to do?" I plead, attempting to regain my breath.

He sits across from me. "You can do anything you want."

I drop my head and cover my face in my free hand. "But if I quit, I'll be burning bridges." I look up at him. "The art world is enormous, but in New York, it's a tight community. *Oh, crap.* What do I say to them? They're counting on me. What will my dad say?" Panic has gripped my throat, squeezing.

"Tell them thanks, but you have a better offer," he says, as if it's no big deal. "Sorry to say this, but you're a blip in a big-ass company. They'll survive. And your dad? It's your life, your future, not his. You've been down this road with him before. He'll understand."

I drop my head below my knees, fighting for air. "I can't believe this is happening."

"Tess, it's okay." He rubs a hand up and down my back. "Come here." He coaxes me onto his lap. "Breathe, okay?" I try to relax against him, but find it hard. "Have you tried applying to galleries? That's where you wanted to work originally."

He thinks this is about the job. This is so messed up. How do I follow my passion for art and live here?

"No. I haven't applied since interning at Sotheby's. Working there full-time became an easy, almost natural progression. I figured I'd work my way up to something reputable, but that could take forever. I don't want to live there anymore. And I don't want to be someone's errand girl." I stare into his eyes, my nerves close to shattering. What the hell am I supposed to do? I can't have it both ways.

"Hey. It's okay." His hand slides under my hair to the back of my neck and grips me there. "You don't have to do anything you don't want to do. You hear me?"

"Yeah. But it doesn't make it any easier." I touch my forehead to his.

"No. I don't expect it does, but you're not alone in this, remember? Life throws us changes, big and small, good and bad. We gotta roll with 'em. Same way you'll roll with this. It's not life or death. Remember that."

His words make me think of Josie and what they all went through. Next to that, this is nothing. "You're right." I touch my lips to his. "But I'm still scared." I'm terrified at what my realization will mean.

"Life's too short. You need to be happy. Call them and decline the position and stay here. At least until you decide your next step." I take in my surroundings, this time with a deep sense of longing. "Is it the job or living in New York City?"

The sun is high in the sky now; the birds awake and chirping loudly. "Both. This is the only place that's ever felt like home. Am I crazy?"

"No. Not if you're happy here."

"Did I just waste four years of education?"

"*Of course not.* There are other places we can explore. What about Europe? The art scene there is huge, right? Paris? I loved Paris. I told you I can fix cars anywhere. I want to be wherever you're going to be happy."

"How did I get so lucky?"

I snuggle my head under his chin, suddenly hopeful that

anything is possible. I'd like to enjoy the summer here, spend time together. I'm twenty-two. My trust fund went into effect on my twenty-first birthday, so money isn't an issue, thankfully.

"You know, I've made a lot of friends in the art world. Artists I respect and admire." My mind is spinning with ideas. I lean away from him suddenly, excited about where my thoughts are going. "Do you think your mother would want to open a gallery with me in town?" Twyla said she didn't want to do it alone, not that she wasn't interested.

"Uh . . ." He stalls, looking surprised. "You can ask her." Then a smile slowly spreads across his face. "Actually, I think she'd love it."

"Would you be okay sticking around for a while, maybe forever?"

He touches my cheek. "Would you?"

"It feels right—more than anything in my life. This is home." I touch my lips to his, then look up into eyes that hold more love than I've ever known. "I've come home."

EPILOGUE

COLTEN and I found a vacant house with an empty lot beside it for sale at the end of Main Street. Using the insurance money from the fire, as well as my own, we renovated the main floor into an art gallery and added a studio for Twyla. We turned the second floor into our apartment and built a two-bay garage for Colten on the empty lot. I love that he works close by. It's just like old times and my favorite part of the arrangement.

When Twyla and I agreed to start the gallery, I contacted all the creatives I'd met over the many years of immersing myself in the beauty that became my first love. They were thrilled at my endeavor, and now we exhibit an eclectic array of work from some of New York's finest artists. And just like George Townsend and his drive-in, Twyla and I created something a little over-the-top for this small town, but with tourists, a killer website, and massive social media following, we are beyond busy.

My dad was unsure about the gallery as a business adventure. He also wasn't too thrilled about me getting back together with Colten. But after my dad met him, and seeing how happy I was, he eased up and eventually relented. As far as the gallery . . . He was there for the opening, and told me he couldn't have been prouder, which meant the world to me. Oh, and my dad loves Earl's cooking and keeps offering to back him in his own restaurant in SoHo, which, of course, Earl declines every time.

As I sit next to Colten on the beach with our friends, I realize it's been over a year and a half since I decided to stay in Jasper Creek. I watch as Dawson and Sri take their one-year-old, Marla Rae, out of the stroller and set her on the sand. Sri was pregnant with her when I came back to find Colten. She was going to announce it at the BBQ before we left, but didn't want to take away from our big announcement.

I watch as the baby toddles on unstable feet before falling on her bottom. Squealing in delight, she throws sand in the air, then sputters in surprise when it lands on her face. As she begins to cry, Naomi picks her up, bouncing her on her hip, cooing as she wipes the sand gently away with a towel. Riley's at her side, kissing the baby's adorable, pudgy cheeks until she is giggling once again.

For some people, it's speed, success, money, or power that drives them. For me it's friends, family, and this small out-of-the-way town and a beach called Jumpin' Jack's.

ACKNOWLEDGMENTS

Thank you to my wonderful readers for reading, reviewing, sharing, and encouraging. You are like an extended family and the reasons for doing what I do.

The process by which this novel came to be is mostly a solitary task, but not solely. If it wasn't for the developmental skills of C.L. Walters, this story would have hit some pretty serious pitfalls. Next in line are my editors: copy and line edits from Murphy Rae, proof-reading from Melanie Kirk, and the final stage, my mother, who has a gift of picking out the most obscure mistakes (love you, Mom), beta readers C.L. Walters and Chelle Northcutt.

A huge thank you to my launch team, most of which double as compatriots of the pen: Leanna Floyd, Linda Ganzini, Julia Blake, Mary Ann Tippett, Tam DeRudder Jackson, Kathy Strobos, Laura Langa, Katerina Dennison, Faith, Beatrix Eaton, Karen Crawford, Ginell, Casy & Alyssa, Vashita Q, Amy Noelle, Karen Pokras, Kelly Bachtell, Linda Park, GG London, Yvonne Young, Sherry Grant, and Chris Johnson.

Thank you to my children who are the biggest accomplishments in my life and my husband who, besides my mother, is my biggest cheerleader (he even built me a writing shack, folks).

Made in the USA
Monee, IL
29 November 2022

19042800R00199